W9-BUO-836

Praise for the novels of

"Camp has again produced a fast-paced plot brimming with lively conflict among family, lovers and enemies."
—*Publishers Weekly* on *A Dangerous Man*

"The talented Camp has deftly mixed romance and intrigue to create another highly enjoyable Regency romance."
—*Booklist* on *An Independent Woman*

"Known for creating unforgettable characters, Camp continues to prove herself capable of twisting traditional plotlines into powerful stories to touch readers' hearts."
—*Romantic Times BOOKreviews* on *An Independent Woman*

"Romance, humor, adventure, Incan treasure, dreams, murder, psychics—the latest addition to Camp's Mad Moreland series has it all."
—*Booklist* on *An Unexpected Pleasure*

"Entertaining, well-written Victorian romantic mystery."
—*The Best Reviews* on *An Unexpected Pleasure*

"Camp spins a tale that commands attention."
—*Romantic Times BOOKreviews* on
An Unexpected Pleasure

"Camp brings the dark Victorian world to life. Her strong characters and perfect pacing keep you turning the pages of this chilling mystery."
—*Romantic Times BOOKreviews* on *Winterset*

"All the pieces necessary for a riveting read are here: a cast of endearing, quirky characters, sexual tension, a thrilling climax and a marvelous pair of lovers."
—*Romantic Times BOOKreviews* on
Beyond Compare

"From its delicious beginning to its satisfying ending, [*Mesmerized*] offers a double helping of romance."
—*Booklist*

CANDACE
CAMP
THE Marriage
WAGER

HQN™

ISBN-13: 978-0-373-77243-8
ISBN-10: 0-373-77243-2

THE MARRIAGE WAGER

This edition published by arrangement with Harlequin Books S.A.

www.HQNBooks.com

Printed in U.S.A.

Newly released classics from

and HQN Books

Promise Me Tomorrow
No Other Love
A Stolen Heart

Other books by Candace Camp

A Dangerous Man
An Independent Woman
An Unexpected Pleasure
So Wild a Heart
The Hidden Heart
Swept Away
Winterset
Beyond Compare
Mesmerized
Impetuous
Indiscreet
Impulse
Scandalous
Suddenly

Watch for the next installment of
Candace Camp's Matchmakers series
The Bridal Quest
Coming in spring 2008

THE Marriage WAGER

CHAPTER ONE

LADY HAUGHSTON SURVEYED the throng of people below her, one hand resting lightly on the polished black walnut railing. She was aware that heads turned to look at her. Indeed, she would have been disappointed if they had not.

Francesca Haughston had been a reigning beauty of the Ton for over a decade now—at thirty-three, she no longer cared to be specific about the number of years since her coming out. She had been blessed with a naturally beautiful combination of features—light golden hair and large, deep blue eyes, skin that was as smooth and white as cream, a straight, slightly tip-tilted nose, and well-shaped lips that curled up a bit at the ends, giving her a faintly catlike smile. A small mole sat low on her cheek near her mouth, the tiny blemish only accentuating the near-perfection of her features. She was of medium height, with a lithe, slender form and an elegant carriage that made her appear taller than she actually was.

But even with the natural advantages Francesca had been given, she was always careful to show her looks to the best advantage. One would never find her dressed in anything less than the best, or with a pair of slippers on her feet that did not complement her dress or her hair arranged in a style that did not frame her face becomingly. While always in the forefront of fashion, she was not one to chase after foolish fads but chose only those shades that best suited her coloring and the styles that flattered her shape.

She was dressed tonight in her signature color of ice blue, the neckline of her satin dress low enough to show off her soft white shoulders and bosom in a way that was just a trifle dashing but not at all vulgar. Silver lace adorned the scoop neckline and ran around the hem of her gown, as well as cascading down the demi-train in back. A simple but striking diamond necklace encircled her slender white throat, a matching bracelet was on one arm, and more single diamonds winked here and there in the intricacies of her hair.

No one, she was certain, would have guessed that she hadn't a feather to fly with. The truth was that her late, largely unlamented husband Lord Andrew Haughston, an inveterate gambler, had died leaving her with nothing but debts, a fact that she had been at great pains to conceal. No one was aware that the jewels adorning her were paste copies of the actual ones, which she had sold. Nor did even the most hawkeyed Society matron suspect that the kid slippers on her feet had been maintained with the utmost care so that they were now in their third season, or that the dress she wore had been cut from a different gown worn the year before and resewn by her talented maid into a newer style fresh off the most recent fashion doll from France.

One of the few who knew her true circumstances was the slender, elegant man beside her, Sir Lucien Talbot. He had joined the circle of her admirers during her first season, and though his romantic interest in Francesca was a pleasant fiction in which they both participated, his devotion to her was quite real, for over the course of the years, they had become fast friends.

Sir Lucien was both stylish and witty, facts that, given his perpetual bachelor status, made him a sought-after guest at parties. It was well-known that his pockets were frequently to let, as had always been the case with the Talbot family, but that did not mar his reputation as being "of very good Ton," a quality that was held in far higher regard, at least by hostesses. He could always be counted upon to liven the conversation with an acerbic remark or two; he never created a scene; he was an excellent dancer and his stamp of approval could establish a party-giver's reputation.

"Egad, what a crush," he commented now, raising his quizzing glass to inspect the crowd below them.

"I believe Lady Welcombe adheres to the notion that a rout must have as many attendees as one has floor space," Francesca agreed lightly. She opened her fan and waved it languidly. "I dread going down there. I know I shall get my toes trampled upon."

"Ah, but is that not the point of a rout?" A deep voice came from slightly behind her and to her right.

Francesca knew that voice. "Rochford," she said before she turned her head. "I am surprised to find you here."

Both Lucien and Francesca turned to face the new arrival, and he sketched a bow to them, replying, "Indeed? I would think that you could reasonably expect to find almost everyone you know here."

His mouth tightened in that familiar way that was almost, but not quite, a smile. His name was Sinclair, the fifth Duke of Rochford, and if Lucien's presence was sought after by a hostess, the attendance of Rochford was the star in her crown.

Tall, lean and broad-shouldered, Rochford was dressed in the impeccable black-and-white of formal wear. A discreet ruby nestled in the folds of his snowy cravat and was echoed in the cuff links at his wrists. He was easily the most powerful and aristocratic man in the room at any gathering, and if there were those who did not care for his dark, saturnine good looks, they were rarely heard to say so. His manner, like his dress, was elegant without a hint of showiness, and he was as much admired by men for his excellent horsemanship or his dead aim as he was pursued by women for his fortune, high cheekbones and thickly lashed, Gypsy-dark eyes. He was approaching forty and had never married, and as a consequence he had become the despair of all but the most determined ladies of the Ton.

Francesca could not keep from smiling a little at his retort. "Indeed, you are probably correct."

"You are a vision, as always, Lady Haughston," Rochford told her.

"A vision?" Francesca arched one delicately curved eyebrow. "I notice you do not say a vision of what. One could suppose almost anything to end that sentence."

Something glinted in his eyes, but he said in a neutral tone, "No one with eyes to see could suppose that aught but beauty would apply to you."

"An excellent recovery," Francesca told him.

Sir Lucien leaned in toward Francesca, saying in a low voice, "Don't look. Lady Cuttersleigh is approaching."

But his warning was too late, for a high-pitched woman's voice cut sharply through the air. "Your Grace! What a delight it is to see you."

A tall, almost skeletally thin woman made her way toward them, her short, rotund husband chugging along in her wake. The daughter of an earl, Lady Cuttersleigh had married a mere baron and was never averse to reminding him and the rest of the world that she had married beneath her. She considered it her duty to marry off her gaggle of daughters to someone worthy of intermingling with her own elevated bloodline. However, given the fact that her daughters strongly resembled her in both face and form, as well as overweening pride, she had found it a difficult proposition. She was one of the stubborn few who had not given up on snaring the Duke of Rochford for one of her girls.

A pained expression touched Rochford's face briefly before he turned and executed a perfect bow toward the approaching couple. "My lady. Cuttersleigh."

"Lady Haughston." Lady Cuttersleigh acknowledged Francesca and gave a brief, uninterested nod toward Sir Lucien, whose title fell far below her expectations, before she turned back to Rochford, smiling. "Delightful party, is it not? The party of the Season, I vow."

Rochford said nothing, only giving her a quizzical smile.

"I wonder how many 'parties of the Season' there will be this year," Sir Lucien commented drily.

Lady Cuttersleigh favored him with a look of dislike. "There can be only one," she told him repressively.

"Oh, I should think there will be at least three," Francesca put in. "There is the one with the greatest attendance, which I think this one will surely win. But then there is the party of the year based on how lavishly it is decorated."

"And the one based on *who* attends," Sir Lucien added.

"Well, I know that my Amanda will be sorry that she missed this one," Lady Cuttersleigh said.

Francesca and Lucien exchanged a glance, and Francesca unfurled her fan and raised it to her face to hide her smile. Whatever the subject, Lady Cuttersleigh could be relied upon to somehow bring her daughters into the conversation.

Lady Cuttersleigh went on to describe in detail the fever that had laid low two of her daughters and the touching way her eldest, Amanda, had stayed home to watch over them. Francesca could not help but consider what it said about the woman's own maternal instincts that it had been her daughter who had felt the responsibility to remain with the sick girls.

She continued to babble about the virtues of Amanda until at last Rochford cut in to say, "Yes, my lady, it is clear that your eldest daughter is a saint. Indeed, I imagine that naught but the most virtuous of men would satisfy as a husband for her. May I suggest the Rev. Hubert Paulty? An excellent fellow, and quite suitable for her."

For once Lady Cuttersleigh was reduced to silence. She gazed at the Duke in consternation, blinking rapidly as she tried to recover from this blow to her efforts. Rochford, however, was too quick for her.

"Lady Haughston, I believe you promised to introduce me to your esteemed cousin," he went on smoothly, offering Francesca his arm.

Francesca cast him a laughing glance, but said in a demure voice, "Of course. If you will excuse us, my lady. My lord. Sir Lucien."

Sir Lucien leaned in close to her, whispering, "Traitor."

Francesca could not hold back a small chuckle as she walked away on Rochford's arm. "My esteemed cousin?" she repeated. "Pray, do you mean the one who is far too fond of his port? Or the one who fled to the Continent after a duel?"

A faint smile curved the Duke's dark features. "I meant, fair lady, anyone of any sort who can get me away from Lady Cuttersleigh."

Francesca shook her head. "Dreadful woman. She is ensuring her daughters' destinies as spinsters, the way she goes about trying to marry them off. Not only is she horridly ham-handed about pushing them on people, her expectations far exceed the girls' possibilities."

"You, I understand, are an expert on such matters," Rochford said in a faintly teasing tone.

Francesca glanced at him, her eyebrows lifting. "Indeed?"

"Oh, yes. I have heard that you are the one to consult on one's foray into the marriage mart. One can only wonder why you have not ventured into the lists again yourself."

Francesca released his arm and turned aside, looking out once again over the crowd below. "I find that the status of a widow suits me quite well, Your Grace."

"Your Grace?" he repeated quizzically. "After so many years? I perceive that I have once more offended you. It is, I fear, something I am quite prone to."

"Yes, you do seem to be adept at it," Francesca replied lightly. "But you have not offended me. However, one cannot help but wonder...are you asking for my help?"

He let out a laugh. "No, indeed. Merely making conversation."

Francesca turned to study the Duke's face. She wondered why he had brought up the subject. Could it be that there were rumors about her matchmaking efforts? Over the past few years, she had come to the aid of more than one parent struggling to get his or her daughter into a successful marriage. There had always been a gift of gratitude from the mother or father, of course, after Francesca had taken the daughter under her wing and guided her through the tricky shoals of Society's waters and into the arms of the proper husband. But such gifts had always been dealt with most discreetly by both parties, and Francesca did not know how word could have leaked out that a certain silver epergne or pigeon's-blood ruby ring had found its way to the pawnbroker's shop.

Rochford returned her gaze, and Francesca saw the spark of curiosity begin in his eye. She said quickly, "No doubt you find such a skill quite negligible."

"No, indeed. I have met too many formidable mothers bent on making their daughter a duchess to discount matchmaking efforts."

"It is appalling, really," Francesca went on, "how

many of those mothers go about the matter in precisely the wrong way. Not just Lady Cuttersleigh. Look at *those* girls."

She nodded toward a group below them, standing beside a potted palm. A middle-aged woman, dressed all in purple, stood beside two young women, both clearly her daughters, given the unfortunate similarities of their features.

"Invariably, women who haven't the faintest idea how to dress well themselves insist on choosing their daughters' clothes," Francesca commented. "Look how she has them in lavender, a more girlish shade of the color she wears, and any shade of purple is disastrous with their skin, only making it look more sallow. Moreover, they are dressed far too fussily—all one can see are the ruffles and bows and the explosion of lace. And see how she talks and talks, never letting either of the girls get a word in."

"Yes, I see," Rochford responded. "But surely this is an extreme example. I cannot imagine that there would be much hope for them even without their overbearing mama."

Francesca made a disparaging noise. "I could do it."

"Come now, my dear…." Amusement danced in his dark eyes.

Francesca raised one eyebrow. "You doubt me?"

"I bow to your expert knowledge," he said, a faint smile hovering about his mouth. "But even *you* could not bring out some girls successfully."

His laughing tone raised Francesca's hackles. Without pausing to consider, she said, "I could. I could take any girl down there and get her engaged by the end of the Season."

He controlled a smile in a decidedly annoying way and said lightly, "Care to place a wager on that?"

It occurred to Francesca that she was being foolish, but she could not retreat before his gallingly mocking tone. "Yes, I would."

"Any girl in this crowd?" he posited.

"Any girl."

"And you will take her under your wing and get her engaged—an acceptable engagement—by the end of the Season?"

"Yes." Francesca gazed back at him coolly. She had never been one to back down before a challenge. "And you may choose the girl."

"But what shall we bet? Let me see…if I win, you must agree to accompany my sister and me when we pay our yearly visit to our great aunt."

"Lady Odelia?" Francesca asked with some horror.

His eyes twinkled as he replied, "Why, yes. Lady Odelia is quite fond of you, you know."

"Yes, as a hawk is fond of a fat rabbit!" Francesca retorted. "However, I shall agree because I know that I will not lose the bet. But what will I get when *you* lose?"

He looked at her consideringly a moment before

saying, "Why, I think a bracelet of sapphires the color of your eyes. You are, I believe, fond of sapphires."

Francesca's gaze locked with his for a moment. Then she turned away, saying blandly, "Yes, I am. That will do nicely."

Her hand tightened a little on her fan. She lifted her chin and gestured toward the partygoers. "Well, which girl will you choose?"

She expected him to take one or the other of the unattractive young women they had been discussing. "The one with the large bow in her hair, or the one with the dispirited-looking feather?"

"Neither," he replied, surprising her, nodding toward a tall, slender woman in a simple gray dress who stood behind the two girls. It was clear from the plainness of her dress and hairstyle that she was there in the capacity of chaperone, not as a debutante. "I choose *that* one."

CONSTANCE WOODLEY WAS bored. She supposed she should be grateful, as Aunt Blanche frequently told her, to be in London during the Season and to have the opportunity to go to grand parties such as this. However, Constance could find little joy in chaperoning her foolish cousins through countless balls, soirees and routs. There was, she found, a great deal of difference between actually having a Season, such as Georgiana and Margaret were, and watching someone else have a Season.

Her own chance at a Season had come and gone long ago. When she was eighteen and it was time for her coming-out, her father had fallen ill, and she had spent the next five years taking care of him as his health steadily declined. He had died when she was twenty-three, and as his estate had been entailed and he had had no male heirs, the house and lands went to his brother, Roger. Constance, unmarried and with no means of support other than the small amount of money that her father had left her, all of it conservatively invested in the Funds, had been allowed to remain in her home as Sir Roger and his wife moved in, accompanied by their two daughters.

She would always have a home with them, Aunt Blanche had told her somewhat piously, although she did think it would be better if Constance moved out of the bedchamber in which she had always slept into a smaller one in the rear of the house. The larger room, with its lovely prospect of the drive and park, was more suitable, after all, for the two daughters of the household. The move had been a bitter pill for Constance to swallow, but she had consoled herself with the thought that at least she had a room all to herself, rather than having to share with one of her cousins, and she could retreat there for a bit of much-needed peace and quiet.

Constance had spent the last several years living with her aunt and uncle and their children. She had helped her aunt with the children and with the household, wanting to be of use out of gratitude for their having taken her in, but also because it was plain that such help was expected in return for her room and board. Patiently Constance saved and reinvested the small income she received from her inheritance, hoping to one day accumulate enough that she would be able to live off it entirely and therefore be able to live on her own.

Two years ago, when the eldest daughter, Georgiana, had turned eighteen, her aunt and uncle had decided that, given the expenses of a debut, it would be best to wait until the younger girl turned eighteen also and then bring their two daughters out together.

Constance, her aunt told her graciously, could come along to help chaperone. There had been no mention of Constance participating in the annual social rite in any other capacity. Although the London Season was used as a sort of marriage market for mothers of marriageable girls, neither Constance nor her aunt considered Constance eligible to look for a husband. She was not an unattractive woman—her gray eyes were large and expressive, and her hair was a rich, dark brown strewn with reddish highlights—but at twenty-eight, she was decidedly a spinster, long past the normal age to be brought out into Society. She could hardly hope to wear pastels or pin her hair up in fetching curls. Indeed, Aunt Blanche preferred that Constance wear a spinster's cap, but although Constance usually gave in and wore a cap during the day, for parties she refused to don that final symbol of blighted hopes.

Constance did her best to comply with her aunt's expectations, for she knew that her aunt and uncle had not been obliged to take her in after her father's death. The fact that they had done so primarily out of equal parts fear of social disapproval and eagerness to have an unpaid helper for their own children did not absolve her, Constance thought, from a proper gratitude toward them. However, she found it difficult to endure the chatter of her cousins, who were both silly and inexplicably vain about their looks. And though it was also vain of her, she supposed, she despised wearing plain dresses in grays, browns and dark blues, the sorts of colors that her aunt felt befitted an unmarried woman of a certain age.

There was some pleasure to be taken in watching the glittering people of the Ton, of course, and Constance was engaged in that pastime now. She was gazing at a couple who stood at the top of the stairs looking out over the partygoers like monarchs observing their subjects. It was not an inapt analogy, for the Duke of Rochford and Lady Francesca Haughston were among the reigning members of London society. Constance, of course, had never met either one of them, for they normally moved in more elite circles than did Uncle Roger and Aunt Blanche. It was only at large events such as this rout that she even saw them.

They moved down the stairs now, and Constance

lost sight of them in the crowd. Her aunt turned to her, saying, "Constance, dear, do find Margaret's fan. She seems to have dropped it."

Constance spent the next few minutes looking all around them for the errant fan, so she did not notice the approach of two women until her aunt's sharp intake of breath alerted her to something unusual and she looked up from her search. Lady Haughston was walking toward them, and beside her was the beaming hostess of the party, Lady Welcombe herself.

"Lady Woodley. Sir, um…"

"Roger," her uncle supplied helpfully.

"Of course. Sir Roger. How are you? I hope the two of you are enjoying my little party," Lady Welcombe said, gesturing toward the great hall stuffed with people. Her deprecating smile indicated that she realized the humor in her statement.

"Oh, yes, my lady. 'Tis a wonderful rout. The finest of the Season, I'll warrant. I was just remarking to Sir Roger that it was the most splendid thing we had attended yet."

"Well, the Season is still young," Lady Welcombe replied modestly. "One can only hope that it will still be remembered by July."

"Oh, indeed, I am sure it will." Aunt Blanche hurried on to compliment the flowers, the candles, the decorations.

Even the hostess herself appeared to grow bored

with this effusive praise, and at the first opportunity, Lady Welcombe jumped in to say, "Pray, allow me to introduce you to Lady Haughston." She turned to the woman beside her. "Lady Haughston, this is Sir Roger Woodley and his wife Lady Blanche, and these are…uh, their lovely daughters."

"How do you do?" Lady Haughston said, extending one slender white hand.

"Oh, my lady! This is indeed an honor!" Aunt Blanche's face was flushed with excitement. "I am so pleased to meet you. Pray, allow me to introduce you to our daughters, Georgiana and Margaret. Girls, say hello to Lady Haughston."

Lady Haughston smiled perfunctorily at each of the girls, but her eyes moved on to Constance, standing slightly behind the others. "And you are?"

"Constance Woodley, my lady," Constance said with a brief curtsey.

"I am sorry," Aunt Blanche said with a twitter. "Miss Woodley is my husband's niece, living with us since her poor father's death some years ago."

"Please accept my condolences," Lady Haughston said, adding after a slight pause, "on your father's death."

"Thank you, my lady." Constance saw the light of amusement in the other woman's deep blue eyes, and she could not help but wonder if Lady Haughston had not meant to imply something else altogether. She suppressed the smile such a thought brought to her lips and returned Lady Haughston's gaze politely.

Lady Welcombe moved away, but to Constance's surprise, Lady Haughston remained with them for a few moments, making polite small talk. It surprised her even more when Lady Haughston said that she must leave and turned to Constance, adding, "Won't you take a stroll around the room with me, Miss Woodley?"

Constance blinked with surprise, too startled for a moment to speak. Then she moved forward with alacrity, saying, "Yes, I would like that very much, thank you."

She remembered to cast a look at her aunt for permission, though Constance knew that she would have gone with Lady Haughston even if Aunt Blanche had forbidden it. Fortunately, her aunt only nodded somewhat dazedly at her, and Constance moved forward to join the other woman.

Linking her arm through Constance's, Francesca began to stroll around the edge of the enormous room, chatting casually.

"I vow, one can scarcely find someone one knows in the crush. 'Tis well nigh impossible to meet anyone," Lady Haughston commented.

Constance smiled at the other woman in response. She was still too startled by Lady Haughston's interest in her to relax, and she could think of nothing to say, even the most commonplace of comments. She could not imagine what one of the lights of London Society could want from her. She was neither proud enough nor foolish enough to think that Francesca had singled her out because she had realized with a brief glance that Constance was worthy of her friendship.

"Is this your first Season?" Francesca went on.

"Yes, my lady. My father was quite ill when it came time for me to make my come-out," Constance explained. "He passed away a few years later."

"Ah, I see." Constance stole a quick glance at her companion. There was a shrewd look in Lady Haughston's eyes that told her that she understood far more than Constance had said. That she could envision the slow passage of time spent caring for her father, the days of boredom and sadness, interspersed with the rush of hard work and turmoil when his disease took a bad turn.

"I am sorry for your loss," Lady Haughston said kindly. After a moment, she added, "And so now you live with your aunt and uncle? And she is sponsoring you. That is kind of her."

Constance felt the heat of a blush rising in her cheeks. She could scarcely deny the words, for it would seem ungrateful, but to agree that her aunt acted out of kindness was more than she could do. She said merely, "Yes. Well, her daughters are that age now, and so…"

"I am sure you are a great help to her," Lady Haughston replied obliquely.

Constance glanced at her again and had to smile. Lady Haughston was no fool; she understood quite well why Aunt Blanche had brought Constance along, not for Constance's benefit, but for her own. Though Constance wondered what Lady Haughston was up to, she could not help but like her. There was a warmth in her that was all-too-frequently missing in the denizens of the Ton.

"Still," Lady Haughston went on, "you must take time to enjoy your visit to London, as well."

"I have visited some of the museums," Constance replied. "I quite enjoyed it."

"Did you? Well, that is very well and good, I'm sure, but I was thinking more along the lines of, oh, say, shopping."

"Shopping?" Constance repeated, more at sea in this conversation than ever. "For what, my lady?"

"Oh, I never limit myself to one thing," Lady Haughston replied, her lips quirking up into a smile that gave her the faint look of a self-satisfied feline. "That would be far too dull. I always set out with the idea of exploring whatever is out there. Perhaps you would like to accompany me tomorrow."

Constance looked at her in astonishment. "I beg your pardon?"

"On a shopping expedition," the other woman said, a chuckle escaping her. "You must not look at me so. I promise you, it will not be horrifying."

"I—I'm sorry." Constance felt herself blushing again. "You must think me a dolt. It is simply that your kind offer was unexpected. Indeed, I would like very much to go with you—though I fear I should forewarn you, I am a poor shopper."

"No need to worry," Lady Haughston replied, her eyes twinkling. "I can assure you that *I* am expert enough at it for both of us."

Constance could not keep from smiling at the other woman. Whatever was going on, the prospect of a day away from her aunt and cousins was delightful. And she was much too human not to feel a certain low satisfaction at the thought of the look on her aunt's face when she learned how Constance had been singled out by one of the most well-known and aristocratic women in London.

"Then it is settled," Lady Haughston went on. "I shall call on you tomorrow, say around one, and we shall make a day of it."

"You are very kind."

Again that smile flashed, and Francesca took her leave, pressing Constance's hand in farewell before she walked away. Constance watched her go, her mind still humming. She could not imagine why Lady Haughston was so interested in her, but she suspected that it would prove entertaining to find out.

She turned and looked over to where she had been standing with her aunt and uncle. She could not even see them through the crowd of people. It occurred to her that her aunt would not know precisely when she had parted from Lady Haughston. Perhaps she could spend a little more time away without encountering any censure from Aunt Blanche.

Constance glanced around her and spied a doorway opening into a hall. She slipped through it and made her way around the people who had drifted out of the crowded great hall and stood about in small clumps, talking. No one paid her any mind as she walked along the hallway—an advantage, she supposed, of her plain style.

Another, smaller corridor took her past a set of double doors that stood partly open. She saw that it was a library. A smile touched her lips, and she stepped inside. It was a grand library, with bookshelves up to the ceiling filling all four walls except for the space occupied by windows. With a sigh of pure pleasure, she gave herself up to looking at the rows and rows of books.

Her father had been a scholarly man, far more inclined to keep his nose in books of this sort than in the books of accounts for his estate. Their library at home had been crammed full of volumes of every description, but that room had been much smaller than this one and could not have held a third of the books here.

She strolled over to the shelves on the opposite wall and was reading through the titles when she heard the clatter of hurrying footsteps in the marble-tiled hallway outside. A moment later a man burst into the room, looking harried. He checked for an instant when his eyes fell upon Constance, who was standing watching him in surprise.

He laid his forefinger against his lips in a gesture of silence, then slipped behind the door, out of sight.

CHAPTER TWO

CONSTANCE BLINKED IN surprise, not sure what to make of this peculiar entrance. She hesitated, then started toward the open doorway. There was the sound of short, quick steps in the hallway, and Constance came to a halt as a woman now appeared in the doorway.

The new visitor was short and square, a startling vision in a puce overdress of sheer voile above a satin rose gown. Neither the material nor the fashionable color suited the woman's middle-aged body. And the heavy frown she wore did nothing to improve her looks.

She glared somewhat accusingly at Constance and barked, "Have you seen the Viscount?"

"Here? In the library?" Constance raised her eyebrows in a skeptical way.

The other woman looked uncertain. "It does seem unlikely." She glanced back into the hallway and then into the library. "But I am positive I saw Leighton come this way."

"There was a man running down the hall only a

moment ago," Constance lied cheerfully. "He probably turned into the main corridor."

The woman's gaze sharpened. "Headed for the smoking room, I'll warrant."

She turned and bustled away in pursuit of her quarry.

When the sound of her footsteps had receded, the man emerged from behind the door, pushing it halfway closed, and let out an exaggerated sigh of relief.

"Dear lady, I am eternally in your debt," he told her with a charming grin.

Constance could not keep from smiling back. He was a handsome man, his looks enhanced by his smile and easy manner. He was a little taller than average, topping Constance by several inches, and slender, with a wiry body that hinted at hidden strength. He was dressed well but not meticulously in a formal black suit and white shirt, his ascot tied in a simple but fashionable style, with none of the fusses and frills of a dandy. His eyes were a deep blue, the color of a lake in summer, and his mouth was wide and mobile, accented by a deep dimple on one side. When he smiled, as he did now, his eyes lit up merrily, beckoning everyone around him to join in his good humor. His hair, dark blond sunkissed with lighter streaks, was worn a trifle longer than was fashionable and tousled in a way that owed more to carelessness than to his valet's art.

He was, Constance thought, someone whom it was difficult to dislike, and she suspected that he was well aware of his effect, especially upon women. The unaccustomed visceral tug of attraction she felt inside was proof of his power, she thought, and firmly exercised control over the jangling of nerves in her stomach. She had to be immune to flirtatious smiles and handsome men, for she was not, after all, marriage material, and any other option was unthinkable.

"Viscount Leighton, I presume?" she said lightly.

"Alas, I am, for my sins," he responded, and swept her a very creditable bow. "And your name, my lady?"

"It is merely miss," she answered. "And it would be highly improper, I think, to give it to a stranger."

"Ah, but not as highly improper as being alone with said stranger, as you are now," he countered. "But once you tell me your name, we will no longer be strangers, and then all is perfectly respectable."

She let out a little laugh at his reasoning. "I am Miss Woodley, my lord. Miss Constance Woodley."

"Miss Constance Woodley," he repeated, moving closer and saying confidentially, "now you must offer me your hand."

"Indeed? Must I?" Constance's eyes danced. She could not remember when she had last engaged in light flirtation with any man, and she found it quite invigorating.

"Oh, yes." He made a grave face. "For if you do not, how am I to bow over it?"

"But you have already made a perfectly proper bow," she pointed out.

"Yes, but not while I was so lucky as to be in possession of your hand," he replied.

Constance extended her hand, saying, "You are a very persistent sort of fellow."

He took her hand in his and bowed over it, holding it a bit longer than was proper. When he released it, he smiled at her, and Constance felt the warmth of his smile all the way down to her toes.

"Now we are friends, so all is proper."

"Friends? We are but acquaintances, surely," Constance replied.

"Ah, but you have saved me from Lady Taffington. That makes you very much my friend."

"Then, as a friend, I feel I am free to inquire as to why you are hiding in the library from Lady Taffington. She did not seem fearsome enough to send a grown man into popping behind doors."

"Then you do not know Lady Taffington. She is that most terrifying of all creatures, a marriage-minded mama."

"Then you must take care not to run into my aunt," Constance retorted.

He chuckled. "They are everywhere, I fear. The prospect of a future earldom is more than most can resist."

"Some would think it is not so bad to be so eagerly desired."

He shrugged. "Perhaps…if the pursuit had aught to do with me rather than my title."

Constance suspected that Lord Leighton was sought after for far more than his title. He was, after all, devastatingly handsome and quite charming, as well. However, she could scarcely be so bold as to say so.

As she hesitated, he went on, "And for whom is your aunt hunting husbands?" His eyes flickered down to her ringless wedding finger and back up. "Not you, surely. I would think that it would be an easy task if that were the case."

"No. Not me. I am well past that age by now." She smiled a little to soften the words. "I am here only to help Aunt Blanche chaperone her daughters. They are making their come-out."

He quirked one eyebrow. "You? A chaperone?" He smiled. "You will forgive me, I hope, if I say that sounds absurd. You are far too lovely to be a chaperone. I fear your aunt will find that her daughters' suitors call to see you instead."

"You, sir, are a flatterer." Constance glanced toward the door. "I must go."

"You will abandon me? Come, do not leave just yet. I am sure your cousins will survive a bit longer without your chaperonage."

In truth, Constance had little desire to leave. It was far more entertaining to exchange light banter with the handsome viscount than it would be to stand with her cousins watching others talk and flirt. However, she feared that if she stayed away too long, her aunt would come looking for her. And the last thing she wanted was for Aunt Blanche to find her closeted here with a strange man. Even more than that, she had no desire for her aunt to meet Lord Leighton and become another of the pack of mothers who hounded him.

"No doubt. But I am neglecting my duty." She held out her hand to him. "Goodbye, my lord."

"Miss Woodley." He took her hand in his, smiling down at her. "You have brightened up my evening considerably."

Constance smiled back, unaware of how her enjoyment had put a sparkle in her eye and a flush in her cheeks. Even the severity of her gown and hairstyle could not mask her attractiveness.

He did not release her hand immediately, but stood, looking down into her face. Then, much to Constance's surprise, he bent and kissed her.

Startled, she froze. The kiss was so unexpected that she did not pull away, and after a moment she found that she had no desire to do so. His lips were light and soft on hers, a mere brushing of his mouth against hers, but the touch sent a tingle all through her. She thought he would pull away, but to her further surprise, Leighton did not. Instead, his kiss deepened, his lips sinking into hers and gently, inexorably, opening her lips to him. Her hands went up instinctively to his chest. She should, she knew, thrust him away from her with great indignation.

But without any conscious thought, her hands

instead curled into the lapels of his jacket, holding on against the swarm of sensations assaulting her. His hand went to her waist, wrapping around her and pulling her into him, and the other hand cupped the nape of her neck, holding her as his mouth worked its way with her.

Frankly, Constance was glad for his steadying support, for her knees seemed about to give way. Her entire body, in fact, suddenly was weak and melting and seemingly beyond her control. She had never felt anything like this before, not even when she was nineteen and in love with Gareth Hamilton. Gareth had kissed her when he asked her to marry him, and she had thought nothing could be as sweet. It had made things even harder when she had to turn him down in order to nurse her father through his last illness. But Lord Leighton's embrace was not sweet at all; it was hard and demanding, and his kiss seared her. And though she scarcely knew the man, her body was trembling and her thoughts scattered to the winds.

He lifted his head, and for a long moment they stared at each other, more shaken than either cared to admit. Leighton drew a breath and stepped back, releasing Constance. She gazed at him, eyes wide, unable to speak. Then she turned and hurried from the room.

THERE WAS NO ONE IN THE hallway outside the library, for which Constance was very grateful. She could not imagine how she must look. If it was anything like the way she felt inside, then she was sure that anyone who saw her would stare. Her heart was galloping in her chest, and her nerves were thrumming.

There was a mirror on the wall halfway down the corridor, and Constance walked to it to take stock of herself. Her eyes were soft and lambent, and her cheeks were stained with color, her lips reddened and soft. She looked, she realized, prettier. But was it as obvious to anyone else as it was to her what she had been doing?

With hands that trembled slightly, she tucked a stray hair or two back into the neat bun at the nape of her neck, and she drew several deep breaths. Her thoughts were not so easily brought out of turmoil. Thoughts and sensations tumbled madly about in her, resisting all attempts to bring them into order.

Why had Lord Leighton kissed her? Was he nothing but a rake, a vile seducer seeking to take advantage of a woman in a vulnerable position? She found it hard to believe. He had been so likeable, not only handsome, but with that charming twinkle in his eye, that easy sense of humor. But then, perhaps that was how rakes were. It would make sense. It would be far easier to seduce someone, no doubt, if one were charming.

Still, she could not quite believe it about Lord Leighton. And there had been that look of surprise on his face when he had pulled back from her, as though he had not quite expected what had happened, either. And he had not gone forward with any seduction—even though she would certainly not have put up any resistance, as lost in his kiss as she had been. Surely his breaking off the kiss was proof that he was too gentlemanly to press the advantage.

He had meant to kiss her, of course, even if it had been an impulsive gesture. But she remembered how the kiss, a light touch at first, had deepened into passion. Had he meant only a mischievous little kiss, but then desire had overtaken him, just as it had her?

That thought brought a small, satisfied smile to Constance's lips. She would like to think that she had not been the only one swept away by ardor.

She looked again at her image in the mirror. Could it be that Viscount Leighton had found her pretty in spite of her plain clothes? She studied her face. It was a pleasant oval shape and her features were even. She did not think she looked much older than she had at twenty. And there had even been a man or two besides Gareth who, when she was young, had called her gray eyes beautiful and her dark brown hair lustrous. Had Leighton seen past her current dullness to the pretty girl she had once been?

She would like to think so, that he had found her attractive, even desirable, that he had not simply thought her an easy target for his attentions.

Of course, how was she to know what Lord Leighton felt, she thought, when she did not even know how she felt herself! She had liked the man immediately. He had made her laugh, and she had enjoyed talking to him. But there had been something more…something she had felt as soon as he entered the room. The way he had looked at her, the way he had smiled, had set up an unusual warmth inside her, an odd fizz of interest, even excitement. And when he had kissed her, she had been prey to feelings she had never had before, never even dreamed of having. What she had felt, she thought, was lust, the very passion that young women were forever being warned about, the thing that would lead them down the path to ruin.

She had never felt it before. She had assumed she never would. She was, after all, twenty-eight, long past the possibility of romance. But, she thought with another little secretive smile, apparently she was not past the age to feel desire.

Constance started back down the corridor and slipped into the great room. The crowded room was stifling, and the noise was loud and grating on her ears. She wound her way through the people, coming at last back to her aunt and uncle.

To her surprise, her aunt did not take her to task for the length of time that she had spent away. Instead she beamed at Constance and wrapped her hand around her arm, pulling her closer.

"What did she say?" Aunt Blanche asked eagerly, leaning close to hear above the noise. Then, without waiting for a response, she charged on. "To think of

Lady Haughston taking notice of us! I could have dropped dead in my tracks when Lady Welcombe introduced her to us. I'd no idea that such a one as she had even noticed us, let alone wanted to make our acquaintance. What did she say? What was she like?"

It took a little effort for Constance to pull her mind back to her stroll about the room with Lady Haughston. What had happened afterward had driven it completely out of her head.

"She was very nice," Constance said. "I liked her a great deal."

She wondered whether she should tell her aunt about Lady Haughston's offer to take her shopping the next day. It seemed, in retrospect, unlikely that the woman had actually meant what she said. The conversation had been pleasant, but it was absurd, surely, to think that a woman of Lady Haughston's position in the Ton would make such an effort to befriend her. Constance came from a respectable family, certainly, one that could trace its ancestors back to the Tudors, but her father's title had been merely that of a baronet, and her family was not wealthy. She and her father had lived a quiet life in the country; she had never even been to London before this Season.

Constance could not imagine what had driven a woman like Lady Haughston to seek her out. She had not seemed inebriated, but Constance could only think that she had tippled too much punch. Whatever the reason, by tomorrow, Constance suspected, it would be forgotten…or, if remembered, it would be regretted. In any case, she doubted that Lady Haughston would call on her the next day, and she did not want to tell her aunt that Lady Haughston wanted to take her shopping and then be proven wrong.

"But what did she say?" Aunt Blanche asked in some irritation. "What did you talk about?"

"Commonplaces, mostly," Constance said. "She asked if I had been to London before and I told her no, and she said that I must be sure to enjoy myself while I was here."

Her aunt gave her an exasperated look. "Surely you did not keep all the conversation on yourself."

"No. Lady Haughston said that it was kind of you to bring me here," Constance told her, hoping that Aunt Blanche would be well enough pleased with that information that she would cease her questioning.

But Constance's words only seemed to cement Aunt Blanche's determination to discuss Lady Haughston. She continued to talk about the woman the rest of the time they were at Lady Welcombe's rout and all the way home in their hired carriage, extolling Lady Haughston's looks, lineage and virtues—though what her aunt could have known about the latter, Constance could not imagine, since she had talked to the woman for no more than three or four minutes.

"Such a lady," Aunt Blanche said enthusiastically.

"There are some would say she is a trifle showy. But I would not. Not at all. Her appearance is exactly what is pleasing. Her dress was clearly sewn by the best modiste. I have heard that she favors Mlle. du Plessis. She is always in the forefront of fashion. Her family is the very finest. Her father is an earl, you know." She paused, looking almost starry-eyed. "And to take an interest in us…well, it is just the most complete luck. When I think of what her patronage will do for Georgiana and Margaret!"

Constance had not noticed any particular interest on Lady Haughston's part in Georgiana and Margaret. Indeed, it had been Constance herself whom she had singled out, though she had no idea why. But she thought it prudent not to point this out to her aunt.

Aunt Blanche looked at her eldest daughter, Georgiana. "You were in your best looks tonight, my dear. No doubt that is why she noticed us. That dress is the loveliest we bought. Although I do think it would have been better with that extra ruffle the dressmaker would not put on."

Again Constance held her tongue. As far as she was concerned, Georgiana's dress was far too ruffled as it was, and if it had drawn Lady Haughston's attention, it would only have been because that elegantly dressed woman had been appalled. Her aunt and cousins were given to flounces, ruffles and bows, bedecking the girls' frocks with far more ornamentation than was attractive. It seemed to Constance that the ruffles usually served to make Georgiana look stouter than she was, just as the fussy curls she wore around her face only served to draw attention to its roundness.

But Constance had learned long ago that any attempt to convince the girls and Aunt Blanche that a little more simplicity would favor them had only ended up with all three of them vexed with her and certain that Constance spoke only out of jealousy.

So she said nothing as Aunt Blanche and the two girls happily speculated upon what knowing Lady Haughston would do to improve their status and on how they might improve their gowns for their next outing. Indeed, she scarcely listened to them all the ride home, for her own thoughts were far away from the carriage and her family. Nor did she think of the mystery of Lady Haughston's interest in her, or whether she would in fact call on her the next day, though under normal circumstances she would have wondered about these things a great deal.

But tonight, as she left the carriage and climbed the stairs to her small room in their rented house, as she undressed for bed and brushed out her long, thick hair, her mind was on the laughing blue eyes of a certain viscount, and the question that would not let her sleep for a good hour after she had retired was whether she would ever see him again.

CONSTANCE DRESSED WITH some care the following morning. Though she refused to let herself get carried away by the thought that Lady Haughston had said she would call on her, neither was she going to ignore the possibility and therefore possibly wind up riding out with the woman in her second-best day dress. So she put on her best afternoon dress, made of brown jaconet muslin. And though she wore the little spinster's cap her aunt assured her was suitable for her age and station in life, she pulled a few strands out from it and twisted them into curls to frame her face. Her pride would not allow her to be seen at Lady Haughston's fashionable side looking like a dowd.

At one o'clock, when Lady Haughston had not arrived, Constance tried not to be too disappointed. After all, she had known that the introduction last night had been a fluke. Perhaps Lady Haughston had assumed she was someone else or had taken pity on a poor wallflower of a girl, but this morning she would have had no interest in actually pursuing the relationship.

Still, it was difficult not to feel somewhat downcast. Constance had liked Lady Haughston and, she was truthful enough to admit, she had felt a degree of pride at being singled out for attention by one of the leaders of the Ton. But most of all, meeting her had enlivened the boredom of life in London.

In truth, Constance was finding that she preferred life

in the country to the glittering world of the capital. The parties, it was true, were far grander and more lavish, but she knew scarcely anyone at them, and she spent most of her time simply standing or sitting with her aunt and cousins. As a chaperone, she was paid no more attention than the furniture or the wallpaper. She was not asked to dance, and she was rarely even included in the conversations that her aunt or cousins conducted with others. Had her relatives been attentive to her, then she supposed that others would have talked to her, as well. But what few people the Woodley women knew they guarded jealously, hopeful that these relationships would help them in their quest for husbands.

Constance therefore found little pleasure in the parties except to look at the beautiful rooms and lovely dresses, or to observe the foibles of the various party-goers. It was an amusement that wore thin, and she often grew bored and wished she were at home reading.

During the days, she was equally bored. She had become accustomed from an early age to running her father's household. When his estate passed to Sir Roger, while Aunt Blanche had been happy to assume the titular reins of the household, she was equally happy to leave most of the actual work of seeing that everything ran smoothly to Constance. But the house and the number of servants here were much smaller, and the housekeeper whom they hired in the city ran the place with such efficiency that Constance had very little to do with its daily operation. Nor did she have any of the social chores to occupy her that had taken up part of her days in the past. She had been wont to pay duty calls to her father's tenants and various people in the village, such as the vicar and his wife, and the now-retired attorney who had in the past handled her father's affairs. She was accustomed, as well, to visiting with her friends and neighbors. But here in London she knew no one besides her family, and, to be truthful, she usually found them poor company. Aunt Blanche, Margaret and Georgiana talked of little except husbands, marriage and dresses, and Uncle Roger talked little at all, spending most of his time at his club and, when he was at home, retreating to the study, where, Constance suspected, he passed the hours by napping.

Worst of all for Constance was the fact that in London she was not free to go on long rambles as she had at home. Here, her aunt and uncle ruled, it was far too unseemly, not to mention dangerous, to go walking out without a maid to accompany her, and they could not spare a maid for what her aunt and uncle considered Constance's foolish and unladylike behavior.

Bored and restricted, Constance had looked forward to the prospect of Lady Haughston's offer of an afternoon's expedition with more eagerness than she would have admitted. Her spirits lowered greatly as the afternoon ticked away.

But then, shortly before two o'clock, just as Constance was thinking of going upstairs to escape the argument that Georgiana and Margaret were having over which of them was more favored by a certain baron—who had never shown the slightest interest in either of them that Constance had seen—the parlor maid announced the arrival of Lady Haughston.

"Oh, my!" Aunt Blanche jumped up as though someone had pinched her. "Yes, yes, of course. Show her ladyship in."

She quickly patted at the cap that covered her hair and smoothed down her skirts, muttering that she wished she had worn a better dress. "Pin up that curl, Margaret. Stand up, girls. Constance, here, take my needlework."

Constance moved over to pick up the embroidery hoop that had fallen from Aunt Blanche's hands when she leapt up from her chair, and she neatly tucked it into her sewing basket. Because of that, she was leaning over and slightly turned away when Lady Haughston entered the room. Aunt Blanche hurried forward, reaching out eagerly to take Lady Haughston's hands in both hers.

"My lady! What an honor. Do sit down. Would you care for some tea?"

"Oh, no." Lady Haughston, a vision in a pomona green silk walking dress, smiled at the older woman as she pulled her hands back. She nodded vaguely toward Margaret and Georgiana. "I cannot stay. I am here for only a moment to fetch Miss Woodley. Where is she?"

She looked past Lady Woodley. "Ah, there you are. Shall we go? I must not leave the horses waiting long or the coachman scolds me." She smiled at the absurdity of her statement, her blue eyes twinkling. "I hope you have not forgotten about our shopping expedition?"

"No, of course not. I wasn't sure…well, that you meant it."

"Whyever not?" Lady Haughston's eyebrows lifted in astonishment. "Because I am late, you mean? You mustn't mind that. Everyone will tell you that I am always shockingly late. I don't know why that is so."

She shrugged prettily, and Constance suspected that few people were ever able to sustain any annoyance at Lady Haughston's tardy arrivals.

"You are going shopping? With Constance?" Aunt Blanche gaped at Lady Haughston.

"I hope you will not mind," Lady Haughston replied. "Miss Woodley promised she would help me choose a new bonnet today. I am quite torn between a pair of them."

"Oh." Aunt Blanche blinked. "Yes, well, of course."

She turned to Constance, the look on her face a mixture of confusion and annoyance, as she said, "It is very kind of you to invite my niece."

Constance felt a trifle guilty for not having told her aunt about Lady Haughston's invitation. However, she could scarcely explain her doubts with Lady Haughston standing right there. She said only, "I am sorry, Aunt

Blanche. I quite forgot to tell you. I hope you do not mind."

Aunt Blanche could do nothing but agree to the expedition if she hoped for Lady Haughston's favor, and Constance was banking on it that she would realize that fact. Otherwise, her aunt would probably have refused out of irritation.

But Lady Woodley was wise enough to nod and say, "Of course, my dear. You deserve a treat." She turned to their guest. "I scarcely know what we would do without dear Constance's help. It is so good of her to come to London to help me chaperone the girls." Aunt Blanche cast a fond glance at Constance's cousins. "It is difficult to keep up with two lively girls—and so many parties!"

"I am sure it must be. Are you planning to attend Lady Simmington's ball tomorrow? I hope that I will see you there."

Aunt Blanche's smile remained fixed on her face, though at Francesca's words she looked as though she had perhaps swallowed a bug. Finally, she said, "I, ah, I fear that I have lost our invitation."

"Oh, no, do not say so. Well, if you care to go, you may have mine," Francesca replied carelessly. "I should hate not to see all of you there. "

"My lady!" Aunt Blanche's face turned pink with happiness. Lady Simmington was a hostess of importance, and Aunt Blanche had spent much of the week bemoaning the fact that she had not received an invitation to her ball. "That is generous of you indeed. Oh, my, yes, of course, we shall be there."

Her joy was such that she beamed at her husband's niece with actual good will as she bade them goodbye. Constance quickly put on her hat and gloves and followed Lady Haughston out of the house before her aunt could think of some way to try to foist her two cousins on them.

However, glad as she was to make her escape, Constance could not help but wonder what Lady Haughston was doing. Francesca's generous gift of an invitation to one of the most exclusive balls of the Season would, of course, result in no great loss on her part. No one, Constance was sure, would deny Lady Haughston entrance to a party without her invitation. But why, Constance wondered, had she done it? She seemed a friendly and kind person—she had, after all, pretended to believe her aunt's face-saving fabrication about a lost invitation. But a friendly nature could not explain the odd interest she had taken in Constance's family.

It seemed beyond belief she would have been so intrigued by the look of Constance, Aunt Blanche or her daughters that she arranged to be introduced to them. And Constance had barely spoken two words to her when the woman had asked her to stroll about the party with her, as if they were bosom friends, capping this extraordinary action with an invitation to take her on a shopping expedition. Even more bizarrely, she had actually followed through on her invitation, then had expertly put Aunt Blanche in her pocket by giving her an entrée to Lady Simmington's ball.

What sort of game was Lady Haughston playing? And even more perplexing, really, was the question of why?

CHAPTER THREE

THE TWO WOMEN CLIMBED into Lady Haughston's waiting carriage, a shiny black barouche. Constance knew, from listening to her aunt's chatter yesterday evening that this barouche, a slightly outdated equipage for someone usually so slap up to the mark as Lady Haughston, was one of the woman's well-known and charming eccentricities. The barouche had been given her by her late husband when they were first married, and since his untimely death six years ago, she had refused to buy a new carriage, preferring his gift.

"I have been, in truth, looking at two hats at the milliner's," Lady Haughston said. "But we have ample time to stop elsewhere. Shall we go to Oxford Street? What would you like to shop for?"

Constance smiled at her. "I am quite happy to go wherever you wish, my lady. I have nothing particular I wish to buy."

"Oh, but we cannot neglect you," her companion said gaily. "You must at least need ribbons or gloves or some such thing." She looked consideringly at Constance. "A bit of lace for the neckline of that dress, for instance."

A little surprised, Constance glanced down at her chocolate brown dress. It would be prettier, it was true, with a ruffle of lace around the neckline and the small puffed sleeves—champagne-colored lace, for instance.

She shook her head, unaware of letting out a tiny sigh. "I fear it would not be plain enough then."

"Plain enough?" A faint look of consternation marred Francesca's pretty features. "You are not a Quaker, are you?"

Constance let out a chuckle. "No, my lady, I am not a Quaker. It is just that it is not appropriate, is it, for a chaperone to call attention to herself?"

"Chaperone!" The other woman exclaimed. "My dear, whatever are you talking about? You are far too young and pretty to be a chaperone."

"My aunt needs my help. She has two daughters out."

"Help? To watch them talk or dance? I think you are far too serious about the matter. I am sure she would not expect you to sit out every dance. You must dance at Lady Simmington's ball. Her musicians are always excellent. I will speak to your aunt about it."

Constance felt a blush begin in her cheeks. "I doubt I would be asked, my lady."

"Nonsense. Of course you will. Especially when we brighten up your wardrobe a trifle. I have a deep blue satin gown—I have worn it far too many times already, and I fear I must give it up, but it would look wonderful on you. My maid can change something here and there, spruce it up a bit so no one will recognize it. You must come to my house before the party and let her make it over for you."

"My lady! That is much too kind of you. I cannot accept such a generous gift."

"Then do not consider it a gift. 'Twill be a loan, and you may give it back to me when the Season is over. And, please, that is quite enough of 'my lady.' I am Francesca."

Constance stared at her, dumbfounded. "I—I don't know what to say."

"Why, what should you said but 'Thank you for the dress, Francesca?'" the other woman retorted, smiling.

"I do thank you. But I—"

"What? You do not wish to be friends with me?"

"No!" Constance hastened to assure her. "I would like that very much. Indeed, I should very much like to have a friend. But you are too generous."

"I am sure that you would be able to find a number of people who would tell you that I am not generous at all," Francesca retorted.

"You make it very difficult to say no," Constance told her.

Francesca's white teeth flashed in a mischievous grin. "I know. I have worked at it for many years. Ah, here is the millinery. Now, stop all these protestations and come help me decide between these hats."

Constance put away her doubts and followed Lady Haughston into the store. They were greeted with a smile and pleasant words from the girl behind the counter, and a moment later, an older woman who was obviously the proprietress of the store, swept out from the curtained rear of the shop to help them herself.

Francesca modeled both of the hats in which she was interested. One was a soft, dark blue velvet with a jockey brim, a delicate lace veil hanging down to cover her eyes. The other, a straw cottage bonnet, was lined with blue silk and tied fetchingly under the chin with a matching blue ribbon, Gypsy style. Both did wonderful things for her blue eyes, and Constance declared herself as unable to decide as Francesca was.

"You try them on," Francesca suggested. "Let me see how they look."

Constance made a token protest, but, in fact, she had been itching to see how the blue-lined straw would look on her. When she tried it on, she could not help but smile at her reflection.

"Oh!" Lady Haughston cried, clapping her hands together. "It looks perfect on you! You must get it, not I. I will take the velvet."

Constance hesitated, gazing at her image in the mirror. The blue silk lining did as much for gray eyes as for blue, she decided. It was an excessively pretty bonnet, and she had not bought a new hat this year. Surely it would not hurt to spend a little of her money.

Finally, with a sigh, she shook her head. "No, I fear it must be too dear."

"Oh, no, I am sure it is not. I believe it is on sale, is it not, Mrs. Downing?" Francesca turned and looked significantly at the store owner.

Mrs. Downing, who was well aware of the benefits of Lady Haughston's patronage, smiled and agreed. "Indeed, it is. You are right, my lady. It is, um…" She shot another glance at Francesca. "…one-third off the price on the tag." At Francesca's smile, she nodded. "Yes, that's right. One-third off. A true bargain."

Constance looked at the price, quickly calculating. She had never spent even as much as two-thirds of this price for a hat at home. But, then, none had been as becoming or carried quite the elegant panache as this one.

"All right," she agreed, saying goodbye to her pin money for the month. "I will take it."

Francesca was delighted with Constance's purchase and took the velvet hat for herself. Then she insisted on purchasing a spray of tiny silk buds as an ornament for Constance's hair.

"Nonsense," she said when Constance protested. "It will look perfect with the blue gown you are borrowing. It is a gift. You cannot refuse it."

Their hats in boxes, they went back out to their

waiting carriage. When they had gotten in and settled into their seats, Constance turned to Francesca.

"My lady—Francesca. I do not understand. Why are you doing this?"

Lady Haughston turned a look of supreme innocence upon her. "Doing what, my dear?"

"All of this." Constance made a vague gesture around her. "Inviting me out with you this afternoon. Offering me a dress. Inviting us to Lady Simmington's party."

"Why, it is because I like you," Francesca answered. "Why would I have any ulterior motive?"

"I cannot imagine," Constance retorted candidly. "But neither can I believe that you spotted me or my aunt and cousins across the great hall at Lady Welcombe's and were so enchanted with us that you had Lady Welcombe introduce us to you."

Francesca looked consideringly at Constance, then sighed. "Very well. You are right. I had a reason for meeting you. I do like you—you are a very pleasant young woman, and you have a certain laughing look to your eyes that I know means you see the humor in the world. I would like to be your friend. But that is not why I came over to meet you. The fact is…I made a wager with someone."

"A wager?" Constance stared at her, dumbfounded. "About me? But what? Why?"

"I was boasting. I should learn to mind my tongue,"

Francesca admitted in a vexed tone. "Rochford had the gall to challenge me. And, well, the fact is that I bet that I could find you a husband before the end of the Season."

Constance's jaw dropped. For a moment she could think of nothing to say.

"I am sorry," Francesca said earnestly, leaning forward to lay a placating hand on Constance's arm. "I know I should not have, and I regretted it as soon as it was done. And you have every right to be angry with me. But I beg you will not. I did not mean you any harm. I still do not."

"Not mean me any harm!" A variety of emotions rushed through Constance, hurt followed almost immediately by anger and resentment. "No, of course not. Why should I mind that I am held up to ridicule by the leaders of the Ton?"

"Ridicule!" Lady Haughston looked at her with alarm and concern. "No, how can you think that?"

"What else am I to think when I have been made the object of a public wager?"

"Oh, no, no. It was not public at all. It was between Rochford and me alone. No one else was privy to it, I assure you. Well, except Lucien," she added honestly. "But he is my closest friend, and I can assure you that he would never tell a soul. He knows the secrets of half the Ton. I promise you that I shall not spread it about, and I can assure you that Rochford will not tell anyone.

A tighter-lipped man I have never met." She looked rather exasperated at the fact.

"And is that supposed to make it all right?" Constance asked. She had liked Francesca, and now she felt betrayed. Though she had had her reasonable doubts, she found it was a lowering thought indeed that Lady Haughston had not sought out her friendship but was only using her as a test of her matchmaking skills. "Why was I chosen? Was I the most unmarriageable of all the women at the ball? Too plain and old for any man ever to wish to marry me?"

"No, please, you must not think that!" Francesca exclaimed, her lovely features tightening in distress. "Oh, I have made such a muddle of this. The truth is, we made the wager, and then Rochford chose the woman. When he picked you, I was greatly relieved, for I had thought he was going to give me one of your cousins, and that would have been a formidable task, indeed. I am not sure why he chose you, other than that you were so clearly relegated to the background by your aunt and cousins that he must have been sure that I would get no help from them in bringing you out."

"That is certainly true." Constance could not keep the bitterness from her voice.

"My dearest Constance—I hope you will not mind if I call you that." Francesca slipped her gloved hand into Constance's and squeezed it gently. "I knew at once that he had foolishly chosen the easiest of you to turn into a *belle.* It is very difficult to give a person wit or beauty when they have none. But a want of fortune is not the hardest thing to overcome, at least when it is accompanied by style, intelligence, and a lovely face and figure."

"I will not let you get around me with flattery," Constance warned her, but in truth she found it difficult to dislike Lady Haughston. The woman was disarmingly candid, and her smile was hard to resist.

"I am not trying to get around you," Francesca assured her.

"Then what do you want?" Constance asked bluntly.

"I am suggesting that you and I join forces. We shall work together to find you a husband."

"You want me to help you win the bet?" Constance's voice was incredulous.

"No. Well, I mean, yes, I do, but that is not why *you* would wish to help me."

"I *don't* wish to help you," Constance pointed out.

"Ah, but you should. I might win a bet, but the advantages for you are far greater."

Constance looked at her skeptically. "You don't honestly expect me to believe that I will get a husband out of this."

"Why not?" Francesca replied calmly.

Constance wrinkled her nose. "I have little liking for listing my liabilities, but surely they must be obvious. I have no fortune. I am past the age of marrying and I am no beauty. I am here only to help my cousins achieve marriages. I am a chaperone, not a young girl on the marriage mart."

"A lack of fortune is an obstacle," the other woman agreed. "But it is certainly not impossible to overcome. As for your looks, well, if you took off that silly cap and dressed your hair attractively and wore something to show off your looks instead of hiding them, you would be a very attractive woman. You would also look scarcely older than your cousins. Tell me something, who decided that you should wear drab browns and grays and such?"

"My aunt felt it would be more appropriate for a spinster. She did not make me dress so."

"But you, of course, are under obligation to her, as you live with them."

"Yes, but…it is not only that. I do not wish to appear foolish, either."

"Foolish? Why?"

Constance shrugged. "I am used to living in the country. I have no town bronze. Indeed, I have never even been to London before. I have no desire to make a misstep before all the Ton. To embarrass myself by dressing in something unsuitable for a woman of my age."

Lady Haughston's face assumed an expression befitting a woman with generations of earls behind her. "My dear Constance, if you dress according to my guidance, I assure you that no one would think you appeared in any way unsuitable."

Constance could not hold back a chuckle. "I am sure not, Francesca. But the truth is, I have given up hope of marrying."

"Do you want to spend the rest of your life with your aunt and uncle?" Francesca asked. "I am sure you are quite grateful to them, but I do not think that you are…very happy with them."

Constance cast her a rueful look. "It is that obvious?"

"The differences between you are clear," Francesca told her flatly. "One could hardly expect to live a happy life with people with whom one has so few traits in common. Nor can I think that your aunt and uncle have done well by you. You told me last night that you did not have your come-out because of your father's illness. That was a good and properly filial thing to do. But when your father passed on and you came to live with your aunt and uncle, how old were you?"

"Twenty-two. Too old for my coming out."

"Not too old to have a Season," Francesca retorted. "Had they done the right thing by you, they would have given you a Season. I am sure it is what your father would have wanted, and it is what you deserved. Oh, yes, I know, you were older than the silly little seventeen- and eighteen-year-old girls being presented to the Queen. But, really, it isn't necessary to have the presentation. Many do not. You could have had a Season.

There are still a number of girls who are unmarried at that age. I know I should not malign your relatives, but I must tell you that I think your aunt and uncle acted selfishly. They saved themselves the expense of a Season, and they kept you at their beck and call for the past few years. Looking after their children, no doubt, and running errands for them. Doing the little things that no one else wanted to do. Now instead of letting you enjoy yourself at these parties, your aunt has forced you into the role of chaperone, making you wear dull clothes and dull hair."

She cast a shrewd look at Constance and added, "Of course, she would want you looking as plain as possible. You outshine her daughters as it is."

Constance stirred uncomfortably in her seat. Lady Haughston's description of her life with Aunt Blanche was uncannily accurate. Constance herself had thought the same things many times. Aunt Blanche had used Constance's sense of duty and obligation toward her, taking advantage in countless ways of her gratitude and her good nature.

"You cannot want to spend the rest of your life with them," Francesca said, pressing her advantage. "Besides, you seem to me to be a rather independently minded young woman. Do you not wish for your own house, your own life? A husband and children?"

Constance's thoughts turned to that brief time, many years ago, with Gareth, when she had let herself believe, at least for a little while, that such a life might be hers.

"I have never wanted to marry just to achieve a position in life," Constance told her quietly. "Perhaps you will think me foolish, but I would like to marry for love."

Constance could not read the look in Lady Haughston's eyes as she regarded her. "I hope you do find love," she said gravely. "But whether one loves or not, marriage gives a woman independence. You will have a place in life, a status that one can never find even in the happiest of situations, living with loving and wealthy parents. There is certainly no comparison to living under the thumb of a selfish and demanding relative."

"I know," Constance answered quietly. She knew, she thought, better than the lovely Lady Haughston, the facts of such a life. "But I cannot tie myself to a man for life without love."

Francesca glanced away. Finally, after a long moment, she said lightly, "Well, surely, there is no reason to believe that one cannot find a husband one loves during the Season. No one will force you to marry any man who asks you. But would you not like to have the chance? Don't you think it is only fair for you to taste some of what you missed?"

Her words struck a chord with Constance. She had stayed with her father through his years of illness, and she had done her best not to pine for what might have been. But she could not deny that there had been times when she had wondered what would have happened if she had been able to have even one London Season. She could not help but yearn to experience a little of the glamour and excitement herself.

Francesca, seeing Constance's hesitation, pressed her argument. "Would you not like to have a Season? To wear pretty dresses and flirt with your beaux? To dance with the most eligible bachelors in England?"

Constance's thoughts went to Viscount Leighton. What would it be like to have a chance to flirt with him? To dance with him? She wanted, quite badly, to meet him again, this time wearing something pretty, her hair falling about her face in curls.

"But how can I have a Season?" she asked. "I am here to act as chaperone. And my clothes…"

"Leave it all to me. I will make sure that you receive invitations to the right parties. I will be there to guide you through the treacherous waters of the Ton. I will make you the most sought-after woman in London."

Constance chuckled. "I do not think that I could be made into such a creature, no matter what your efforts."

Francesca cast her another haughty look. "You doubt my ability?"

Constance could not imagine even Francesca pulling off what she promised. But if anyone could do it, she supposed, it would be Lady Haughston. And even if she did not make her the most popular *belle* of London, Constance had little doubt that she would enable Constance to have a far better taste of a real Season than what she was experiencing now. Aunt Blanche would dislike it, of course. That thought gave Constance a wicked little spurt of amusement.

"I will deal with your aunt," Francesca went on, as if guessing Constance's thoughts. "She, I think, will not complain. Your family will, after all, receive the same invitations. And she will not want to go against me. If I choose you as my special friend, I do not think she will fight it. As for the clothes, you may not believe it, but I am rather good at economizing. We will look over your dresses and see what we can add to make them more attractive. The gown you wore last night, for instance—a slightly lower neckline, a bit of lace and it will do well enough. My maid Maisie is a wonder with a needle. She could raise it in the front and add an underskirt. We would just have to buy some material. I will send my carriage for you tomorrow, and you must bring your best dresses with you. We will go over your things and see what can be done, and I will see what dresses of mine we can use."

Constance felt excitement starting to bubble up in her. She thought of her small hoard of money. She had saved as much as she could every year from the income left her by her father, hoping one day to increase her principal enough that she would be able to live off it, no longer dependent on her aunt and uncle for a place to live.

She could use some of that money, she thought, to buy a pretty gown or two. Something that would bring a man—someone like Lord Leighton, say—rushing to her side from across the room. So what if it meant that she had to spend a few more months, even years, scrimping and scraping her money together? She might have to live with her aunt and uncle for longer than she'd hoped, but at least she would have had a wonderful summer to remember, a time that she could look back on and treasure always. A season of fun and excitement, memories that she could keep forever.

Constance turned to Francesca. "Would you really do all this just to win a bet?"

Francesca's lips curved up in that little catlike smile, her eyes glinting. "This is more than simply a bet. It is with a gentleman I most particularly want to prove wrong. Besides, it will be fun. I have helped a young girl or two through their first Seasons. They ended up engaged, as well, before long. But with you..."

"It is more of a challenge?" Constance asked, smiling to take the sting out of her words.

"In a way, because with them I had free rein to spend any amount of money for gowns and balls and such. But then I had to worry so much about covering up this problem or that—dresses that brightened a sallow complexion or how to make a short, squat girl look taller and more willowy. With you, that aspect is much easier. We just need to show off what is already there." She leaned a little closer. "Will you do it, then?"

Constance hesitated for a moment, then took a breath. "Yes. Yes, I want to have a real Season."

Francesca grinned. "Wonderful. Then let us begin."

CONSTANCE SPENT THE REST of the day in what was, for her, an absolute orgy of shopping. To Constance's surprise, Lady Haughston turned out to be quite skillful at shopping for bargains. It took only her smile and a few words to her favorite modiste to have the woman quickly lowering her price on the dresses in which Constance was most interested. Mlle du Plessis also brought out a ball gown that had been ordered but never picked up or paid for, and which she was willing to sell to Constance for only a fraction of its original price.

When Constance quietly commented with surprise on the modiste's willingness to discount her goods, Francesca merely smiled and replied, "Mademoiselle's well aware of how much good it does her to have her wares shown on an excellent figure. It makes those less fortunately endowed believe that if they wear Mademoiselle's dresses, they will look as tall and willowy in them as you do. Besides, she values my patronage. Now...this shawl. It is lovely, is it not? And look at this little flaw. I am sure Mademoiselle will reduce the price for that."

Even at the discounted prices, the things that she bought at Mlle Du Plessis's put a serious dent in Constance's savings, so they moved on to less expensive means of supplementing her wardrobe. Their next stop was Grafton House, where they purchased laces, ribbons, buttons and such to enliven the dresses Constance already owned, as well as several yards of cambric and muslin from which, Francesca assured her, a talented seamstress whom she knew could whip up several quite respectable and attractive day dresses. There were, as well, gloves and dancing slippers to be bought, and they also made a stop at a fan shop, where they spent a good many minutes admiring a variety of fans before Constance reluctantly decided that the prices were too dear, and she would simply have to make do with the ivory-handled fan she already owned. Last, but certainly not least in importance, there were hair ornaments to be purchased, not to mention adornments such as silk flowers or a cluster of wooden cherries with which to brighten a plain, inexpensive bonnet.

By the time they finished late in the afternoon, Constance was exhausted but almost giddy with excitement. She could hardly wait to get home and go through all her purchases again.

"I feel positively decadent," she told Francesca, smiling, as they left the shop and started toward their carriage. "I have never splurged so."

"You should do it more often," Francesca counseled, grinning. "I find that splurging is a wonderful restorative for the soul. I make sure to do it frequently."

The coachman took Constance's most recent purchase from her and stowed it up on the seat where he rode, for they had already filled up the rack behind the coach and had even taken up a good portion of the space inside the barouche. Francesca took his proffered hand and started up the step into the carriage when a masculine voice rang out behind them.

"Francesca!"

Lady Haughston paused in midstep and turned toward the voice. Her face lit up, and she smiled in welcome. "Dominic!"

"Francesca, my dear. Buying out Oxford Street again?"

Constance turned to the man who was walking toward them, sweeping off his hat and reaching out to take Francesca's hand. He smiled down warmly at Lady Haughston, affection evident in his handsome face.

Constance stared, surprised. He loves her, she thought, aware of a sinking feeling of regret.

"Apparently it is the only way I can see you," Francesca laughed. "Since you never call on me. You are the rudest man alive."

He chuckled. "I am incorrigible, I know. I detest paying calls."

"There is someone I want you meet," Francesca told him, turning toward Constance.

The man followed her gaze, and his eyes widened when they fell on Constance. "Miss Woodley!"

"Lord Leighton."

CHAPTER FOUR

"YOU KNOW EACH other?" Francesca asked, astonished.

"We met last night," Constance told her, hoping that she sounded more natural than she felt. It was absurd that her spirits should be so lowered by the fact that Viscount Leighton and Lady Haughston were clearly close. It was not as if she had actually thought she had any chance of attracting him. Anyway, he was clearly something of a rake, going about stealing kisses from young ladies whom he scarcely knew.

"Miss Woodley is too modest," Leighton said, his blue eyes alight with amusement. "She saved my life last night at Lady Welcombe's rout."

"Hardly that," Constance murmured.

"Ah, but you did," he insisted, turning toward Francesca and explaining. "Lady Taffington was in hot pursuit of me last night, and Miss Woodley was so kind as to throw her off the scent."

Francesca chuckled. "Then I am doubly your friend, Constance. I fear my brother is often in need of such aid. He is entirely too softhearted and cannot bear to be rude. You should take lessons from Rochford, Dom. He is an expert at damping pretensions."

Constance scarcely heard Lord Leighton's reply to Lady Haughston's jest. *The Viscount was Francesca's brother!* She told herself that it was absurd to be swept with relief upon learning of their relation. It could make no difference to her that the familiarity and affection between Lord Leighton and Francesca came from family ties, not a romantic understanding.

"Come with us," Francesca urged her brother. "We are done with our shopping, so you needn't worry about being dragged into any stores."

"In that case, I will accept your kind offer," Leighton answered, extending his hand to help his sister up into the coach.

He then turned to Constance, offering her the same assistance. She slid her hand into his, very aware of his touch, even though their flesh was separated by both his gloves and hers. She glanced up into his face as she stepped up into the carriage. She could not help but remember that moment in the library when he had kissed her, and something in his eyes told Constance that he was thinking of it, too.

Heat rose in her cheeks, and she glanced away from him, quickly getting in and sitting down beside Francesca. Leighton climbed in and dropped into the seat across from them, laughingly shoving aside the profusion of boxes.

"I can see that you have had a successful afternoon," he told them. "I trust that not all of these belong to you, Francesca."

"No, indeed. Miss Woodley made a good accounting for herself, as well. We intend to dazzle everyone at Lady Simmington's ball tomorrow evening."

"I am sure that both of you will do that in any case," Leighton responded gallantly.

Constance was painfully aware of how plain she must look beside Francesca's elegant loveliness. She wished that she had put on her newly purchased bonnet for the remainder of their shopping trip and relegated her old hat to the box. At least then, however dull her dress might be, her face would have been becomingly framed, the blue satin lining complementing her skin and eyes.

"Are you attending Lady Simmington's ball?" Francesca went on. "You should escort us. Constance is to come to my house tomorrow to prepare for it, and then we shall go together."

"That would be a pleasant duty indeed," Leighton responded easily. "I would be honored to escort you."

"We shall guard you from matchmaking mamas," Francesca teased.

Leighton answered her back in the same light vein, and their banter continued as the carriage made its slow way through the streets of London. Constance contributed little to the conversation. She knew few of the people of whom they spoke, and she was, in any case, quite content to watch and listen.

She had thought that perhaps she had remembered the viscount as handsomer than he actually was, that, in thinking about him, she had made his eyes a deeper blue or added a brightness to his hair or infused his smile with more charm. But, looking at him now, she thought that she had, if anything, imagined him less handsome than the reality.

He was not one who needed the soft glow of candlelight. Here in the bright light of daytime, his jawline was sharp and clean, his eyes an arrestingly dark blue, his hair glinting under the touch of the sun. Tall and broad-shouldered, he filled the barouche with his masculine presence. Constance was very aware of his knee only inches from hers, of his arm resting on the seat of the barouche, of the way the sun slanted across his face and neck.

It was not, she thought, surprising if matchmaking mothers—and daughters—were in pursuit of him. He was handsome and titled and no doubt wealthy, as well. If she remembered correctly what her aunt had said about Lady Haughston's background, their father was an earl, and as viscount was typically a title given to the heir to the earldom, then he would someday possess the greater title of earl. For that title alone, he would have been sought after. To have good looks and charm, as well, must make him hunted like hounds after a hare.

It was all the more impossible, of course, that she

should have any chance with him. Even if Francesca were right in her optimistic assumption that Constance could find a husband this Season, she knew that her patroness doubtless aimed lower than a title for her. And Lord Leighton's kiss, however wonderful she had found it, was not anything on which Constance would be foolish enough to build her hopes. It had meant nothing to him, she was sure. At best it had shown that he was attracted to her; at worst that he simply was in the habit of kissing any young woman he caught alone. It did not mean that he had any serious interest in her; indeed, in all likelihood, it meant precisely the opposite. A gentleman, after all, did not make improper advances to a woman whom he would consider marrying. He made them to women he would not marry, but only dally with.

Of course, she had no intention of dallying with him. But a little light flirtation...now that was a different matter.

Constance turned her head toward the window to hide the secret smile that curved her lips. She was quite looking forward to tomorrow, she thought. It would be pleasant, indeed, to face Lord Leighton looking, for once, at her best.

The carriage rolled to a stop in front of a spacious redbrick house, and Leighton glanced out the window. "Ah, here we are." He opened the door and stepped down, then leaned back in to say, "Thank you for a most enjoyable ride." He made a general bow toward them. "I look forward to seeing you tomorrow evening." His eyes went to Constance and he added, "I am very glad to have found you again, Miss Woodley. Promise you will give the first waltz to no one but me."

Constance smiled back at him. It would be hard, she thought, not to return his smile. "I will."

"Then I will bid you goodbye." He closed the door and stepped back, and the carriage began to roll again.

"Your brother is a very personable man," Constance said after a moment.

"Yes." Francesca smiled fondly. "It is easy to like Dominic. But there is more to him than people assume. He fought in the Peninsula."

"Really?" Constance looked at Francesca in surprise. "He was in the army?" It was an uncommon venture for the eldest son, the heir to the estate.

Francesca nodded. "Yes. The Hussars. He was wounded, in fact. But fortunately, he survived. And then, of course, when Terence died and Dom became the heir, he had to sell out. I think he misses it."

Constance nodded, understanding now. It was common for younger sons to enter the military, or the diplomatic corps or the church, but if the oldest son died and the younger one became the heir, his future would change. He would one day inherit all the wealth and responsibilities of the estate, and the career he had been engaged on would have to be put aside. Besides, it would not do to have the heir to an estate risking his life in a war. Among noble families, the inheritance was all.

"And so now that he is the heir, he is fair game for all the marriageable young ladies."

Francesca chuckled. "Yes, poor boy. He does not enjoy it, I can tell you. I suppose there are men who thrive upon that sort of popularity, but not Dom. Of course, he will have to marry someday, but I suspect he will put it off as long as he can. He is a bit of a flirt."

Constance wondered if Francesca was giving her a subtle warning about her brother, telling Constance, in essence, not to endanger her heart with him. She looked at the other woman, but she could see nothing in Francesca's lovely face to indicate any hidden meaning. Still, Constance did not need a warning. She was well aware that a man of Lord Leighton's standing would not marry someone like her.

But, Constance told herself, as long as she was aware of that, as long as she knew not to give her heart to him, there would be nothing wrong in flirting a little with the man. She could dance with him, laugh with him, let herself have a little fun. And, after all, that was all she could reasonably expect from this Season.

When they reached the house that her aunt and uncle were leasing, Lady Haughston went inside with Constance. Aunt Blanche goggled at the sight of Lady Haughston's coachman bringing in a number of boxes, with Constance carrying several more and even Lady Haughston herself helping out with the last few bags.

"My lady! Oh, my goodness. Annie, come here and take these things from her ladyship. What—" Aunt Blanche stumbled to a halt, looking from her niece to Lady Haughston in befuddlement.

"We haven't bought out all the stores, Lady Woodley," Francesca assured her gaily. "However, I do think that your niece and I put something of a hole in Oxford Street's wares."

"Constance?" Aunt Blanche repeated. "You bought all this?"

"Yes," Constance replied. "Lady Haughston assured me that my wardrobe was sadly lacking."

"Constance!" Francesca exclaimed, laughing. "I never said such a thing. You will have your aunt thinking that I am the most lack-mannered woman imaginable. I merely suggested that you add a few things here and there."

Francesca turned toward Lady Woodley. "I find that girls rarely realize how many frocks they need for a Season. Don't you agree?"

As she expected, Lady Woodley nodded her head, not daring to disagree with one of the foremost members of the Ton. "Yes, but I—well, Constance, this is a little unexpected."

"Yes, I know. But I am sure I have enough room in my dresser for everything. And Lady Haughston has kindly agreed to help me sort through my gowns and decide what to do with them."

At the news that one of the most elegant and highborn ladies in the land was going to be upstairs in her niece's tiny room rummaging through her small store of decidedly ordinary dresses, Lady Woodley appeared torn between elation and embarrassment.

"But, my lady, surely… I mean, Constance should not have asked such a thing of you," she said finally, stumbling over her words.

"Oh, she did not ask me," Francesca assured her. "I volunteered. There is little I like more than dressing up one's wardrobe. It is such a challenge, don't you think?"

She swept up the stairs behind Constance, with Lady Woodley following them, babbling offers of tea and other refreshment, interspersed with admonitions to Constance not to impose on Lady Haughston.

At the door to Constance's room, Aunt Blanche hesitated. The little room, barely large enough for the dresser, bed and chair that occupied it, seemed even smaller now with the piles of boxes and bags. There was hardly enough room for the three of them, as well, yet Lady Woodley clearly hated to leave Lady Haughston.

So she hovered by the door, looking uncomfortable and chattering on, while Francesca and Constance pulled out Constance's dresses and laid them out on the bed.

"Such a small number of gowns, my love," Aunt Blanche tittered. "I told you that you should bring more to Town. But, of course, a girl never foresees how very many gowns one will need." She turned toward Francesca with a confidential look that suggested that the two of them were old hands at the social whirl. "And, of course, Constance is merely chaperoning the girls."

"But what nonsense," Lady Haughston said briskly. "Constance is much too young to be a chaperone…as no doubt you told her."

"Oh, my, yes, of course!" Aunt Blanche exclaimed. "But what can one do? Constance's nature is rather retiring, and she is, after all, well past the age of coming out herself."

Francesca made a noise of disdain. "There are a good many years before Constance reaches that point. One has only to look at her to see how ridiculous it is to place an arbitrary age on a girl's come-out. Some women are far more beautiful at this age than they were when they left the schoolroom. You have noticed that yourself, I am sure."

"Well…" Aunt Blanche trailed off uncertainly. She could scarcely disagree with Lady Haughston's pronouncements, especially given the way she so graciously linked Aunt Blanche's thoughts with her own.

Lady Woodley watched as Francesca and Constance matched up ribbons and lace to some dresses and discarded others as unfit for anything but the most mundane daily wear, and talked of lowering necklines and adding overskirts or demi-trains, of replacing dull sleeves with others slashed with contrasting color.

Constance, too, had experienced a certain embarrassment at exposing her unimpressive wardrobe to Lady Haughston, but Francesca's manner could not have been more matter-of-fact or uncritical. Her eye for color and style was unerring, which did not surprise Constance. One need not look at her long to realize that she was an artist when it came to clothes. But Constance did find it rather peculiar that someone like Lady Haughston should be so conversant with ways to modify, update and generally renew one's wardrobe. It was as odd as her knowing where to buy ribbons, lace and other accessories at the best prices. Constance could not help but wonder if Lady Haughston might not suffer from something of a lack of funds herself. She had heard no rumors to that effect, of course, but clearly Francesca was quite adept at hiding such a thing, at least in regard to one's wardrobe.

Before long, Georgiana and her sister drifted down the hall and stood with their mother, looking awestruck as they watched Francesca bustle about the little room. When, finally, Francesca left, reminding Constance that she was to come to her house the following afternoon before the ball, the two girls turned to their mother, their voices rising in a wail.

"Why is *she* going to Lady Haughston's?" Georgiana cast a disparaging glance toward Constance. "Why can't we go, too?"

"I am going because Lady Haughston asked me," Constance told her calmly, refraining from pointing out the obvious corollary that Georgiana and Margaret were not going because Lady Haughston had *not* invited them.

"I know that," Georgiana snapped. "But why? Why does she want you there? Why did she take you out today?"

Constance shrugged. She was not about to tell her relatives of Francesca's plans for her.

"And how did you buy all these things?" Margaret added, looking at the dresses and adornments scattered all over the bed."

"I used money I'd been saving."

"Yes, well, if you have so much money, you might have thought to help us a little," Aunt Blanche sniffed. "We have been giving you a roof over your head and food to eat for the past six years."

"Aunt Blanche! You know I give you money every month!" Constance cried. "And I always pay for my clothes and personal items."

Her aunt shrugged, as though Constance's argument had nothing to do with what she had said. "I cannot see why Lady Haughston has such a preference for you. It is most inexplicable. Why does she not ask to take out Georgiana?"

"What about me?" Margaret asked indignantly.

"I am the eldest," Georgiana told her sister haughtily.

The two girls began to squabble, and Constance turned away to begin to fold and put away the things that now lay all over her bed. After a few minutes, her aunt and cousins moved out of her room, continuing their conversation in the more comfortable arena of the sitting room.

But the subject did not die. Georgiana and Margaret brought it up again at the dinner table, until finally their normally lax and imperturbable father snapped at them to be quiet. The two girls lapsed into a sullen pout, but they took up their grievances again as soon as their father had retired to his port after dinner. Their mother, of course, agreed with them that it was neither right nor fair that they had not been taken under Lady Haughston's wing instead of Constance. Constance retired early, claiming a headache—which was indeed the truth, after listening to the other women harp on the subject of Lady Haughston all evening. The next day she stayed to herself as much as possible, working quietly in her room on the various small things that she and Francesca had determined could be done to her dresses. The larger alterations, of course, she would have to take with her to Lady Haughston's for the more skilled hands of Francesca's maid.

Constance even considered foregoing her luncheon. Sir Roger always went to his club during the day, so there would be no one to put a stop to Georgiana's and Margaret's complaints. Their mother rarely reined them in, and in any case, Constance knew that Aunt Blanche also disliked the fact that Lady Haughston preferred Constance to the rest of them. Her worst fear was that Aunt Blanche would forbid her to go to Francesca's house, even though it would clearly work against her own best interests. Aunt Blanche was often as slow-witted as her daughters, and much more stubborn.

However, Constance reasoned that if she did not show up for the meal, her aunt would decide that she was feeling ill and should not go either to Lady Haughston's or to the ball this evening. So she went downstairs, vowing to keep a rein on her tongue and her temper, an ability that was often sorely tested by her cousins and aunt.

Just as she had feared, Georgiana and Margaret started in on what they saw as injustice before they even sat down at the table. Constance did her best to disregard them, but she could not ignore it when her aunt at last said to her, "Constance, I am thinking that, if the matter is going to cause this much dissension and misery in the house, perhaps you should not go to Lady Haughston's this afternoon."

Constance looked at her, trying to hide her alarm, and pondered briefly what would be the best tack to take with her aunt. "I should not like to offend Lady Haughston, Aunt. She is very powerful in the Ton, and she seemed most adamant about my joining her this afternoon."

"Yes, well, I am sure that she would understand if

you sent her a note telling her that you were feeling a trifle under the weather and could not come." Lady Woodley's face brightened. "In fact, the girls and I could call on her and deliver your regrets personally." She nodded, looking pleased with herself. "Yes, that might be best."

Anger flared up in her, but Constance firmly thrust it down. "But I am not feeling at all ill, and I should like to go to Lady Haughston's this afternoon," she replied calmly. "And I am not sure whether she would like anyone else to go to her house, uninvited."

Her aunt's eyebrows shot up. "She has called here. That makes it perfectly acceptable for me to call on her."

"She will not like it if I do not come," Constance told her aunt firmly. "She might very well retract the invitation to Lady Simmington's ball tonight if she is displeased."

"She can hardly expect you to come to her house if you are ill." Aunt Blanche looked at her, her eyes hard.

"I am not ill." Constance looked back at her, making her gaze as obdurate as she was able.

"Lady Haughston will not know that," her aunt reasoned.

"Yes, she will," Constance replied flatly.

Her aunt's eyes opened wider in surprise. It was a moment before she could speak. "Are you— Do you defy me?"

"I intend to go to Lady Haughston's this afternoon,"

Constance replied calmly. "I do not wish to defy you, of course. Therefore, I do hope that you will not forbid me to go."

If possible, Aunt Blanche looked even more astounded. She gasped, then opened and closed her mouth without saying anything, looking remarkably like a fish.

Constance took advantage of her aunt's momentary speechlessness to lean forward and say earnestly, "Lady Haughston is very important. Her father is an earl. She is friends with the Duke of Rochford. She can do much for you and the girls, as you well know. But it would be equally ruinous for you to cross her. Pray, however angry you may feel at me, do not offend Francesca."

Her aunt had been swelling with ill-feeling during Constance's words, and Constance knew that she wanted to break into a long, loud tirade against her niece. But even as she opened her mouth, something flickered in her eyes, some bit of reason or caution, and she closed her mouth.

"Francesca?" she said at last. "She gave you the use of her first name?"

Constance nodded. She had spoken Francesca's given name deliberately, for the use of it indicated a close relationship. She was glad to see that her aunt had noticed that fact.

"Please," Constance said. "I know you do not like this. But think about the ball tonight. Think about telling your friend Mrs. Merton what Lady Haughston said to you when she called on you yesterday. Then think about not being able to say such things in the future."

"You ungrateful wretch," Aunt Blanche spat at her. "After all that I have done for you!"

"I am well aware of all that you have done for me, and I have told Lady Haughston about it. I have no desire to be on bad terms with you." Constance forced herself to keep her voice firm, and her gaze equally calm and unyielding. She had often yielded to Aunt Blanche out of a sense of obligation and a desire to live in peace. But this time she was determined not to bend, even if it meant coming to a complete break with her aunt. She was discovering that she wanted this Season very much. "I am sure that Lady Haughston's friendship will not last past this Season, and then our lives will return to normal. But think of how much you can accomplish for your daughters in the next few months, if only none of us act foolishly."

Aunt Blanche's nostrils widened, her lips thinning with fury, and for a moment Constance was afraid that her aunt would be unable to control herself. But after a moment the older woman swallowed hard, unclenched her fists and let out a long breath. Turning back to her food, she said in a cold voice, "Naturally, I would not stop you from going to Lady Haughston's this afternoon, despite your insolence toward me. I shudder to think how your poor dear father would have felt had he seen you address me in this manner."

As Constance was well aware that her "poor, dear father" had disliked his sister-in-law intensely and thought up any excuse to be absent when she came to visit, Constance rather thought that he would have applauded her actions. However, she refrained from saying so to her aunt and merely finished her food as quickly as she could, aware of her cousins' amazed gazes upon her. As soon as she was done, she asked to be excused and was granted her request in frosty tones.

She fled upstairs, where she put the dresses for Francesca's maid to redo into some of the boxes and bags that she had brought home the day before. Then she sat down to wait for the Haughston carriage. Fortunately, she did not have to wait long before Jenny, the downstairs maid, knocked on her door and announced with some awe that a grand carriage waited for her in the street.

Constance forced herself to stop and bid her aunt and cousins a pleasant goodbye. She was met with three silent, furious stares. Obviously, she thought, it would take some time to mend her relationship with them. Still, she could not regret what she had done, no matter how chill the air might be around the household for the next few weeks.

It was no surprise that Haughston House, an elegant white stone mansion in the classic Palladian style, lay in the center of Mayfair, that most fashionable of London districts. Constance, stepping out of the carriage and gazing at the imposing black iron fence railings and the enormous house beyond them, felt rather daunted. It was easy to forget when one was with Francesca that she was a descendant of men and women who had moved among kings and princes—as well as the widow of a man from another such family.

She wondered for a moment about the man who had been Francesca's husband. Francesca had not mentioned him to Constance, even when they were talking about marriage and love. Constance was not sure exactly what that meant. She knew that the man had died several years ago, and that Francesca had never remarried. The romantic rumor was that she had loved Lord Haughston too much to ever marry another man. However, Constance thought that precisely the opposite might be true—that her first husband had given her a profound distaste for marriage.

Whatever anxiety the house inspired in Constance was erased, however, when Lady Haughston herself came sweeping down the staircase, hands extended in friendship. "Constance! Come up to my room. Maisie has worked her usual wonders. I cannot wait until you see."

A wave of her hand sent one of the footmen hurrying to take Constance's boxes, while Francesca herself took Constance's hand and led her up the wide, curved staircase to the floor above.

"You have a lovely home," Constance told her admiringly.

"Yes. Lady Haughston—my husband's mother, that is—had excellent taste. The decoration is all owing to her. Had it been left to the old Lord Haughston, I am afraid it would have been all hunting scenes and enormous dark Jacobean furniture." She gave an exaggerated shudder. "Of course, it is far too enormous to keep up. I have the east wing entirely closed off." She waved vaguely toward the other side of the stairs.

She led Constance into her bedroom, a large and pleasant room overlooking a quiet back garden. With windows on two sides, it was filled with light and soft summer air. It was femininely decorated without being fussy, the furniture elegant and graceful, and there was ample room to move around in it, for Francesca had eschewed the habit many matrons had of stuffing as many pieces as possible into every space.

A neatly dressed maid was waiting for them, a blue gown laid out on the bed beside her. She turned and bobbed a curtsey toward Constance and Francesca.

"Oh, excellent, Maisie," Francesca said, moving forward to look at the dress. "Constance, come see. This is the dress I was telling you about. Maisie has already changed it. She took off that ruffle with the Vandykes." She pointed to a swath of material on which were sewn dark blue triangular shapes. "And she took off the sleeves—they were long. And, of course, the matching band of Vandykes around the bottom of the bodice. Then she made an overdress of lighter blue voile and the little puffed sleeves—it is a younger look, I think, more suitable for you."

"Now, if you'll just try it on, miss," Maisie told Constance, "I can see how deep a band of lace we need at the hem."

"It's beautiful," Constance told her, entranced by the frothy confection.

With Maisie's help, she took off the dress she was wearing and put on the one that the maid had redone. She turned to look into the mirror as Maisie fastened the buttons up the back and drew in a quick breath at the sight of herself. She looked younger and prettier. Constance beamed, unaware of how much of the youth and beauty she saw in the mirror was due to the happiness that glowed in her face.

"It's perfect. Oh, Lady—Francesca, I cannot begin to thank you enough."

Francesca clapped her hands in delight. "There is no need. The way you look is reward enough. I knew that dress would be exactly right for you. Did I not tell you that Maisie was a genius with a needle?"

"Indeed, you were right." Constance could not resist looking at her image in the glass as Maisie knelt, pinning on the wide band of lace around the bottom.

The blue did wonderful things for her eyes and her skin, and her breasts pushed up over the deep scoop of the neckline in a way that would have been, perhaps, too provocative, had it not been for the demure trim of blond lace and the almost girlish look of the small puff sleeves.

"A very simple little something around your neck, I think," Francesca said, studying her. "A locket, say. And I have a shawl that will look perfect with that." When Constance began to protest, she shook her head firmly, saying, "I will lend it to you, and that will make it perfectly all right, won't it?"

When Maisie had finished pinning the dress, Constance and Francesca laid out the clothes that Constance had brought over and discussed with the maid their plans for altering them, bringing out the materials they had bought the day before. They spent the rest of the afternoon cheerfully discussing hems and necklines and overdresses and petticoats. Then Maisie left to finish her work on the dress that Constance would wear that evening, and Constance and Francesca settled down to cut the narrow blue ribbon they had bought the day before into pieces and make tiny bows for Maisie to sew on at regular intervals around the deep lace ruffle.

They took time out for tea, which they had in the shade in the pleasant little garden in back, then went back inside to begin their preparations for the party. They chatted and laughed as Maisie helped them into their clothes and did their hair. Constance could not remember when she had enjoyed herself so much. This, she thought, must be what it was like to have a sister—or what it might be like getting ready with her cousins if she did not spend all her time helping them into their clothes or putting up their hair or finding their lost gloves and fans.

Then, at last, Maisie was done and they were ready. As Francesca beamed at her like a proud mother, Constance went to the mirror for one last look at herself.

"Oh, my." She could not hold back the soft exclamation.

Her hair was pulled up and caught in a cluster of curls, and feathery wisps curled softly around her face. Her dark brown tresses gleamed in the soft glow of the candles, warm and lustrous, the red highlights catching the light. The spray of tiny blue silk rosebuds that Francesca had bought for her the day before was pinned into her hair at the base of the cluster of curls.

The blue dress fitted her perfectly, the bodice cupping her breasts, then falling from the high waist in graceful folds that swayed with her movements as she walked. Excitement stained her cheeks with color and glowed in her large gray eyes. She knew that she had never looked lovelier.

"Ah, I think I hear Dom's voice downstairs," Francesca said, and they left the room, walking down the curved staircase together.

Lord Leighton stood in the entryway at the foot of

the staircase, and he turned at the sound of their approach, looking up the stairs. He stiffened, and his eyes widened as he saw Constance.

Unconsciously, he took a step closer, and the slightly stunned expression on his face was everything that Constance could have hoped for.

"Miss Woodley," he said, recovering himself and sweeping her a bow. "You take my breath away."

Francesca laughed and said lightly, "Watch out for this one, Constance. He can charm the birds from the trees."

"I am well aware that he is a terrible flatterer," Constance replied in the same light vein.

"You wrong me, both of you," Leighton retorted, taking the hand his sister held out and bowing over it, then doing the same with Constance. A thrill sizzled through her at the brush of his lips against her hand, even through the cloth of her glove.

She could feel the color rising higher in her cheeks. She stole a look at Dominic and found him gazing at her. There was a look in his dark blue eyes that set her heart thumping madly in her chest.

"Remember that you have promised the first dance to me, Miss Woodley," he said quietly.

"I would not forget, my lord," Constance replied, and swept out the door before him, anticipation swelling in her chest.

Tonight, she thought, unsure whether her words were of prayer or dread, was the start of a different life.

CHAPTER FIVE

CONSTANCE WAS VERY AWARE of Leighton's hand around hers as he helped her up into the carriage. He was watching her, she knew, despite the dimness of the light, as the coach rolled away from the house and started up the street.

"Are you going to Redfields next week, Dom?" Francesca asked.

The grimace he gave her in response did not indicate that that was a very likely prospect, Constance thought.

"Not if I can find anything better," he replied, adding, "And I shouldn't think that would be difficult."

"You should go. You have a duty to the estate, you know. Now that you are the heir."

He shrugged. "I doubt I will be missed."

"Of course you will be. Everyone always asks about you."

Leighton raised one eyebrow skeptically. "The earl and countess?"

Weren't the earl and countess Leighton's parents?

Constance wondered. It seemed odd that he should refer to them so formally. She supposed that he could be inheriting the estate from an uncle, but, no, she was certain that Francesca had said that Leighton had become the heir when their elder brother died. It did not, she thought, seem that there was much love lost between Dominic and his parents, especially given the fact that Francesca responded to his question with an uncomfortable silence.

Leighton sent his sister a faint twist of a smile. "I cannot imagine why you go, frankly."

"I have a dreary tendency to do what is expected of me."

"And you wish to make me do the same?" he asked lightly.

"No. I wish to make my own time there more lively," she told him, a grin dimpling her cheek. "You know Mother and Father invite the most dreadfully dull group of people. I merely attempt to liven it up."

Her eyes lit up, and she turned to Constance excitedly. "You must come with me."

Constance looked back at her, surprised. "To visit your parents?"

"It isn't just a family gathering," Francesca assured her. "They have a large party at Redfields every year. That's our country house. It's a huge, old rambling place, and they have dozens of guests."

"Our father and mother and a dreadfully dull guest

list hardly make it sound appealing, Francesca," her brother pointed out, grinning.

"Oh, but it won't be dull," Francesca told Constance earnestly. "You mustn't think that. I will make sure to invite a number of interesting people."

Her eyes were bright; one could almost see the thoughts spinning through her head. Constance had the suspicion that what Francesca meant by "interesting people" was marriageable men.

Her suspicion was confirmed when Francesca added, "It will be a perfect opportunity for you to meet people."

"But your parents do not even know me," Constance protested automatically, although the prospect of attending a country party was quite alluring.

"That won't matter. And there will be people you know. I will attend, and my friend, Sir Lucien Talbot. I will introduce you to him tonight. And Dominic will be there."

"I will?" he repeated, sounding amused.

"Yes, of course, you will. You have avoided them long enough. It is high time you went to visit them, and you know it. Far easier, don't you think, with a house full of people?"

"You may have a point."

Constance wondered what trouble lay between Lord Leighton and his parents. It sounded as though he had been avoiding them for some time, and she could not help but be curious about what manner of thing could have so separated his father from the heir.

Their barouche drew up behind a line of carriages that were disgorging their finely dressed occupants. Leighton stepped out and handed first his sister, then Constance, out of the carriage. A woman from another vehicle immediately swooped down upon Francesca, pulling her along as she talked animatedly.

Lord Leighton offered his arm to Constance, and they followed at a more leisurely pace. She hoped that the viscount could not feel the slight trembling of her fingers upon his arm. Being this near to him did funny things to her insides, she found, and her mind was peculiarly blank.

The silence grew, and Constance felt awkward. She cast about anxiously for something to say. "Will you go then to the party at Redfields?"

"Perhaps." She could feel his shrug. He looked down at her and smiled, a wicked light gleaming in his dark blue eyes. "If you will be there, the idea of going has much more appeal."

Constance felt a little breathless at his words, but she struggled to appear nonchalant. "I fear, sir, that you are a terrible flirt."

He chuckled. "You misjudge me, Miss Woodley."

She noticed that he had not actually denied her words, and that fact made her feel a little downcast. She told herself not to be foolish. It was clear what sort of man Lord Leighton was. She had known it from the moment he kissed her at the party the other night. Even his own sister had warned her of it, however lightly Francesca had said it.

But that was precisely what she wanted, after all—fun and flirtation. That was the purpose of her one Season. To dance and laugh and enjoy herself. Whatever Francesca thought, Constance did not intend to look for a husband. She wanted only to have something to remember.

They caught up with Francesca at the door to the Simmingtons mansion, and the other woman turned to them with relief, leaving her voluble companion. They joined a line of people snaking up the stairs and into the grand ballroom. Francesca and her brother were greeted by the people around them, and there was a steady stream of guests coming up to say hello before returning to their places in line. Constance was aware of the multitude of curious glances turned in her direction.

Francesca introduced her to a dizzying number of people. Constance was sure she would never be able to remember all the names. Francesca turned to her and leaned closer to whisper, "You are causing quite a stir tonight."

"I am?" Constance looked at her in surprise. She knew she had received a number of looks, but she had assumed that people were simply curious about why someone as unknown as she was with Lady Haughston and Lord Leighton.

"Oh, yes." Francesca nodded with a satisfied little

smile. "They are wondering who that beautiful woman is with us."

Constance chuckled. "I am sure not."

"It's the truth!" Francesca protested. "Why do you think so many people have felt the need to stop to say hello? They are all hoping to meet you."

Constance suspected that Francesca was exaggerating, but she could not help but feel a little pleased at her words.

"Ah, look, there is Lucien." Francesca waved to a man who had just entered the house.

He smiled and made his way over to them, pausing to chat with people on the way. He was, Constance thought, the epitome of the world-weary, fashionable gentleman, from the top of his brown locks, carefully styled in the Brutus fashion, to the tips of his black shoes made of butter-soft leather. His ascot was exquisitely tied; his suit jacket had been cut to fit him perfectly. And Constance was certain that everything on him, from the heavy onyx ring on his right hand to the silk stockings below his formal black breeches, had been chosen by him for just the right effect.

Francesca introduced him to Constance and he swept her an elegant bow. Next to Sir Lucien, Constance thought, Lord Leighton looked a trifle thrown together—his hair too long and unstyled, his long, strong fingers devoid of any ornamentation, his ascot tied in a simple manner, and his clothes, though of excellent cut and quality, not so perfectly coordinated as Sir Lucien's. But Constance could not help but prefer Leighton's unstudied masculine good looks and easy-going manner. Leighton was clearly not a man who spent much of his life in front of his mirror, and he seemed all the more compelling because of that.

"Well, Lady Simmington is living up to her reputation," Sir Lucien commented, casting a glance around them.

The house had been decorated beautifully, with garlands of ivy and ribbons twining up the banisters of the stairs, fragrant flowers nestled here and there among the leaves. Flowers were massed in colorful clumps in great urns at the top of the stairs, and everywhere candles blazed, burning in sconces along the walls and in chandeliers that hung from the ceiling, as well as in tall stands of candelabras. The glow of the candlelight caught on the jewels that glittered at the throats and wrists of the women, casting back their brilliance, and in its golden warmth, the colors of the gowns seemed deeper and richer and the lines softened. From the ballroom beyond came the strains of music rising above the babble of voices, faint and inviting.

"The cream of the Ton is here tonight," Sir Lucien went on. "Of course, no one dares not accept—people might think they were not invited."

At the top of the stairs, Lady Simmington bid them welcome in a grave way, as though she were bestowing an honor. Francesca introduced Constance to her, but Constance felt sure the woman barely heard her name as she smiled and regally gestured with her hand toward the ballroom, moving the line along.

"Is she always so…?" Constance struggled to think of the right word to describe Lady Simmington.

"Arrogant?" Leighton supplied with a smile.

Francesca and Lucien chuckled.

"Oh, no," Sir Lucien replied. "Sometimes she is far worse. Lady Honore was old Montbrook's youngest daughter."

"The Duke," Francesca elaborated.

"The old codger who sleeps in his chair at White's all day?" Leighton asked.

"I don't know about that, but he's marvelously old and deaf as a post, and I understand he still wears white wigs and shoes with diamond buckles," Francesca said.

"Yes. He looks as if he's about to be presented at Court every day," Leighton told her. "Must take him two hours to get dressed."

"My dear fellow," Lucien stuck in, "it takes *me* two hours to dress in the morning."

"Anyway, Lady Honore expected to marry a duke herself and was mightily disappointed that there were none available when it came time for her to come out. She had to settle for an earl, and I can tell you that she feels it was quite a comedown. Fortunately, however, Simmington is enormously wealthy, which allows her to spend as though she were a duchess—a royal duchess, even. So between those two things—her family line and Simmington's money—she is of the opinion that almost everyone in the Ton is beneath her. Although I believe she would admit that the Prince outranks her."

"Really?" Leighton countered. "I distinctly remember her referring to the royal family as those German upstarts."

Her attention only partially on her companions' conversation, Constance glanced around the enormous ballroom. It was far larger than the great hall in which Lady Welcombe had held her rout. Like the staircase and entryway, it was lavishly decorated with flowers, garlands and candles. Tall windows, framed with plush velvet drapes, lined one wall and chairs were placed along the opposite long wall. At the far end of the room, on a small raised platform, was a small orchestra. Overhead hung three large glass chandeliers, blazing with the reflected light of their candles. People were clustered around the edges of the room, talking and watching the dancers, while in the middle of the room, lines of dancers went through the opening quadrille.

Over by the wall of windows, Constance caught sight of her aunt and uncle and their daughters, looking awed. It was, she thought, quite different from the small assemblies and balls that she and her family were used to in the country. And none of the other parties they had attended since they moved to London had prepared them for this.

As Constance and her companions stood watching, the quadrille ended, and Lord Leighton turned to her. "I believe this dance was promised to me."

Her heart beating fast, Constance put her hand on his arm and walked with him out onto the dance floor as the orchestra struck up a waltz. Her stomach was clenched with nerves. She had danced the waltz before, but not often. Assemblies and balls in the country were more conservative than those in London, and the waltz was still regarded somewhat askance there. Certainly she had not danced it with anyone but men whom she had known since childhood. She was afraid that she would make a mistake, that she would slip or stumble or tread on Leighton's toe, and he would think her oafish.

He turned to face her, putting his hand on her waist and taking her other hand in his. Constance's mind went suddenly blank, and she realized that she had quite forgotten the steps. Then he swept her out onto the floor, and all thoughts and fears fell away. He moved with a grace and strength that was missing in most of Constance's usual partners, guiding her expertly about the floor. It felt heavenly and natural to be in his arms, and she moved without thinking, feeling only the joy of the music, the excitement of his closeness.

She looked up into his face and smiled, unaware of how her smile dazzled. He drew in a sharp little breath, and his hand tightened for an instant on her waist.

"I cannot think why I have not seen you before the other night," he said. "Did you just recently come to town?"

"We have been here for three weeks."

He shook his head. "I could not have seen you and not noticed."

Constance felt sure that he could have; until tonight, she had always been in the background, drab and unnoticed in her spinsterish clothes. But she did not want to point that out, so she said only, "Perhaps we attended different parties."

"Clearly I have been in the wrong places."

She laughed. "You are too smooth-tongued by half, sir."

"You are unjust," he responded, his eyes twinkling. "I have only spoken the truth to you."

She cast him a cynical glance. "You forget, my lord, I know—from your own words—how much you are pursued. Can you expect me to believe that among all those girls, you would notice each and every one?"

"Not each and every one," he replied. "Only you."

Constance tried to suppress the warmth that flooded her at his words, but she could not. When he smiled at her like that, it made it difficult to remember that she needed to keep her head around him. Yet how could she not smile and flush when he said such things to her?

Forcing a certain tartness into her voice, she countered, "And all the ones with whom you try to dally in the library—do you remember all of them?"

"Ah." He cast her a knowing glance. "I see that you are holding my sins against me. Please, believe me when I tell you that I do not, in fact, usually dally with young ladies—in the library or elsewhere."

"Indeed?" She arched an eyebrow.

"No. The truth, Miss Woodley, is that there is something about you which makes me act…out of the ordinary."

"I am not sure whether you are complimenting me or disparaging me," she told him.

"'Tis no disparagement, I assure you."

Constance could think of nothing to say. There was a warm look in his eyes that did strange things to her insides. It was difficult to be witty or aloof; all she wanted was to dance in his arms, to gaze into his eyes, to live in the moment and the music.

But all too soon the music was over. They whirled to a stop. There was the briefest of hesitations, then Leighton dropped his arms from her and stepped back. Constance drew a shaky breath, glancing away from him as she pulled herself back into the real world.

She took his arm, and he walked her back to where his sister stood waiting. As soon as they arrived, Sir

Lucien asked Constance to dance and led her out to the floor. When they returned, Constance saw to her disappointment that Lord Leighton was no longer with Francesca.

However, she was far too busy for the rest of the evening to miss his presence. There were always a number of men dancing attendance upon Lady Haughston at any party, but tonight their number doubled. Francesca was besieged with young gentlemen seeking an introduction to her new companion, and she was happy to oblige. Before half the evening was over, Constance's dance card was filled. She was certain that the reason for her sudden popularity lay in the fact that Lord Leighton and Sir Lucien had asked her to dance. There was nothing that established a woman's desirability like the attention of other men.

Constance, however, was enjoying the evening far too much to quibble about the reasons behind it. As she danced and talked and flirted, she did not feel at all like a chaperone—or even like a spinster. She felt young and as attractive as her admirers were telling her, and she could not remember when she had enjoyed herself as much. It had been years, she thought. Since her father's death, in fact.

While she could not accuse her aunt and uncle of cruelty or mistreatment, there was no love for her in their house; she was less a loved member of the family than a sort of high-class servant. Nor did she, frankly, enjoy their company. Her happiness came from small things—a walk in the spring, a visit with a friend in the village or an hour spent alone reading. It did not spark and fizzle as it did tonight, making her want to bubble over with laughter. She had not realized until now just how gray her world had become. She would, she thought, always be grateful to Francesca for this feeling, and she knew that, whatever happened, she had been right to join in Francesca's scheme.

The only thing that marred her happiness was a moment when she glanced to the side and found a woman staring at her with an intense look of dislike. Startled, Constance stared back at her for a moment. The woman was tall and dark-haired, with very light blue eyes. Constance took her to be a few years younger than herself, and she would have been attractive if it had not been for the cold, disdainful expression on her face. She stood beside an older woman who looked so much an older version of her that Constance assumed they must be mother and daughter. The mother, as much as the daughter, was gazing at Constance with a venomous look.

Constance turned away, shocked and uncertain. She was sure that she did not know either woman. Indeed, she did not think she had ever even seen them before, though she supposed she might have come across them at some other party and not remembered them. But she could not imagine why the two would have taken such a dislike to her.

She turned to ask Francesca who they were, but Francesca was chatting with a young man, whom she promptly introduced to Constance. By the time he left, the women Constance had seen were no longer standing there. With a mental shrug, she dismissed the thought of them and took the floor with her next dance partner.

FRANCESCA SPENT MOST OF the evening watching Constance like a proud mother. She had asked Sir Lucien to dance with Constance, as Constance had suspected, but she was pleased to hear him say, after the dance was over, that her protégé was both pretty and charming.

"What are you about with this girl, anyway?" he went on, looking at Francesca shrewdly. "I know she is not one of those chits whose parents ask you to establish them. From what I have heard, she is a poor relation of that dreadful Woodley woman."

"Why, Lucien, you wound me," Francesca teased him. "Do you think me entirely mercenary?"

"My dear girl, I know you are not. You could have had your pick of a wealthy husband any time these last five years, and you have not snapped one up. But I cannot understand why you came to choose this girl. She is long past the age of coming out. I believe she is a veritable ape-leader."

"She is younger than I, so let us not talk of age, sir. But if you must know, it is because of Rochford."

"Rochford!" Lucien looked surprised. "What has he to do with it?"

"He challenged me."

"Ah." Lucien smiled faintly. "You could not, of course, fail to take up the glove with him."

She cast him a dampening look. "A sapphire bracelet rides on my success, and I should rather like to have it."

"I see." He paused, then went on. "And what have you committed yourself to do?"

"Find Constance a husband this Season."

"Ah, a mere trifle, then." He made an airy gesture. "She has no fortune. Her relations are clearly not an advantage. And she is older than most of the marriageable girls by five years, wouldn't you say? That should be wonderfully easy, no doubt. And what does it matter that almost a month of the Season has already passed? I feel no doubt you will be able to pluck out an earl from somewhere…or, at the very least, a baron."

"I did not say it had to be a brilliant marriage," Francesca retorted. "Only an acceptable one."

"Ah, well, then." Sir Lucien favored her with a smirk.

"All right, I will admit that it may prove something of a difficulty. But that is precisely why it was so important that you showed her favor tonight," Francesca went on, smiling at him. "It will take at least two weeks off the time to establish her since *you* have approved of her."

Her friend looked at her suspiciously. "What do you want from me?"

"Lucien! As if I must want something from you to pay you a compliment."

He said nothing, merely waited, one brow raised.

"Oh, very well. I thought you might accompany me to Redfields next week."

He looked pained. "To the country? Francesca, dear, you are the love of my heart, but to travel into the country?"

"It's in Kent, Lucien. It isn't as if I am asking you to trek off to the wilds."

"No, but a house party? It's bound to be dreadfully dull."

"No doubt it will be, since my parents are giving it. But that is why I particularly need you to go—so it will be more interesting."

"But why?"

"Because I decided that this house party would be the perfect thing to introduce Constance to a number of eligible men. Because she has no fortune, I must make sure that several men have a chance to spend a goodly amount of time with her, and fall in love with her wit and her smile."

"I don't know why you would need me for that. I would just be taking up space that could go to one of your bachelors."

"Because I need to get the bachelors to come. How many young gentlemen are going to want to attend if they think that they will be sitting around with Father and Lord Basingstoke and Admiral Thornton, drinking port and decrying the state of today's youth? Or playing whist with the Dowager Duchess of Chudleigh?"

"Good Gad, is *she* going to be there?"

"She is my mother's godmother, and I have never known her to miss it. So I need to reassure them that there will be someone livelier there. I think Dominic may attend. He seemed somewhat more amenable to it tonight."

"Then you don't need me."

"I daren't count on him. Even if he comes, there is nothing to say he and Father won't have a row the first night, and Dom will ride back to London. Besides, it would be better to have more than one man who is interesting. Dom will provide good sport, and you will provide entertaining conversation."

"My dear Francesca, I suspect that your fair face and form will be more than enough to ensure that an adequate number of bachelors will be happy to attend," Sir Lucien told her. "However, I will come, as well. It will provide some amusement, after all, to watch your machinations."

"I knew I could count on you."

"And what about your—I scarce know what to call him—your nemesis? Your friend?"

Francesca looked puzzled.

"The deliverer of your challenge," Sir Lucien clarified. "Rochford."

"Oh." Her expression cleared. "Him." She shrugged. "I suppose he will drop by at least for the ball, if he is at home at Dancy Park," she said, naming the Duke's country house, one of many, which lay not far from the house in which she had grown up.

"And do you expect him to try to thwart your efforts?"

"Sinclair?" Francesca laughed. "I cannot imagine him bothering to attempt to influence events. He prefers to observe in a godlike manner as we petty mortals scurry around trying to direct our lives."

Sir Lucien raised his brows at the touch of bitterness in her tone. "Well, it appears as though he has descended from Mount Olympus for the moment, at least."

He nodded, and Francesca turned to look in the direction of his nod. The Duke of Rochford was moving toward them, his passage winding and desultory as he paused to speak to this person or that. But he looked up, and his eyes met Francesca's, and she felt certain that she was his ultimate destination. She pivoted back to watch the dancers, the picture of indifference.

But she knew immediately when he drew close, and she did not even turn her head when he stopped beside her and gazed out onto the dance floor, too.

"Quite a swan you have made out of your duckling, my lady," he said after a moment, amusement curling through his voice.

Francesca glanced at him then. His saturnine face was, as always, unreadable. "It required little effort on my part, I assure you. I am afraid, Rochford, that you may have chosen the wrong subject for your bet."

A thin smile touched his lips. "Expect to have an easy time of it, do you?"

"Not easy, no," Francesca responded. "But she has far more possibilities than the other two."

"Mmm. I may have chosen rashly," he admitted. He looked at her, and Francesca thought there might be a hint of laughter in his eyes. It was always so hard to tell with him. "No doubt you will take advantage of my weakness."

"But of course."

The dance had ended, and Constance and her partner made their way across the floor to where Francesca stood between Sir Lucien and the Duke. Francesca saw Constance's eyes go somewhat apprehensively to Rochford.

Francesca introduced Rochford to her protégée. She presumed that was why he had come over to her. But she was a little surprised to hear the Duke, after bowing to Constance, ask her for the next dance. Constance's eyes widened, and she glanced over at Francesca, then back at Rochford.

"I, um, I fear the dance is already taken, Your Grace," she said, looking more relieved than regretful.

"Ah, I see." His eyes flickered over to the man who

was walking toward them, and he went on, "To Micklesham?"

Constance looked confused. "What?" She turned to look in the direction Rochford indicated. "Oh, yes, that's right. Mr. Micklesham."

Rochford's smile was a trifle vulpine as he greeted the new arrival. "Ah, Micklesham. I'm sure you would be willing to give up your claim to Miss Woodley's hand for the next dance, wouldn't you?"

Micklesham, a short, rather pudgy young man with carefully styled ginger-colored locks and a sprinkling of freckles across his nose and cheeks, looked startled at being addressed by the Duke. He flushed, his expression changing to one of awe. "Oh. Um…to you? Why, y-yes. Of course." He bowed to the Duke. "My pleasure. That is, I mean…well…beg pardon, Miss Woodley." He looked somewhat entreatingly at Constance.

"Very good, then. Miss Woodley?" Rochford extended his arm to Constance, who hesitated, then put a smile on her face and accepted.

Francesca watched the pair walk out onto the dance floor.

"Now what the devil is he up to?" she murmured.

"Perhaps he means to frighten your little bird away," Sir Lucien offered.

"No, Rochford would not try to hinder my plans," Francesca said. "I was quite correct when I said he would consider it beneath him to try to influence the outcome."

She watched the Duke put his hand on Constance's waist and sweep her into the steps of the waltz. He was smiling down at her. Francesca felt a distinct twinge of irritation.

"The devil take the man," she said and turned away.

Sir Lucien cast a measuring look at her. "What do you think he is doing, then?"

"In all probability, just trying to annoy me," Francesca responded.

"Then it appears he has succeeded."

"Oh, hush, Lucien," Francesca said crossly, "and ask me to dance."

"Of course, my love," he replied with a bow.

CHAPTER SIX

CONSTANCE FELT AN ICY trickle of perspiration snake down her back. Never in her life had she expected to dance with a duke. Indeed, she had not even thought she would ever so much as *meet* a duke.

Lord Leighton would be an earl someday, of course, but his infectious grin and easy-going manner made one quickly forget about his title and his lineage. But Rochford was every inch a duke. His demeanor was not exactly stiff, but his spine was as straight as a board, and he carried himself with the kind of confidence that came only from generations of aristocratic breeding. His angular countenance was every bit as intimidating as his demeanor—high, swooping cheekbones and black slashes of brows, beneath which his deeply set black eyes looked out upon the world watchfully. He was not, Constance thought, a man with whom it would be easy to feel comfortable.

Certainly *she* did not feel comfortable with him. He did not speak for some time, and she was glad, for she was concentrating upon her steps, feeling that it would be far worse to stumble or make a wrong move with this man than with any of the others who had partnered her this evening.

He, apparently, did not find the silence unusual. She supposed he was accustomed to the effect he had on people. Nor did he make any effort to ease the situation; he simply watched her with that vaguely unsettling black gaze.

"I see that Lady Haughston has taken you under her wing," he said at last.

His words startled Constance a little, as she had grown accustomed to their lack of conversation.

"Yes," she answered somewhat cautiously. "Lady Haughston is quite kind."

Constance did not understand why the Duke was dancing with her. Surely he must realize that his asking her to dance would raise her social standing immeasurably, which could only help Lady Haughston's plan for her and therefore increase the possibility of his losing the bet. Perhaps he was simply curious about her, or maybe the bet was, for him, such an insignificant amount that he did not care. But she could not help but worry that he had some ulterior motive in dancing with her, that he hoped to gain some knowledge from her or trick her into doing something that would ruin her chances in Society.

A faint smile touched his lips, and Constance had the suspicion he knew the direction of her thoughts.

"Indeed," he said, a wry twist in his voice. "I have heard that she is."

Constance glanced at him, wondering a little at his tone. She was unsure whether the Duke and Francesca were friends, mere acquaintances or perhaps even enemies. It was difficult to tell; she had quickly discovered that in the *beau monde,* the most vicious of enemies often smiled at one another like the dearest friends. Even the ladies who ruled Almack's together often made mercilessly unkind remarks about each other.

The Duke asked her then where she was from, and she told him, explaining that she lived with her aunt and uncle.

"And are you enjoying your time in London?" he went on.

"Yes, thank you. Very much. It has been a great deal more fun since I met Lady Haughston."

"That is generally the way."

It was, Constance thought, the most prosaic conversation one could imagine. She still could not understand why he had asked her to dance. Certainly it had not been for a scintillating discussion.

"If you follow her ladyship's advice, you will do quite well, I am sure," the Duke continued.

"I hope so," Constance replied, adding, "I would not think that would suit Your Grace, however."

She was surprised at her own daring, but frankly, she

was growing a little tired of the way they had tiptoed about the subject that connected them.

He raised his brows in a way that she was sure dampened most pretensions. "Indeed? And why would you think I wished you ill, Miss Woodley?"

"Not ill, precisely. But I am aware of your bet with Lady Haughston."

"She told you?" He looked surprised.

"I am not entirely stupid," Constance retorted. "And it is a trifle difficult to make a new woman out of someone without revealing what you are about."

"I suppose it would be," he commented. Constance was almost sure that she had seen the flash of a smile in his eyes. "And you are agreeable to her plan?"

"I do not expect that Lady Haughston will win her bet," Constance told him. "I am not counting on that. However, I found the idea of a Season…appealing."

It definitely was a smile this time, for it touched his lips, if only briefly. "Then I hope it will turn out to be so for you, Miss Woodley."

They finished the dance in silence, though Constance thought that it did not seem so uncomfortable anymore. When the waltz ended, the Duke escorted her back to Francesca. Francesca, however, was about to take the dance floor herself. Constance glanced around, thinking that she should seek out her aunt. She had been having far too enjoyable a time to even think about her aunt and cousins, and she felt a trifle guilty about that fact.

As she looked over the room, she caught sight again of the young woman whom she had seen staring at her so balefully earlier in the evening. She was no longer standing with her mother but was walking out onto the dance floor on the arm of Lord Leighton.

Could it be that the young woman had been looking at her with such dislike because Lord Leighton had danced with her earlier? It seemed rather absurd, Constance thought; they had, after all, merely danced one waltz together. Still, she could not deny that she was feeling a certain pinprick of jealousy herself as she watched Leighton take the floor with another woman.

In any case, there was nothing that she could do about the matter, she thought, and she tried to put it out of her mind as she continued looking for her aunt and cousins. She strolled through the room, winding her way around the small clumps of guests. She was vaguely surprised at the number of people who nodded to her or bowed. Some were men whom she had met and danced with earlier, and she recognized a few women who had come up to talk to Lady Haughston, as well, but there were several others whom she was rather sure she did not know at all. It was amazing, she thought, the influence that Lady Haughston's friendship brought.

As she circled around a large group of people standing and talking at the edge of the dance floor, she saw her uncle's family at last. She made her way over to them, noting that her aunt was watching her with a grim expression. Constance sighed inwardly. It was clear that Aunt Blanche was not pleased with her; she presumed that the woman was still smarting from their argument the day before about Constance's attending the party with Lady Haughston. Aunt Blanche had not tried to stop her, wisely realizing how foolish it would be to cross Lady Haughston, but Constance was sure that she had thoroughly disliked not being in control of her niece's actions.

Constance greeted Aunt Blanche with a smile, but the older woman was having none of it.

"Well, so you have decided to grace your family with your presence at last," Aunt Blanche said sourly. "But then I suppose we are not nearly important enough for you now. Lady Haughston and her friends are all you care about."

"That's not true, Aunt," Constance said, striving to maintain her calm. "But as Lady Haughston was kind enough to favor us with an invitation to the party and to bring me here herself, it seemed only proper that I should remain with her during the ball."

Aunt Blanche greeted this sensible reply with a disapproving sniff. "Oh, yes, very proper indeed—making a show of yourself. Dancing with half the men here. Acting as if you were a green girl instead of a grown woman. Dressing like that. I am sure that everyone was laughing at you, the way you are behaving."

Constance's cheeks flamed—whether from embarrassment or anger, she was not sure. "Aunt Blanche! You wrong me. How have I been making a show of myself? I was properly introduced by Lady Haughston to every gentleman with whom I danced. I am sure there was nothing wrong with my dancing with them if Lady Haughston approved of it. And as for my dress..."

She cast a glance down at herself, then looked pointedly at her aunt's gown, which exposed more bosom than her own. "There is nothing indecent about my dress."

"It is far too young a color for you," Aunt Blanche said flatly. "You are not a girl anymore, Constance. A woman of your age dancing so, flirting with men the way you have been...well, it's disgraceful."

"I was not aware that one could not dance past a certain age," Constance responded coolly. "I am sure there are a number of women on the dance floor whom you should inform of that rule."

"I am not speaking of married women," Aunt Blanche told her. "Of course, if one is married it is perfectly proper to dance with one's husband or a friend. But for a spinster, it is simply not the thing."

"Why?" Constance asked.

Her aunt looked startled. "What do you mean, why?"

"Exactly that," Constance responded, her eyes flashing now with temper. "Why is it not the thing to dance if one is unmarried? At what age does a woman have to stop dancing if she has not married? Twenty? Twenty-five? And does that apply to men, as well? Are bachelors not allowed to dance?"

"Of course not. Don't be foolish." Aunt Blanche bridled. "There are no hard-and-fast rules. It is simply understood that if a woman has not married, she—"

"Ceases to exist?" Constance asked. "Really, Aunt Blanche, you make it sound as if a woman must retire from life ashamed if she has not caught a husband."

"Well, if you have not caught one by your age, there is little likelihood you will now," her aunt retorted, scowling. "You came to London to help me with Georgiana and Margaret, but instead you are—" She made a gesture toward the floor with her fan, apparently too overcome by emotion to speak. "You danced with all those men, and you introduced none of them to your cousins. Not a single one." Lady Woodley had now, apparently, reached the crux of the matter. "You danced with the Duke of Rochford—a duke!—and you did not make the slightest push to bring my daughters to his notice."

"Oh." Constance glanced at her cousins, who were regarding her with pouting expressions, and she felt a twinge of guilt.

Her aunt was right in saying that she had not spared a thought for her cousins. She had been too caught up in her own excitement. She could have returned to her aunt's side after dancing and introduced her family to the men with whom she had danced. It was not the girls' fault, after all, that their mother stuffed them into dresses so bedecked with ruffles and bows that they resembled over-decorated wedding cakes. They would need every bit of help they could get, and Constance knew that she could at least have brought them into the proximity of some eligible bachelors.

"Yes, we would have liked to talk to a duke," Georgiana whined.

"Jane Morissey would have been ever so jealous of us then," Margaret added, and the two girls giggled together at that thought.

Of course, Constance reminded herself, bringing a gentleman within the girls' orbit would scarcely guarantee them any success. A few minutes of Margaret and Georgiana's vapid conversation was apt to send any gentleman with wit hurrying away.

"I am sorry," Constance apologized. "I should have introduced you. I will introduce my next partner to Margaret and Georgiana. However, the Duke, Lady Haughston told me, is quite the confirmed bachelor."

"Well, the man has to marry someday, doesn't he?" Lady Woodley countered. "He has to have an heir. And it might as well be one of my girls as anyone else, eh?"

Wisely, Constance refrained from answering. It was this sort of baseless reasoning that was the hallmark of Aunt Blanche's thought processes, and she had learned long ago that any attempt to point out the errors and inconsistencies in something her aunt said was not only useless but also tended to arouse her ire.

"It is a beautiful party, is it not?" Constance asked cheerfully, deciding that the best course of action was to steer the conversation in a new direction.

Lady Woodley looked as though she would have liked to pursue the subject of Constance's neglect of her proper duty to her cousins, but after a moment she gave in to her even greater love of gossip and began to relate to Constance each influential member of the Ton whom she had seen tonight and what she knew about each one.

Constance listened with more attention than she normally did in an effort to placate her aunt, but it was not long before her thoughts began to wander. She cast a look about the room, hopeful that she could find something to distract Aunt Blanche.

It was with some relief that she saw Francesca strolling toward them, and she straightened, smiling at her. "Lady Haughston."

Aunt Blanche turned and beamed at Francesca, her voice raised as she said, "Lady Haughston! I am sorry to have missed you earlier tonight. So many people, you know. Girls, say hello to Lady Haughston."

Georgiana and Margaret obediently chorused a hello to Francesca, who acknowledged them all with a smile and a nod. "How do you do, Lady Woodley? It is so nice to see you again."

They exchanged a few pleasantries, remarking on

the warmth of the June evening, the excellence of the punch and the loveliness of the ballroom. Aunt Blanche, Constance thought, could go on all night about such commonplaces. However, when she reached the subject of her daughters' gowns, calling upon Lady Haughston to note the fine French lace that adorned the bodices, Francesca cut into the flow of Lady Woodley's speech.

"Has Constance told you that I have invited her to Redfields next week?" Francesca asked as Lady Woodley paused to take a breath.

Aunt Blanche looked at Francesca blankly. "What? Where?"

"It is my father's estate in Kent. They hold a house party there every summer. It is not far from London, only a few hours' drive. I asked Constance to go with me. I hope you will not mind. It is for two weeks, and I vow I shall be quite bored without her company."

Aunt Blanche turned toward Constance, and Constance could see the deep dislike in her eyes. She was going to refuse to allow her to go, Constance thought, and she wondered what she would do in response. If she were to defy her aunt and go without her permission, she feared that her aunt would have no qualms in casting her adrift.

"Oh, my lady, how very kind of you," Aunt Blanche said, turning back to Lady Haughston. "But I am afraid that I cannot allow Constance to go off on her own in that way. It would be most improper for her to be alone among strangers for two weeks. I must think of her reputation, after all."

Francesca's eyebrows went up delicately, and she said in a cool voice, "She would be with me, Lady Woodley. She would not be unchaperoned, and I can assure you that the Earl's parties are quite respectable affairs."

"Oh, I am sure they are, Lady Haughston," Aunt Blanche told her, her voice somehow managing to be both fawning and obdurate. "And your reputation, of course, is above reproach. But I am afraid that I take my responsibilities to Constance very seriously. I could not possibly let her travel or be on her own for such a length of time without a member of her family there."

"Indeed." Francesca studied Constance's aunt, and Aunt Blanche returned her gaze steadily.

It was all too clear, Constance thought, what her aunt was after, and she squirmed a little inside with embarrassment. She was afraid that Francesca might simply give up on taking her to the party at Redfields. Constance was aware suddenly of how very much she wanted to go to it. She waited, holding her breath.

"I see," Francesca said after a moment, giving Lady Woodley a steely smile. "Well, of course, when I extended the invitation, I did not mean Constance alone. You and Sir Roger and your daughters are invited, as well."

"You are too kind, my lady," Aunt Blanche replied, casting down her eyes to hide the triumph therein.

So it was that a week later Constance was in a post chaise with her aunt and uncle and cousins, rolling out of London and down the road to Kent.

It had been a trying week. The house had been full of little except talk of Redfields and the treat that lay before them. Even Sir Roger, normally a most unexcitable sort, was filled with anticipation at seeing the house. One of his hobbies was architecture, and he had told them, a light gleaming in his eyes, that Redfields was one of the finest examples of Elizabethan architecture in the country.

Aunt Blanche, of course, had rolled her eyes at such a peculiar notion of why they would enjoy Redfields. The house itself was of little importance, in her opinion—provided, of course, that it was grand. What mattered was the people who would be there. She spent most of her time that week calling upon her friends to impress them by dropping casually into conversation that she would be out of town for a while, as they were attending a party at Redfields. Her secondary purpose, of course, was to extract all the gossip she could about Lord and Lady Selbrooke, their family, the estate and all the people who were likely to be there with them.

Aunt Blanche's frequent absence, of course, meant that nearly all the work of planning, packing and preparing for their two-week sojourn was done by Constance. Between helping Georgiana and Margaret go through their gowns and choose what to take—doing her utmost to try to talk them out of their ugliest choices—and sewing back on buttons and flounces, and repairing rips to their clothes, as well as giving instructions to the housekeeper for the time they would be gone and guiding the maids in the packing of the family's clothes, Constance barely had time to get her own things in order to take.

Much to her delight—and dwarfing all the other problems that cropped up—the clothes that she had ordered at the dressmaker's, as well as the ones she had ordered from a more ordinary seamstress, arrived before they left. She could hardly restrain her excitement.

Aunt Blanche, predictably, looked over the new dresses lying on Constance's bed and gave a loud sniff of disapproval. "These are much too young looking for you, Constance. Not at all suitable for a chaperone. I cannot imagine what you are thinking these days. I only hope you will not embarrass us at Redfields."

Anger spurted up in Constance as she turned to look at her aunt. She had done her best for many years to please her. She had never expected her aunt to share her interests or be someone she would consider a friend; she knew they were far too different. But her aunt and uncle and their daughters were the only family she had, and she had thought that perhaps her aunt would have come to regard her with some affection. But over the last few days, since she had met Lady Haughston, it had been borne in on her that the only thing her aunt cared about in regard to Constance was Constance's doing things for her. The moment she deviated from the path Aunt Blanche had set out for her, the woman was quick to belittle and hurt her.

"I will strive not to humiliate you," Constance said flatly, looking her aunt in the eye. "However, I feel I must tell you that I am not a chaperone. I have helped you with Margaret and Georgiana, and of course I will continue to do so. But chaperoning your daughters lies with you, Aunt, and not me. I was invited by Lady Haughston to Redfields to enjoy myself, and that is what I intend to do. I will not spend my time fetching and carrying for you and the girls, or hovering over them."

Her aunt's eyes sparked with anger. "Well! You have become most insolent. I daresay it is Lady Haughston's influence. I do not believe that she is a good companion for you."

"Indeed? No doubt you think it would be better if Lady Haughston removed herself from our lives." Constance cast a challenging look at her aunt.

Aunt Blanche drew a breath, but she seemed to think better of what she was about to say. She pursed her lips, then, after a moment, went on. "What is perfectly acceptable behavior in a woman of Lady Haughston's stature is not necessarily attractive in an unmarried woman, especially one with no fortune or high name to recommend herself."

"I believe the Woodley name is good enough for anyone," Constance said stoutly. "I cannot believe that you think differently."

Her aunt looked nonplussed. "I did not mean… The Woodleys are as fine a family as one could find." She stopped and scowled at Constance. "I don't know why we are standing here talking about such things. We had better get back to packing."

She cast a last sour look at the garments on the bed and left the room.

Constance finished packing, doing her best to put her words with her aunt out of her mind. She was going to enjoy this visit, and she was determined not to let her aunt spoil it for her.

They left the next day, after spending a trying morning getting the luggage loaded onto the post chaise. It was not a long journey, which was fortunate, as Georgiana was not a good traveler, and they had to stop often to allow her queasy stomach to subside.

They arrived at Redfields in the late afternoon, driving through a pleasant park of old spreading chestnuts and pink-flowered hawthorns, emerging at last to see the main house spread out before them.

"Oh!" Constance sucked in a quick breath of admiration, leaning her head out the carriage window to get a better view.

The setting sun washed the redbrick house in a warm glow, sparkling on the glass of its many windows. Three stories tall, with a peaked roof and three tall pinnacled gables jutting out from the front in a classic E pattern, it was a house that was at once both stately and welcoming. A multitude of chimneys adorned the steeply pitched roof of the central section, and a long wing, only one story in height, ran off the east side of the house, topped by a balustraded walkway.

It was a beautiful home. How, Constance wondered, could Lord Leighton be so reluctant to visit it? She thought that if she were heir to such an inviting home, she would spend all her time here.

Their vehicle pulled to a stop before the central gable, which jutted out a little more than those on either side of it, forming an enclosed porch leading to the heavy wood door. They disembarked, looking up in some awe at the house, which was even more impressive up close. Three sets of coats of arms were carved into the stone above the porch, and more carvings adorned the stone archway leading to the front door.

The door was opened immediately by a liveried footman, who led them through the large entryway to the drawing room. Constance walked along the marbled hallway, following the stiff back of the footman, her stomach tightening with nerves. *What if Francesca was not here to greet them?* She did not even know Lord and Lady Selbrooke, and even though their daughter had invited Constance and her family, she could not help but wonder if they resented the intrusion of a group of people whom they had never even met before.

She was much relieved to see Francesca sitting on a sofa in the drawing room, conversing with an older woman who resembled her enough that Constance knew it must be Francesca's mother. Constance's gaze traveled across the room. There, standing by the window, was Lord Leighton. He had turned at their entrance, and the light from the window fell across his handsome features. Constance's heart gave a thud as he smiled at her.

Francesca jumped up with a little cry when she saw them and hurried forward to take Constance's hand. She turned, leading Constance to the woman with whom she had been talking, and began her introductions.

Lady Selbrooke—for Constance had been accurate in her guess as to the older woman's identity—was, up close, still quite similar in looks to her daughter, though her blonde hair was streaked with gray, and tiny lines fanned out beside the blue eyes and bracketed her mouth. There was, however, none of the animation in her features that so brightened Francesca's face; her expression was carefully controlled—even, Constance thought, a trifle icy. Lady Selbrooke nodded to Constance and her family politely, and murmured a welcoming comment, but there was no real interest in her features.

Lord Selbrooke rose from his chair to greet them, as well. His manner was as reserved as his wife's, and though he was a handsome middle-aged man, there was none of the laughter in his eyes or the ease of manner that made his son so appealing.

"Are you acquainted with Lady Rutherford and Miss Muriel Rutherford?" Francesca went on, turning toward the other occupants of the room. "Lady Rutherford, Miss Rutherford, may I present Sir Roger and Lady Woodley? Miss Constance Woodley."

Constance turned in the direction Francesca indicated and saw a dark-haired middle-aged woman, and a younger woman with equally black hair sitting beside her. They regarded Constance coolly. She realized, with some shock, that they were the two women who had stared with such dislike at her at the dance the other evening.

Constance gave them her curtsey, murmuring a polite greeting, and discreetly looked them over as Francesca went on to introduce her cousins. Muriel Rutherford was sitting, spine straight and not touching the back of the chair, her hands folded in her lap. She was dressed in an afternoon frock of sprigged muslin, ruffled at the hem and around the neckline, its soft, girlish lines at odds with the rather severe set of her face. Her eyes were a very pale blue, adding to the icy quality of her demeanor. She was a younger version of her mother, down to the narrow nose and straight mouth.

"Miss Woodley!" Lord Leighton's voice jolted her from her study of Miss Rutherford, and she turned to face him as he came forward from his position near the window. His lips were curved and his eyes twinkling in that slightly mischievous way he had. He reached her and bowed over her hand, holding it for a moment longer than was necessary.

Out of the corner of her eye, Constance saw Muriel Rutherford's lips thin with displeasure.

"It is a pleasure to see you again," Leighton told her.

Constance promptly forgot all about the Rutherford women as she smiled up at him. "Lord Leighton. Pray allow me to introduce you to my aunt and uncle."

He turned to the other members of her family, smiling with an easygoing charm. "Sir Roger. Lady Woodley. Miss Woodley. Miss Woodley. I hope you had a pleasant journey."

Georgiana and Margaret promptly fell into blushes and giggles at his smile, and Aunt Blanche looked to be equally susceptible to his charm.

"Oh, yes, indeed, thank you, my lord," Aunt Blanche said, her manner almost coquettish. "So good of you to ask."

"I am sure you must be exhausted, however," Francesca said. "Shall I take you to your rooms now?"

Francesca swept them upstairs, her arm linked companionably through Constance's. "Purlew could have shown you to your rooms," she said, leaning in confidentially. "But I wanted to get away from there. I suppose dryer conversation could be had somewhere, but I would not like to hear it. I do feel a bit guilty, though, about leaving poor Dom to endure it."

Constance smiled. "I suspect that if he wishes, Lord Leighton will have little trouble extricating himself from the conversation."

Francesca chuckled. "So soon you know him."

Constance was grateful to discover that her room was next to Francesca's and thus half the length of the hallway from the two rooms belonging to her aunt and uncle, and her cousins. She suspected that Francesca had seen to that arrangement, and she blessed her silently. It would be far easier to avoid assisting her cousins with their wardrobe if she was not right next door.

Her trunk had already been brought up to her room, and there was a maid pulling clothes out of it and putting them away in the dresser. She bobbed a curtsy to Constance, saying, "I'm Nan, miss. If you want anything, just call me." She gestured toward the bellpull hanging beside the door. "Lady Haughston said her Maisie would be doing your hair, but I'm to help you with your clothes. Supper is at eight. Would you like a little lie-down first?"

Nan helped Constance out of her pelisse as she talked, inspecting it for any spot that might need cleaning, and hung it up in the large mahogany wardrobe, then took her bonnet and gloves, as well. She dug through Constance's trunk for the dress that she would wear that night and hurried off to press the wrinkles from it while Constance washed the dust of travel from her face and hands. She took down her hair, as well, and brushed it out, feeling the slight headache that had built during the journey fade now into nothingness.

She stretched out on the bed, not really meaning to sleep, just thinking how blissful it was to have utter peace and quiet after the journey filled with rattles and shakes and unceasing chatter. She did not even realize that she had fallen asleep until she awoke sometime later, drawn from her slumber by the sound of the maid reentering her room. Nan carried the gown Constance had chosen to wear that night, freshly pressed. It was a white lace dress over a white satin slip, with a bodice of rose and white satin in broad vertical stripes. The neckline was low and square, trimmed in the same white lace.

Nan helped her into the new dress, and she was just finishing buttoning it up the back when there was a knock on the door and Francesca bustled in, followed by her maid.

"Oh, Constance!" Francesca drew a breath of admiration. "It is lovely. Madamoiselle Plessis did a beautiful job. How pretty you look. Now sit down and let Maisie do your hair."

Constance did as she was bade, and Maisie began to work her usual magic with her hair, pinning and twisting until it fell in a profusion of curls about Constance's face. While Maisie worked, Francesca pulled up a chair and watched, talking all the while.

"There will be more interesting company this evening," she promised Constance, then paused for a moment before letting out a little sneeze. "Goodness. Excuse me. Cyril Willoughby—you remember him—you danced with him at Lady Simmington's ball—is here. And Alfred Penrose. Lord Dunborough."

Constance listened with only half an ear as Francesca rattled on, detailing all their visitors, especially the eligible males, and describing their looks and personalities. Constance's thoughts were on the evening ahead and, especially, on seeing Lord Leighton again. Excitement bubbled inside her, combined with a nervous uncertainty. This party seemed to her a time set apart, a special moment in which she could live a different sort of life—not the unmarried niece with whom her aunt and uncle were burdened, striving to please and to help them out of gratitude for their charity, but an attractive woman enjoying the sort of life she had been born to, the life she would have had, had her father not fallen ill when she was eighteen.

Yet she could not keep from her mind a certain degree of worry. What if she was being an embarrassment, as her aunt had said? What if the others looked at her and thought that she should not be here, or that she was too old to be acting and dressing like a young woman?

"There!" Francesca exclaimed, beaming at her. "You look beautiful. Absolutely perfect. Just look at yourself."

Constance did as Francesca told her, going to the cheval glass standing in the corner of the room. She could not keep from smiling as she looked at her reflection, for the woman who gazed back at her was not only pretty, but sophisticated looking, as well. No one, she thought, would mistake her for a chaperone.

Francesca came to stand beside her, looping her arm about Constance's waist. "Ready?"

Constance nodded. "Yes. I think I am."

"Good. Then let's go downstairs and capture some hearts."

CHAPTER SEVEN

EVERYONE HAD GATHERED IN what Francesca told Constance was the anteroom to the formal dining room. It was a smaller room than the drawing room, in which the family had sat earlier, but it was empty of furniture, except for a few chairs around the edges of the room. The anteroom was full of people, conversation rising in a buzz. Constance halted at the doorway, startled by the number of guests. The room seemed a blur of unknown faces.

"Don't worry. It won't be long before you know everyone," Francesca assured her. "Come. We must first introduce you to the Dowager Duchess of Chudleigh. She is the eldest lady here and my mother's godmama. She cannot hear a thing, so she will just look at you disdainfully and nod, like this." Francesca demonstrated, raising her chin to look down her nose at Constance and then lower her head fractionally. "She does it to everyone, so you must not take offense."

The Duchess was seated beside Lady Selbrooke against the far wall, surveying the people before her with a sour expression on her face. Her hair was iron gray and swept up in a high, old-fashioned style, though not powdered. Her black dress, too, seemed to be from another era, boned and hooped in a way that had not been fashionable in fifteen years or more. Her reaction when Francesca curtsied to her and introduced Constance was so much what Francesca had predicted that it was all Constance could do not to laugh.

Then Francesca swept Constance away on a tour of the room, introducing her to everyone. It was dizzying, and Constance feared she would not remember half the names she was told. It was a relief to see Cyril Willoughby, whom she remembered from the dance, and there were two more men whom she had danced with at the Simmington ball, though she did not remember who they were and was grateful when Francesca greeted them by name. There were several young women who seemed far pleasanter than Muriel Rutherford, for which Constance was also grateful. With luck, she thought, she might be able to avoid spending much time in the company of Miss Rutherford or her mother.

As they made their way around the room, she saw Lord Leighton enter and, as she and Francesca had done, go to his mother and her companion, the Duchess, to pay his respects. She turned away, not wishing to be caught staring, but a few moments later she glanced up and found Leighton's gaze on her. He smiled at her before turning back to the man beside him and murmuring something to him, then breaking away from him.

Leighton's journey was slow and meandering, with many a pause to greet this guest or that, but Constance was sure that he was making his way to where she stood. Though she continued to talk to Francesca and a rather languid young man named Lord Dunborough, she was aware every moment of where Leighton was, and she had a great deal of trouble keeping her mind on Lord Dunborough's account of his journey from London.

She felt Leighton's presence beside her an instant before he spoke. "Dunborough. Ladies."

"Leighton!" Francesca turned to greet her brother with an expression of relief.

Lord Dunborough nodded. "Hallo, Leighton. Didn't expect to see you here. Lady Rutherford told me this morning you were coming, but I said I was sure you were not. 'Saw him Saturday a week ago,' I said to her, 'when I took a toddle down to White's, and I'm certain he said he would not be here.' She would have none of it and insisted that she had it from Lady Selbrooke herself, who should, of course, know, as it's her house and you're her son."

"Quite," Leighton broke into the other man's story with the expertise of long practice. "It happens that I changed my mind."

"One does," the other man agreed. "I did so this morning. Thought I would wear my blue jacket down here, told my man to lay it out, and so he did. But then, this morning when I got up, I thought, no, it should be the brown. Better for traveling, don't you see?"

"Of course it is," Leighton agreed quickly. "Just what I would have done. Have you spoken to Mr. Carruthers yet? He is interested in a pair of grays for his carriage, and I know you looked at that pair Winthorpe's trying to sell."

"Really?" Lord Dunborough's eyes lit with interest. "Wouldn't advise him doing it. No, not at all." He glanced around. "I should speak to him."

"No doubt you should," Francesca agreed.

It took him several more sentences to excuse himself from their presence, but at last he started across the room toward Mr. Carruthers.

Francesca let out an enormous sigh. "Thank you, Dom, you are our savior."

"Was Dunny entertaining you with the tale of his broken wheel?" Leighton asked, his eyes dancing in amusement.

"Yes, though we had scarce reached the actual breaking point," Constance told him.

"Quite true," Francesca agreed. "We spent ten minutes on loading the carriage. If his journey was as dull as his recounting of it, it is a wonder he did not expire on the way."

"What possessed you to inflict him on Miss Woodley?" Leighton asked.

"I have avoided him for so long I had forgotten how

horridly longwinded he is," Francesca admitted. "Please forgive me, Constance. We shall cross him off the list." She looked toward the door and said, "Ah, there are your aunt and uncle. I should make introductions. Keep Miss Woodley company, will you, Dom?"

"It will be my pleasure," Leighton assured her.

Francesca left them, and Lord Leighton turned to Constance. "List? What list are you and Francesca keeping?"

Constance blushed a little under his regard. "'Tis nothing. Lady Haughston has taken me on as her newest project. She is determined to find me a husband."

"And are you seeking a husband?" he asked quizzically, raising one brow.

Constance shook her head. "No. You need not worry that I have been added to your bevy of pursuers. I have no interest in achieving the married state."

"You prefer not to marry, then?"

"It is not that. But I prefer not to marry where I do not choose. And a woman with little dowry has equally little choice." She gave a shrug and a smile to take the sting from her words.

"Ah, then we are compatriots, Miss Woodley," he said with a smile. "Fellow fugitives from the marriage mart."

"Yes. Though I do not have to hide from my pursuers," she countered teasingly.

"I can scarce believe that. Are there so few men of discernment among us?"

"Perhaps, like you, they have no interest in marriage," she pointed out. "And interest of any other kind is dangerous for a woman."

She was enjoying their repartee, the light feint and thrust of social discourse, but she glanced away at that moment and encountered the icy gaze of Miss Rutherford. The woman's antagonism deflated some of the buoyant feeling. What was it about her that the woman so disliked? She could not help but think that it had something to do with Lord Leighton, and she wondered if there was some sort of attachment between him and Miss Rutherford.

Constance glanced back up into Leighton's face. He was watching her, and his face showed nothing but the same lighthearted enjoyment in their conversation that she felt. Surely this was not the look of a man attached to another woman. Nor did his joking comments about escaping from the marriage mart give any indication that he was engaged or even close to that state. She must be wrong about the reason for Muriel Rutherford's dislike of her, or else Muriel was this disagreeable about possible competition for any man she happened to favor. Whatever the reason, Constance made the firm resolve to ignore the woman in the future.

Leighton started to speak again, but at that moment supper was announced, and he had to excuse himself to escort his mother in to dinner. Lord Selbrooke was leading the way to the double pocket doors at the far end of the room, now slid back into the wall to reveal the large dining room beyond. The Dowager Duchess of Chudleigh tottered along on his arm. After them came Lord Leighton and Lady Selbrooke, and the rest of the company fell in behind them.

Sir Lucien, whom Constance had not seen until this moment, appeared beside her to offer his arm, and she smiled at him gratefully. Without Francesca around, she felt a bit lost among all the strangers. She was seated near the end of the table, at some distance from either Francesca or Lord Leighton, who were seated near the other end. Fortunately, however, she was between Sir Lucien and Cyril Willoughby, a pleasant man in his thirties with intelligent brown eyes. She had been a little worried about making conversation at dinner, but Sir Lucien, she knew, was capable of making enough entertaining conversation for both of them, and she had spoken with Mr. Willoughby before, and found him both well-spoken and kind.

The meal, therefore, a protracted affair with so many courses and choices that it lasted well over an hour, was pleasantly spent. Sir Lucien supplied her with a murmured social history of everyone at the table, and during the gaps when he turned to entertain Miss Norton on his other side, Constance and Mr. Willoughby discussed one of her father's favorite periods of history, the long and tangled War of the Roses.

Mr. Willoughby, she found, was an admirer of

Edward IV and, like her father, an avid student of history. He owned a small manor house in Sussex, he told her, describing with obvious affection the sleepy village of Lower Boxbury near which it was located. Constance enjoyed her talk with him, and she could easily see why Francesca had included him as a potential suitor. Intelligent, well-read and refined, he was a man of substance—the sort, Constance thought, that any woman should be pleased to marry.

The problem, of course, was that she felt not the slightest speck of attraction to him. She could see that his features were without exception, his form and dress just as they should be. His manner was polite and polished, and if he was not possessed of the sort of biting wit that characterized, say, Sir Lucien, he was, at least, not without some sense of humor—and his comments were far kinder than those of Sir Lucien. But the realization of all these attributes did not give rise in her to even a fraction of the sort of sizzle and excitement that pulsed through her whenever Lord Leighton approached.

Of course, she expected nothing of Lord Leighton, and she had no intention of making the mistake of falling in love with him; for she was well aware of how forlorn any hope of marrying him was. But she could not conceive of marrying a man for whom she did not feel any sort of passion. Her friend Jane was fond of saying that love required nurturing and care, but Constance felt that there must be something there in the first place in order to nurture it. Likeable though Mr. Willoughby was, Constance could not see herself spending her life with him.

And though she had not spent much time with any of them, she suspected that the same would prove true of all the men whom Francesca had invited to this house party. Alfred Penrose was another whom she remembered from Lady Simmington's ball, and though he was an excellent dancer, most of his conversation had been about horses, hounds and hunting. And Lord Dunborough! Well, she had not been able to bear ten minutes in that gentleman's company, let alone a lifetime. There were three other men, of course, whom she had met tonight; two whose names she could not remember at the moment. Perhaps she would feel a spark of something for one of them if she got to know them better, but knowing herself as well as she did, she had the lowering suspicion that she would not. She sincerely hoped that Francesca would not be too disappointed when Constance did not become engaged.

She had warned her, after all. Constance knew that she was considered to be insufferably particular when it came to men, a quality that was difficult enough in a marriageable woman but almost impossible to overcome when one was a portionless spinster. Her cousins were apt to wax enthusiastic over nearly every man they met, overlooking such trifles as a lack of conversation or a predilection for port. However, what Constance had come to think was not that she was so unreasonable about what she wanted in a man—she would admit, after all, that Mr. Willoughby would make a good husband—but that she simply was not one who fell in love easily. Or, when she was feeling especially low, she thought perhaps that she might not be one who could fall in love at all.

She had been in love once. It had been after her father's illness had overtaken him, and they had removed to Bath for a few months in the hopes that the waters there might banish, or at least mitigate, his illness. While they were there, she had met Gareth Hamilton. There had been a few bright weeks of happiness as he courted her, and for a time she had been filled with eagerness and hope. But that had foundered upon the shoals of reality. He had asked her to marry him, and she had had to say no, not while her father still lived. Her duty was to him, and she could not leave him while he was so ill. And so they had parted.

Jane liked to say, with a romantic sigh, that Constance had been pining for her lost love ever since. Constance did not really think so. She did not still yearn for Gareth, did not, in fact, ever think of him in the normal course of things. But she did wonder if perhaps the experience had wounded her in some way, cutting her off from the ability to love.

After dinner, while the gentlemen retired to the

smoking room for port and cigars, the women moved into the music room. Lady Selbrooke suggested that Miss Rutherford entertain them on the piano, and the dark-haired girl obliged, going to the piano and searching through the sheet music, then sitting down to play.

Muriel Rutherford was an accomplished player, Constance had to acknowledge. But her playing, while technically perfect, was without passion, and the piece she chose was dark and slow. Given the music and the heavy meal they had all just consumed, Constance found herself battling to keep her eyelids open. The Duchess, she saw, had lost the battle already; her eyes were closed and her head nodding. The two dyed plumes the Dowager Duchess wore in her hair bobbed with the motion of her head, and periodically she jerked awake, her head flying up, and stared wildly about her for an instant before closing her eyes again and returning to slumber.

Beside Constance, Francesca sighed, wafting her fan gently. She raised her fan to cover the lower half of her face and murmured, "Mother keeps early hours. I think she likes to encourage her guests to do the same, and so she has Muriel play."

A smile twitched Constance's lips, and she quickly bowed her head to hide it. Raising her face, she answered, "You are wicked."

"But truthful. What I would not give to be a man right now, just to escape this."

"Will they stay in the smoking room until this is over?" Constance asked, surprised.

"If they know Muriel is playing, they will," Francesca retorted. "And since Mother always asks her to…" She trailed off, sneezing. She sneezed twice more in quick succession, doing her best to muffle the sounds. "Blast! I keep doing that. I hope I have not come down with a cold."

Lady Rutherford, who was seated in front of them in a chair close to the piano, turned around, frowning, to see who was interrupting Muriel's performance with her sneezes. Francesca smiled at her apologetically. A moment later, she straightened suddenly and cast a glance over at Constance, a look of mischief in her eyes.

Raising her fan again, she leaned closer to Constance, whispering, "Follow my lead."

Constance nodded, mystified. Francesca settled back into her chair, wafting her fan and looking suspiciously angelic. Then she began to cough. First it was one cough, then a series and after that a sneeze, followed by a veritable paroxysm of coughing. It was done so realistically that even Constance felt a stab of worry.

"Are you all right?" Constance asked in a hushed voice, leaning closer to her in concern.

Francesca, covering her mouth, could not answer, only shook her head. She started to stand up, and Constance quickly moved to help her, taking her arm. Murmuring their apologies, Constance led Francesca, still stifling her coughs, from the room.

Once outside, Francesca coughed a few more times for effect as she hurried off down the hall, glancing back at Constance with a grin. Constance suppressed her laughter and hastened after her friend.

"Are you all right?" she asked again as they reached the bottom of the staircase.

Francesca grinned wickedly, then hastily covered her face with her handkerchief as she sneezed again. "I'm not sure," she answered honestly. "The coughing was pretense. But this sneezing…" She cleared her throat and dabbed delicately at her eyes. She sighed. "Oh, dear, I hope I shall not be forced to miss the outing tomorrow."

"What sort of outing?" Constance asked as they climbed the stairs.

"Only a trip to the church in the village." Francesca wrinkled her nose. "The rector is going to give a little talk about its history. It is, apparently, a very good example of a Norman tower— Oh, and there are a number of other things that I cannot remember. Deadly dull, I'm sure, but at least it is an outing, and the Duchess, my mother and Lady Rutherford will not be there, which should make it more appealing."

Constance chuckled, and Francesca smiled, adding, "However, your aunt volunteered to my mother that she would be happy to chaperone the party, never having seen the church, which Mother was quick to take her up on. Still, I think there should be some opportunity for talking and, perhaps, a little flirting?"

She cast a sideways glance at Constance that was at once both hopeful and questioning.

"I am not averse to that," Constance answered.

"I saw you were seated next to Mr. Willoughby," Francesca went on. "How did you like him?"

"He is very nice," Constance replied, then paused.

"But…?" Francesca supplied.

"I hope you will not think me ungrateful, Francesca, but I must tell you that I think there is little hope that he—that I—well, I am sure that it will seem quite vain of me even to say this, for we have scarcely met and I doubt that he would ever actually offer for me, but I truly do not think that if he did, I could accept. He is a very nice man, but I do not feel that I could love him, and—"

"Hush, now, do not look so anxious," Francesca told her, taking her hand and squeezing it. "I shall not be upset with you if you do not become engaged. And certainly I would not expect it to happen in the next two weeks! There is ample time before us—and many more men in the world besides Cyril Willoughby. Why, he is only one of several men here—there are Alfred Penrose and Mr. Kenwick and Mr. Carruthers. Sir Philip Norton. Not Lord Dunborough, of course—I cannot imagine why I thought he might do. And when we return to London, there are hundreds of eligible men there."

The clutch of anxiety in Constance's stomach eased considerably. "It is good of you to say so. I know how much you have done for me, and, indeed, I am very grateful."

"Nonsense. I have been having worlds of fun. Why, what have I done except go shopping with you and cast about a few invitations? I should be the one thanking you for giving me something to enliven this house party. It is always excruciatingly dull."

They had reached Francesca's room by now, and she decided to ring for her maid and get undressed. "Given my little performance downstairs, I suppose I had better go on to bed."

So Constance went on to her own room. Its peace was preferable to listening to Muriel Rutherford play the piano, but she was not ready to go to bed yet, and she had nothing to do. She decided to go down to the library and find a book to read. She had noticed the library on her way to supper with Francesca, and it was a large room with hundreds of books. She was sure that she could find something with which to pass the evening.

After lighting a candle, she slipped back down the stairs and along the hallway to the library, careful to move as quietly as a mouse. The last thing she wanted was for anyone in the music room to hear her and look out, for then courtesy would require her to rejoin them. It was fortunate, she thought, that the music room lay beyond the library, so she would not have to pass it on her way.

There was an oil lamp burning low on a table just inside the library. Constance stepped inside, closing the door silently behind her, and turned up the lamp. She went to the shelves on the right, holding up her candle to better see the spines, and began to trail along the wall, studying the titles.

There was a noise behind her, and she whirled, her heart pounding furiously. She gave a start and let out a squeak when she saw a man sitting on the sofa and gazing over the back of it at her. In the next instant she recognized the man as Lord Leighton, and she sagged with relief, letting out a sigh, her hand going to her heart.

"We simply have to stop meeting like this," he told her lightly. "Someone is sure to talk."

"You scared me to death," Constance retorted, the rush of fright making her cross. "Where were you? I didn't see you when I came in."

"Lying down," he told her, sliding off the sofa and crossing the room toward her. "Hiding out again, are we? Who is it this time? The dread aunt? No, wait, I know the answer. No doubt it is the same reason I am here. Muriel is torturing the piano."

Constance let out a giggle, though she tried to adopt a stern look as she said, "She is an excellent pianist."

"No doubt. But you are right. I misspoke. It is actually her listeners she tortures."

"Surely you were safe in the smoking room with the other men," Constance said.

"Oh, no, for my father was there," he pointed out.

Constance raised her brows a little at this statement. Clearly there was some sort of estrangement between Leighton and Lord Selbrooke, as she had suspected from the formal way by which he referred to his parents and the fact that he apparently rarely visited Redfields. She wondered why, but, of course, it would be terribly rude to ask, so she did not.

"I am sorry to have intruded on you," she said instead.

"Your presence could not be an intrusion," he assured her gallantly. "Come. Stay and talk with me." He gestured toward the sofa and chairs grouped in the middle of the room.

Constance glanced at the closed door. It was scarcely proper to be alone at this time of night with a man, with the door closed, even if they were in so public a room as the library.

He came closer to her, saying teasingly, "Afraid to be alone with me? I promise not to compromise your virtue."

Constance's pulse beat a little faster. She remembered the last time that she had been alone with Leighton and what had happened then. She looked up into his eyes and saw them light suddenly, and she knew that he had thought of that kiss, as well.

He reached up, skimming his knuckles along the line

of her jaw. "I know. I could not resist you last time, so how can you trust me now? That is what you think, is it not?"

"A valid question, surely," she retorted a little breathlessly. Her skin felt warm where his fingers had touched it, and her heart was hammering so hard it seemed a wonder that he could not hear it.

"That time was a lark," he replied softly. "I did not know you, never thought to see you again. It was just…a foolish moment, a bit of pleasure."

"And now?" Constance could not pull her eyes away from his. She felt strangely both bold and filled with trepidation.

"Now it is different, isn't it?" He brushed back a stray curl from where it clung to her cheek, and his eyes traveled over her face, coming to rest on her mouth. His eyes were a dark, velvet blue, so intent and warm she could almost feel them upon her skin.

As though he had actually touched her, her flesh tingled, and some wild, primitive heat blossomed in her abdomen. It seemed suddenly difficult to breathe; Constance was aware of the flow of air as she took a breath, and she realized that her lips had parted slightly.

"Because I am your sister's friend, you mean?" she asked, struggling to sound unaffected by his gaze.

"Because it would mean something."

They stood for a long moment, looking into each other's eyes. Constance thought that he might kiss her again. It was a little shocking, she thought, just how much she wanted exactly that. Her breasts were full and heavy, aching, the nipples prickling, and suddenly her mind was filled with the image of his hands on her breasts. She flushed with heat, unsure whether the blood rushed up through her in embarrassment or desire.

The very air seemed to sizzle between them. Then Dominic dropped his hand and stepped back.

Constance swallowed, turning aside. "I—I had better return to my room."

"But you have not chosen a book," he pointed out.

"Oh." She turned back to the shelves and blindly pulled out a volume. Holding it tightly against her chest, almost like a shield, she murmured, "Good night, my lord."

"Good night, Miss Woodley. Sleep well."

There was little chance of that, Constance thought to herself as she hurried away down the corridor and trotted up the stairs toward her bedchamber. She was so thrumming with nerves, so aware of her senses, her mind filled with thoughts of what had just happened, that she was sure she would not be able to go to sleep for hours.

Because it would mean something. What had he intended by that? *What* would it mean? Love? Marriage? No, clearly that was absurd; they barely knew one another. Yet it would not, presumably, mean something shallow and fleeting, not "a lark." Then would it, in contrast, mean something deep and profound? Or at least a step in the direction of something deep and profound?

Constance entered her room and closed the door, going over to the window to gaze out into the darkness. Perhaps what he had meant had simply been that if they kissed again, she would be taking a step down a road that could lead only to her social ruin.

The heir to an earldom did not marry the penniless daughter of a baronet. She had noticed tonight that when Francesca had been listing the available suitors at Redfields, she had not mentioned Lord Leighton. Francesca liked her, Constance knew, but clearly she did not consider Constance an acceptable bride for her brother. Certainly the stiff and formal Lord and Lady Selbrooke would not.

So his words had likely been a warning to her, she thought. Yet they had not sounded like a warning. They had sounded, quite frankly, like an invitation.

She leaned her head against the frame of the window, closing her eyes, and she remembered their kiss—the touch of his breath against her skin, the full, firm feel of his lips on hers, the heat and hunger that had swirled through her.

She shook her head as though to clear the tangle of thoughts from it and turned away from the window. She noticed that she still clutched the book against her chest, and she lowered her hand to look at the title.

It was *Leviathan* by Thomas Hobbes. A relaxing little bit of nighttime reading, she thought, and a bubble of laughter escaped her lips.

She laid the book aside on the dresser and with a sigh began to unbutton her dress. The maid, Nan, had told her to ring for her help, but Constance had no desire for anyone else's company right now. She wanted to be alone with her thoughts. They might keep her awake too long, but that was all right. For the first time in a long time, she felt vividly alive. And she meant to enjoy the feeling to the fullest.

CHAPTER EIGHT

THE NEXT MORNING WHEN Constance went down to breakfast, Francesca was not there. She had a pleasant conversation with the Misses Norton, a pair of excitable young sisters who had come with their brother Philip from their estate in Norfolk. They were, as best as Constance had been able to make out, some sort of relation to Lady Selbrooke. Living under the somewhat haphazard guardianship of their older brother, who was as placid and introspective as they were outgoing, they had not yet made their debuts, though at seventeen and eighteen they were of an age to do so. It was clear that they regarded their visit to Redfields as a sophisticated treat compared to the county assemblies and small local parties that had constituted their social life heretofore, and they were bubbling with speculation about the outing into the village scheduled for today.

There would be an open air landau for the older ladies and those who did not ride, they told Constance, but those who wished to ride would be provided with horses. This, they agreed, was what they intended to do.

"Though, of course, we shall doubtless look quite gauche compared to Miss Rutherford," Miss Elinor Norton told her with a smile that showed how little she cared.

"She is an excellent horsewoman, I understand. Why, she brought her own mount," added her sister, Lydia.

"She told us yesterday evening that she could not bear to ride any horse but her own."

"I would expect nothing else," Constance replied dryly.

"Do you ride, Miss Woodley?" their brother Philip asked, surprising Constance by showing that he had actually been listening to his sisters' chatter.

She smiled. "I am no expert such as Miss Rutherford, but, yes, I have been known to ride. It has been many years, however, and, sadly, I did not think to bring a riding habit."

Indeed, she had left her riding habit at home, not even bringing it to London, as she had not dreamed of needing it. So, she imagined, she would be consigned to the open air landau along with the "older ladies." Ah well, at least she would not have to be part of the group with Muriel Rutherford, which was some comfort, she thought.

When the meal was over, she went up to Francesca's room, as she found her friend's absence worrisome. Unfortunately, she discovered that her uneasy premonition was correct, for when she knocked upon

Francesca's door, a voice croaked for her to come in, and she stepped inside to see Francesca, swathed in a shawl over her bedgown, sitting propped against her pillows, her face flushed, and her eyes red and watering.

"Oh, Constance," she wailed—if so gravelly a sound could be termed a wail. "I am so sorry. It seems I've caught this wretched cold."

"Heavens, no, don't be sorry," Constance assured her. "It's scarcely as if you caught a cold on purpose."

"I cannot go to the church," Francesca lamented, then paused to sneeze several times.

"Of course not," Constance agreed. "You must stay right here and get better. I shall stay and look after you, why don't I?"

"Oh, no! You mustn't do that!" Francesca cried. "Maisie can fetch my tea and put cooling rags on my forehead. Promise me you'll go!"

Francesca looked so alarmed that Constance hastened to assure her that she would do just as she asked. "But I hate to leave you here, feeling so ill."

Francesca coughed, but shook her head firmly. "No. I didn't bring you here to nurse an invalid. You go and have fun."

Constance felt rather selfish, abandoning her friend, but Maisie entered the room with a bowl of steaming water in which aromatic herbs were floating and placed it by her mistress's bed, then assured Constance that Francesca would prefer that she go.

"Truth is, miss," Maisie told her confidentially as she ushered Constance to the door, "she hates for anyone to see her looking like this. She's used to me, and I know just what to do."

Constance reflected that Francesca's devoted maid had been caring for her for years and doubtless was far better than she would be at nursing Francesca back to health. So it was with a clear conscience that she went downstairs to join the others.

She could not deny that she suffered a pang of envy when she saw Muriel Rutherford mounted on an elegant bay mare, her narrow figure shown off to advantage in her mannishly-cut charcoal-gray riding habit, with a rakish little hat that resembled a military shako perched on her black hair. Miss Rutherford controlled her dancing mount with ease, her eyes almost warm. It was clearly the milieu that suited her best.

Leighton, too, was on horseback, as were most of the young people, and Constance could not help but notice what a striking figure he cut. Tall and broad-shouldered, he looked born to the saddle. She remembered that Francesca had told her that he had been in the Hussars, and she could certainly imagine him on horseback, leading a charge.

Constance resigned herself to riding in the carriage with her aunt and her cousin Georgiana, who could not abide horses, as well as Miss Cuthbert, a solemn, quiet girl who was, if Constance remembered correctly, a grandniece of the Duchess. The ride was exactly what Constance had feared it would be, with Aunt Blanche dominating the conversation, chattering about the excellence of the food, the accommodations and, of course, the entertainment provided last night by Miss Rutherford. She could not, apparently, contain her admiration for that young woman's skill on the pianoforte.

Constance, only half-listening to her aunt's paean of praise to Lady Muriel, was astonished to see Lord Leighton detach himself from the riding party and fall back to ride beside the open carriage, sweeping off his hat and bowing toward them in gallant greeting. Georgiana and Aunt Blanche straightened, greeting him effusively, and Constance noticed that even Miss Cuthbert became somewhat more animated in his presence.

He looked at Constance. "I am sorry, Miss Woodley, to see that you are not riding today."

"Indeed, sir, I wish that I was, but I did not think to bring a riding habit," she responded candidly.

"That can be remedied, I am sure," he told her. "There is bound to be one around the house that will suit you. We must ride out some afternoon. I should like to show you the estate."

"I would enjoy that very much," Constance replied, and from the corner of her eye she could see her aunt and cousin glowering at her.

"I understand you have a very lovely summer house,"

Aunt Blanche put in. "I am sure it would be a treat for the young ones to see it. Wouldn't you like to, Georgiana?"

"Oh, yes, Mama," Georgiana replied eagerly.

"I shall mention that to my mother," Leighton said smoothly. "Perhaps she will set up an outing to the summer house, if, indeed, she does not already have one planned. We have often picnicked there, as I recall."

Constance smothered a smile at his adept avoidance of the implied request to take Georgiana to see the place. "A picnic sounds lovely," she commented, tilting her parasol a little to look at him.

He continued to ride beside their landau, chatting about the upcoming tour of the church and sundry other mundane matters. Constance did not really care about the topic; it was enjoyable just to ride with him. Even the presence of her aunt and cousin was made more enjoyable by his being there.

Constance noted that more than once Muriel Rutherford glanced back at them, her expression icy. Constance felt sure that Miss Rutherford was less than pleased that Leighton was not spending the time with her. She wondered if she was being foolish to feel that Miss Rutherford had taken an especial dislike to her. Perhaps the young woman looked at all other women with such disapproval.

Finally, when the carriage rolled across a small stone bridge over a serene creek and they stopped to admire the view, Miss Rutherford pulled to a halt, then turned and trotted back to join them.

"Is something wrong?" she asked as she rode up, though her voice expressed little tone of concern. "Do you need to return to the house?"

Constance felt sure that Muriel hoped that her surmise was correct. She found herself quite happy to dash her hopes. "No, we simply stopped to look at the view. It's lovely, isn't it?"

Muriel gave her a look down the length of her nose, as if faintly surprised that Constance would address her. She glanced indifferently out over the water, lined with gracefully bending willows along its west bank.

"Yes, I suppose so." She turned toward Leighton. "I am amazed to find you lagging behind, Dominic. Is Arion hurt?"

"No, he's healthy as ever," Leighton replied easily, patting his horse's neck.

"He must be chafing at this slow pace," Muriel commented, a contemptuous smile touching her lips.

Dominic quirked an eyebrow, looking faintly amused. "Are you criticizing my handling of my horse, Muriel?"

Even Miss Rutherford had the grace to blush at his question. "Good heavens, no, of course not. Everyone knows you ride like a centaur. I was merely...surprised at your setting such a slow pace."

"I was simply enjoying a conversation with these

lovely ladies," Leighton replied easily. "Perhaps you would like to join us."

Miss Rutherford glanced at the carriage. Constance suspected that riding alongside the landau ranked very low on her list. However, after a brief mental struggle, she offered a smile to Leighton and said, "Certainly. Why not?"

The remainder of the ride was far less enjoyable, for Muriel did her best to engage the viscount in conversation about people, places and events with which the other women were unfamiliar. Though Dominic time and again brought the conversation back to the others as best he could, Miss Rutherford quickly switched it to another equally unknown topic. It made for a disjointed and boring exchange. However, it was clear to her that Muriel was not interested in conversing so much as in showing Constance and the others that Lord Leighton and she were close friends, part of a group to which the other women did not belong.

The remainder of the ride was mercifully short. Not long after the bridge, they rolled into the quiet village of Cowden. The square stone, battlemented tower of the church was visible above the trees, and they soon pulled to a stop beside the churchyard. A lych-gate led into the graveyard behind the church.

The other members of the party had already dismounted and were standing in the shaded side yard of the church, chatting amongst themselves, having handed over their mounts to the two grooms who had accompanied them.

Leighton dismounted and turned to help the ladies down from the carriage. When they reached the others, they saw that their group had been joined by the black-clad rector, a white-haired, well-rounded gentleman who beamed at them.

"Well, well, welcome to St. Edmund's," he said cheerfully, bouncing a little on his toes. "It is not often that we have so many distinguished visitors. Lord Leighton." He bowed toward Leighton, his smile broadening even more.

He led them into the church, pointing out the Norman tower, which dated from the thirteenth century, and the charming metalwork on the ancient wooden doors. Inside, he continued extolling the historic and architectural virtues of the church in a rich, rolling voice that doubtless stood him in good stead when delivering his sermons. He pointed out the fifteenth-century octagonal font made of brass, and the Flemish stained-glass east window through which the sun filtered, throwing jewel-like colors across the stone floors.

They walked past tombs covered with the effigies of this or that lord or lady, including the apparent focal point of the church, a highly detailed stone rendering of a thirteenth-century Sir Florian FitzAlan, the precursor of all the other Lords Leighton and Earls of Selbrooke whose tombs and memorials lined the east wall of the church. He lay, sword strapped to his side, his hands folded prayerfully on his chest and his feet propped on his faithful staghound.

They admired the medieval wall painting, now faded almost into nothing, of the twelve apostles, as well as the gothic arches, and the Jacobean black walnut pews and high pulpit, the latter topped with a flat sounding board. The enclosed pew belonging to the Earl's family was, Constance noticed, far roomier than any of the others, and its back rose so high as to make the family virtually invisible to the other parishioners behind them.

As the priest led them to the chancel at the front of the church, describing the carved rood screen and the marble altar, Constance trailed along behind the others, looking at the effigies and memorials. Though she admired the unexpectedly fine artistic points of the church, it was these reminders of the departed humans who had lived and worshipped here that most intrigued her.

"The FitzAlans are a disgustingly self-satisfied lot, are we not?" murmured a wry voice behind her, and Constance turned to see Leighton standing there. He nodded toward the brass memorial touting the virtues of the First Earl of Selbrooke.

Constance smiled. "I suspect most tombs and memorials describe their subjects in rather glowing terms."

"Hmm, no doubt. But I have seen the portrait of that fellow, and I can tell you that he looked more like a tyrant than a 'kinde and gentle' father and 'just master.' This one, on the other hand—" he pointed to a brass plaque a few feet ahead of them on the wall "—had a decidedly weak chin and a rather hunted look. It was said that his lady was a virago, which perhaps explains the fearful expression."

Constance chuckled, rebuking him in a playful tone, "I think you are too severe with your ancestors."

"You would not say that if you had seen the gallery of their portraits. I will show it to you tomorrow, and you will understand."

They strolled along slowly, looking at the statues and markers. Dominic pointed out certain phrases and names that had caught his fancy over the years, murmuring sardonic comments about many of them.

"Stop," Constance told him with mock severity. "You will have me laughing most improperly in church."

He cast a glance over at their group, who were clustered in the small side chapel, listening to the priest expound on the perpendicular style of the windows. He took her arm and nodded toward the back of the church. "Then let us walk outside, where we won't disturb the sanctity."

Constance went with him out the side door of the church and into the old graveyard behind. The cemetery was green and cool, shaded by oaks and ancient yew trees, and there was a charmingly unkempt look to it.

Aged tombstones were covered with lichen, and some of them listed in one direction or another, often leaning comfortably against another marker. Ivy covered much of the iron bars of the fence and grew over the curved roof of the lych-gate. Flowers were bursts of color in stone urns, and here and there a rose bush had grown wild over a low fence enclosing a few graves.

They strolled along companionably, not talking much, winding through the old graves and monuments, looking at the statuary that marked them, pausing now and then to read an inscription. Some were so old and covered with lichen that they were almost impossible to read. Some were poignant, even heartbreaking, such as a cherub watching over the tiny grave of a child, while others provided wry commentary on life or death.

Constance felt easy and comfortable with Dominic. They talked about the graves and the occupants whose names he recognized. They talked about the church, the village, about Redfields itself. He asked about her parents, and she found herself telling him about her mother, whose death and life she could not remember, and about the father who had raised her, the bond they had shared.

"You sound as if you loved him very much," he commented.

"Yes. I miss him still. We spent many hours together, talking or reading. I know the vicar's wife often despaired of him. She felt he ought to have made more of a push to get me settled in life. I heard her once scold him for being selfish. But he could not know that if he delayed a year or two taking me to London for a Season, he would fall ill and be unable to do so. And once he fell ill, I could not have left him."

"It must have been painful," Leighton said sympathetically, taking her arm to help her over a rough patch of ground.

She felt a small thrill at his touch, her heart picking up its beat. His gesture was nothing more than polite, yet still it affected her. Constance glanced up at him, wondering if he, too, had felt anything. It was impossible to tell. There was warmth in his eyes, but she could not be sure what that meant about his feelings for her.

"Still," he went on, releasing her arm and looking back in front of him, "it must be a wonderful thing to have that sort of bond with your father."

"You and your father are not close?" Constance asked carefully. She had yet to see Dominic talking with the Earl since she had been at Redfields, and it was clear from what he had said that he was unfamiliar with such closeness himself.

He shook his head, a wry smile quirking up the corner of his mouth. "No, we are not close. That would be a…tactful way to describe it."

They reached a plot marked off from the others by a low stone wall. Carefully tended, it was centered by a large stone vault resembling a miniature Parthenon. Across the top, carvings of angels flanked a coat of arms in the middle. Below the coat of arms was carved the name FitzAlan. Around the central mausoleum were other graves, each with its marble marker.

"The family plot," Leighton told her as they strolled around the low wall bordering it. "The lesser-known members, as well as the more recent ones. We seem to be concerned about not being remembered."

Constance followed him, reading the names and dates on the markers. Dominic stopped at the rear of the plot and stood for a moment, gazing down at one of the graves. For the first time since Constance had known him, his face was somber, his blue eyes dark with sorrow.

She looked at the name on the tombstone: Lady Ivy FitzAlan, Beloved Daughter. Lady Ivy had died twelve years earlier, in the cold of January, and Constance could see from the birth and death dates that she had been young, only sixteen years of age.

"She was my sister," Dominic said in a soft voice. "The youngest of us."

Instinctively, Constance took his hand in sympathy, covering it with her other hand. "I am so sorry. Were you close?"

"Not as close as I should have been," he replied, his tone tinged with bitterness.

Constance glanced at him in some surprise, wondering what he meant. But she could not pry into something so private. She merely squeezed his hand gently. He glanced at her and smiled, returning the pressure of her hand.

"Thank you," he murmured.

Voices carried across the cemetery, and they glanced toward the church. The other members of their party were wending their way through the gravestones. Muriel Rutherford, the long train of her riding habit looped up over her arm, was walking beside Mr. Willoughby, but she was looking all around the graveyard.

Constance had a fleeting impulse to duck behind the large mausoleum of the FitzAlan family so that Miss Rutherford would not see her, but she sternly suppressed the notion. She glanced up at Leighton and thought she saw the corner of his mouth twitch in irritation. Or was she merely imputing to him what she herself felt?

"I suppose we cannot escape any longer," he told her, releasing her hand.

They strolled back toward the others. Muriel saw them, and Constance was quite certain it was irritation, or worse, that she saw cross that woman's features. Her hand firmly around Mr. Willoughby's arm, Muriel stalked toward them.

"Leighton," she said as they grew closer. "Whatever are you doing pottering about here in the graveyard?"

Her gaze swept over Constance dismissively. She released Mr. Willoughby's arm and moved over to stand beside Lord Leighton, linking her hand possessively through his arm. "You must have been desperate to escape the rector's lecture to have allowed yourself to be dragged out here to look at your ancestors. Deadly dull, I should say. But then, I suppose the graves of important families are interesting to others."

She cast a look down her nose at Constance. Her implication was clear: Constance was a person of lesser stature who would be awed by families such as the FitzAlans, though Muriel, of course, would not, being of the same group as Leighton. Constance's hand tightened around the grip of her parasol, and she was aware of a great urge to whack it over the other woman's head.

"But my family is, of course, not important to you, Miss Rutherford?" Leighton asked, his eyebrows raised and his voice faintly ironic.

"What?" Muriel looked surprised, then color bloomed in her cheeks, and Constance was pleased to see that she looked rather disconcerted. "Well, no, of course, I did not mean that I…"

She trailed off, searching for some way to salvage what she had said. Constance regarded her silently, not eager to step in and help the woman out. But after a moment the silence became too strained, and Constance gave in to her better nature.

"No doubt Miss Rutherford knows you and your family too well to be curious about them, my lord,"

Constance offered. "It is those of us who are strangers who want to learn more about them."

Dominic cast Constance a dancing glance, murmuring, "Well put, Miss Woodley."

Muriel, far from appearing grateful for Constance's aid, glared at her. "I think it is time to return to Redfields, Dominic."

"No doubt you are right," Leighton said mildly and nodded to Constance and Mr. Willoughby, who had come up to stand beside her. "Miss Woodley. Willoughby."

He started back toward the church, Muriel's hand tight on his arm. Willoughby looked after them for a moment, then turned to Constance.

"Odd sort of woman," he commented and smiled at Constance. "It was good of you to say what you did."

Constance shrugged. "It was an awkward moment. Perhaps Miss Rutherford did not mean to be insulting."

"Perhaps not," he agreed. "Indeed, her speech is so universally insulting that one must wonder if she does not understand what she says. She more or less told me that I would have to do as an escort through the graveyard, presumably because Lord Leighton and Lord Dunborough were already engaged."

Constance chuckled. "Then I would say that it is you who are very good to have given her your arm."

He smiled. "Well, you see, I was willing to settle

for *her,* as well, as *you* were engaged, so it all worked out." He offered her his arm. "May I escort you to your carriage?"

Constance took his arm, thinking that it was most unjust that putting her hand on Mr. Willoughby's arm caused not a single flutter in her heart.

The ride back to Redfields was uneventful. Mr. Willoughby rode beside the carriage all the way, joined after a time by Margaret. Constance would not let herself watch Lord Leighton, but she was aware, nevertheless, that he spent the entire time at Miss Rutherford's side.

When they reached the house, Constance went first to check on Francesca. She was sleeping, but Maisie told Constance that Lady Haughston was feeling no better. If anything, she was a little worse, having developed a fever during the day.

Constance offered to relieve Maisie for the evening. At first the maid protested, but Constance pointed out that the maid would need to eat and have a few hours' unencumbered sleep if she intended to spend the night on a truckle bed in Lady Haughston's room, as Maisie had told her she planned to do. Maisie gave in to her reasoning and allowed Constance to take over for a few hours.

It was easy enough work, requiring only that Constance sit beside the bed and periodically wring out a fresh cool cloth to put on Francesca's hot forehead. Francesca woke once or twice, and another time Constance awakened her to give her a spoonful of the tonic that Maisie had left on the bedside table. Her fever was not great, so she was lucid, seeming more fretful and irritated that she was stuck in bed than anything else.

"You are good to sit with me," Francesca croaked.

"Nonsense. I would not even be here if not for you," Constance pointed out. "In any case, I am quite content not to spend an evening in company. I have been trapped in a carriage with my aunt for much of the afternoon, and I vow my ears are still sore."

Francesca chuckled, then grimaced as her laughter turned into a cough. When she finally finished coughing, she said, "Why were you trapped with her in the carriage? Why did you not ride?"

"I did not have a riding habit. I did not think to acquire a new one, and I left my old one at home in Wyburn."

"Oh, dear. I should have thought…" Francesca shook her head in regret. "Well, it does not matter. I shall have Maisie lower the hem of mine. When you are on a horse, it will not show if it is a trifle short."

"Oh, no, you must not lend me yours."

"Well, *I* shall not be using it," Francesca pointed out, making a sweeping gesture across her bed. "It looks as though I shall be spending much of my time stuck here. And even when I can get out of bed, I doubt I should do much riding. No, you must have it. What is a party in the country if one is unable to ride?"

Constance gave in, knowing that Francesca was right. But she could not help but feel a niggling tendril of guilt. Would Francesca be so willing to lend her her riding habit if she knew that Constance's main reason for accepting it was the fact that Lord Leighton had asked her to go riding with him?

She could not help but feel that she was deceiving her friend and benefactress by not telling her anything about her interactions with Lord Leighton. But, on the other hand, it seemed remarkably foolish and even presumptuous to tell her that the two of them had talked or that he had asked her to ride with him, as though she believed that Francesca's brother had any serious interest in her. So she kept silent, reminding herself that nothing had happened between them, nor was anything likely to.

Constance spent most of the evening in Francesca's chamber, eating her supper from a tray that one of the maids brought up to her. Late in the evening, Maisie bustled into the room, trailed by one of the footservants, who carried a low cot for Maisie to sleep on.

"There now, miss," she told Constance, smiling. "I'm here, so you can get to bed. You're ever so good to spell me." She rounded the bed and leaned over Francesca, laying her palm on her forehead. "How has she been?"

"Sleeping, mostly," Constance replied. "She was restless for a while, and then she woke up, but after a bit she went back to sleep."

"Well, her fever seems no higher," Maisie said. "That's good. I hope you don't catch it, miss. My lady would be fussed about that something proper."

"I don't imagine I shall," Constance assured her. "I am invariably healthy. So tell Lady Haughston not to worry on that regard."

Promising to look in on Francesca again the next morning, Constance returned to her own room. Once again, she found it difficult to settle down to sleep. She kept thinking of the afternoon and the walk she had shared with Dominic—when, she wondered, had she fallen into the way of thinking of him by his first name?

And why did even thinking about him leave her feeling so odd and aching inside, as if some part of her were not complete? How could she feel excited and scared and yearning all at the same time?

She had only to remember his smile to be suddenly giddy. And when she thought of his hand upon her arm, his long masculine fingers curling around her flesh, warm and strong, she felt again the same surge of heat and hunger that had swept through her then.

Lord Leighton was not for her; she knew that. She should be sober and realistic and put all thoughts of him out of her head right now. But she could not. All she could think of was seeing him again tomorrow.

CHAPTER NINE

AFTER BREAKFAST THE NEXT morning, Constance stopped by Francesca's room again. She learned that Francesca's fever had passed in the night and she was feeling better, though sleeping. Maisie obviously had everything well in hand, and Constance could find no reason to stay.

She made her way downstairs, somewhat at sixes and sevens. The men, she had heard at the breakfast table, had gone out early to hunt, and there appeared to be no other particular entertainment scheduled for today. She felt a trifle out of place without Francesca there, as if she were somehow there under false pretenses. She considered going to the library and finding a book to wile away her time in her room, but that seemed unsociable, perhaps even rude.

In the end she strolled along the central hallway downstairs until she came to a small sitting room, somewhat more casual than the music room or the large drawing room. Several women were seated inside, including her aunt and Lady Selbrooke, as well as Lady

Rutherford and the two Norton sisters, who looked less lively this morning. Constance was not sure whether their silence and heavy lids were the result of overtaxing themselves the day before or merely boredom with the company.

She hesitated at the doorway, thinking of turning back, but the Nortons looked up and saw her.

"Miss Woodley!"

"Do come in and sit with us."

One of the girls stood up and hurried over to her, taking Constance's arm as though she feared she might get away and guiding her over to the sofa upon which the sisters sat. Given their enthusiastic greeting, Constance decided that it was the older women's company that had made the sisters sluggish.

"Did you enjoy the trip to St. Edmund's?" Elinor Norton asked.

"Yes, it was quite interesting," Constance replied.

Before she could go on, her aunt jumped in, exclaiming, "Of course she enjoyed it. How could she not? It was most educational. I vow, my own two girls could talk of nothing else yesterday evening. It is such a lovely church, Lady Selbrooke," she told her hostess, as if St. Edmund's was some sort of personal achievement of her ladyship.

She continued to run on at length about the many delights of the church. Next to Constance, Lydia and Elinor Norton moved restlessly in their seats, and Constance could see Lady Rutherford exchange a look of irritation with Lady Selbrooke. Constance felt her own cheeks burn with embarrassment for her aunt, but it was clear that Aunt Blanche felt none at all, clearly unaware of her audience's reaction.

Trying to save her aunt from herself, Constance reentered the conversation as soon as her aunt paused to draw breath, and asked Elinor what she and her sister planned to do that afternoon.

"We had thought we might go for a walk in the garden," Elinor told her, perking up a little.

"We heard it is quite lovely," Lydia joined in. "Would you care to join us?"

"What a splendid idea," Aunt Blanche chimed in. "You young people should explore the gardens. No doubt my own two would love to go, as well. I took a small stroll myself about them this morning, and it was most delightful."

Her aunt continued on the wonders of the garden at some length. Constance tried another time or two to stem the flow of her aunt's words and bring someone else into the conversation, but each time Aunt Blanche almost immediately turned the talk back to herself. It seemed to Constance that her aunt must have some perverse desire to irritate everyone around her.

At last Lady Selbrooke rose, which did cause Aunt Blanche's river of words to pause for a moment.

"I am sorry, but I hope you will excuse me," Lady

Selbrooke said, offering them a tight smile. "I must speak to the housekeeper about the menu for tonight." With a nod to them all, she left the room.

"Such a distinguished lady," Aunt Blanche commented. "A wonderful woman."

"Yes, poor woman, she has had to bear a great deal," Lady Rutherford agreed.

"Indeed?" Aunt Blanche turned to look at the other woman, her eyes bright with interest.

Lady Rutherford, Constance reflected, had found the best way to quiet her aunt: offer the possibility of gossip.

"There has been a great deal of tragedy in her life," Lady Rutherford went on. "Her youngest child died ten or twelve years ago. She was only sixteen. Then the eldest son, the heir, Terence, was thrown by his horse and broke his neck, only two years past. She was devastated, of course. Lord Selbrooke, as well. Terence was the apple of their eye. Such a handsome man. If he had lived, it would have been he, of course, whom Muriel—" She stopped and shook her head. "But that is neither here nor there. The fact is that he died, and Dominic became the heir."

Lady Rutherford sighed. She looked around at the other people in the room, and it seemed to Constance that her gaze pointedly lingered when it reached her.

"I fear Lord Leighton has been something of a disappointment to them," she went on.

She paused, and Constance suspected that she was

waiting for someone to ask why he had been a disappointment. Constance determinedly said nothing; she was not about to encourage this woman to gossip about Dominic.

Unfortunately, her aunt could always be relied upon to encourage anyone to gossip. "In what way?" she inquired.

"Of course, one could hardly expect him to equal Terence. Terence was head and shoulders above most men—an excellent rider, a sportsman and handsome as a Greek god. He did well at whatever he undertook."

"He sounds like a paragon," Constance commented dryly, the other woman's excessive praise making her feel a certain perverse dislike of the man.

"Yes, he was," Lady Rutherford agreed earnestly. "Dominic could not hope to measure up. Still, one would have hoped for better from him. Gambling, drinking, fisticuffs—Leighton is given to all sorts of vices in London. It is said that he is a rake." Again she turned to look levelly at Constance. "He woos girls whom he would not consider marrying, making them believe that his intentions are serious, but of course they are not, and the girls are then abandoned."

Constance curled her fingers into her palms, the nails biting into her flesh. Lady Rutherford's words, she knew, were directed at her, a warning of what Lord Leighton would do to her, for she would naturally, be one of those young women whom Lady Rutherford had labeled as the sort Lord Leighton would never consider marrying. She refused to show any reaction to

Muriel's mother, neither the anger nor the disbelief she felt. She refused to accept the portrait that Lady Rutherford had painted of Dominic. It was all spite on her part, Constance was certain.

Aunt Blanche, though, was all the audience that Lady Rutherford could ask for. She drew in a long breath of astonishment and disapproval. "No! And he seems such a nice young man."

Lady Rutherford shrugged and said, lowering her voice conspiratorially, "Drink has always been his downfall. Even before he became the heir. He was drunk at his own sister's funeral."

"No!" Aunt Blanche gasped again, her hand flying up to her breast.

"Oh, yes." Lady Rutherford nodded. "I was there. I saw him. He was drunk and loud. It was utterly disgraceful. He even came to blows with Terence when Terence tried to get him to leave the gravesite. Lord and Lady Selbrooke were humiliated."

"I can imagine!" Aunt Blanche's eyes glistened with horrified enjoyment of the tale. "It must have been awful."

"It was. He left shortly after that and bought a commission in the Hussars. I rather think Lord Selbrooke must have banished him from Redfields."

Aunt Blanche tsk-tsked, shaking her head. Constance glanced at the Norton sisters, who were gazing at Lady Rutherford, wide-eyed, taking in her story. Constance wished she had some actual knowledge of what had happened, so that she could refute the other woman. It galled her that the woman was spreading such tales about Dominic, wantonly damaging his reputation, and she could not keep from thinking that Lady Rutherford was telling these stories primarily for Constance's own benefit.

"And yet," Constance said in a level voice, meeting the older woman's gaze, "Lady Muriel is friends with Lord Leighton, I believe. I would not think a woman of her spotless reputation would want to be seen in the company of a roué."

Lady Rutherford's eyes widened, and spots of color flamed suddenly on her cheeks. Her hands tightened on the embroidery hoop that she held in her lap. "That is entirely different," she snapped, giving Constance a searing look.

"Indeed? But I believe you just were saying that a young woman was not safe in his company…."

"I was not speaking of a young woman such as my daughter, of course. Her reputation is unassailable. And he would not prey upon a young woman from a good family."

"Oh. I see." Constance did not drop her gaze before the older woman's angry glare, even though her aunt had now turned to glower at her, as well. "Still, appearances…"

"There can be no appearance of anything wrong," Lady Rutherford shot back, her temper flaring. "Muriel is engaged to Lord Leighton!"

An icy blast swept through Constance. Leighton engaged to Muriel Rutherford? It was all she could do to keep her face blandly unconcerned when everything inside her was screaming that it could not be true. She sensed more than saw her aunt turn her avid gaze on her, hoping for some reaction on her part.

Constance was determined not to let either of them guess how the woman's words had pierced her. "Indeed?" she responded coolly. "One can only wonder that you have pledged your daughter to such a man as you have described."

Lady Rutherford's pale eyes were like a cold blue flame. "Among *our* kind, Miss Woodley, marriages are an alliance between families, not some foolish love-struck joining. The FitzAlans are an important family. Dominic will be the Earl of Selbrooke one day. Those are the important things to consider, not the young man's personal foibles."

"Ah, yes," Constance replied. "I realize that many people consider it more important to marry to improve one's position than to marry a person of character."

Lady Rutherford's eyes bulged, and for an instant Constance thought she might throw her embroidery hoop at her. She rather thought she would have welcomed such a display on Lady Rutherford's part, for it would have shown just how frustrated her own retort had left the woman. Constance had, she thought, rather neatly pointed out that Lady Rutherford's daughter would be marrying up in the social order of things. The Rutherfords were only minor nobility, Lord Rutherford a baron of no ancient title, whereas the FitzAlans' titles stretched back for centuries. The Rutherford name was no more aristocratic than the Woodleys'. Such a reminder would gall Lady Rutherford, yet there was no way she could wiggle out of the betrothal being for position only, given what she had already told them.

"Constance!" her aunt said at last. "Really, such impertinence!"

"Impertinence?" Constance repeated blandly. "Why, I did not mean to be impertinent, Aunt. I am sorry, Lady Rutherford, I thought that was what you were saying."

Lady Rutherford glared at her. "I would not expect you to understand such things."

"Yes, I rather think you are right," Constance agreed. "Now, if you will excuse me, ladies, I think that I shall take a turn around the gardens."

She bade them all goodbye by name, nodding to each, then moving unhurriedly out the door. She would not let it appear that she desperately wanted to sprint out of the room, to run as far away as she could from Lady Rutherford's sharp gaze and painful words.

Dominic was engaged!

She walked down the hall and through the conservatory, finding the door that led out into the garden in the rear of the house. She struck off down the path, not knowing or caring where she was going, only seized by a desire to get away. Once she heard the sound of voices and quickly turned down a side path to avoid whoever might be approaching. She followed that path, taking any narrower walkway that branched off from it, moving ever deeper into the garden.

She sat down at last on a bench that snuggled up against the curving wall of a hedge. The branches of a large tree on the other side of the hedge spread out above, casting dappled shade all around her. It was a peaceful spot, quiet except for the occasional chirp of a bird, and sweet with the mingled scent of flowers. But the thoughts that gripped Constance were anything but peaceful.

Her first instinct, and the one to which she clung for a few desperate minutes, was that Lady Rutherford had been lying. She had to be. Leighton could not be engaged to that cold, disagreeable girl. Lady Rutherford had said that only to hurt Constance, or to warn her away from the man her own daughter so obviously wanted for herself.

But Constance knew how unlikely that idea was. If Lady Rutherford publicly claimed that they were engaged and later it was revealed that they were not, the woman would be humiliated. Surely, no matter how much she disliked Constance or how much she hoped that Muriel would marry an earl, she would not have risked everyone finding out that she had lied. And she would know that the lie had to come out—the first time any of her listeners congratulated the groom or mentioned the wedding to Lord or Lady Selbrooke, the falsehood would be exposed.

So, reluctantly, Constance had to admit that it was extremely unlikely that Lady Rutherford had lied about the engagement. And that meant that Dominic had deceived Constance. The thought made her feel ill.

Oh, he had not lied directly to her, since he had never actually told her that he was not engaged. But the totality of his actions since he met her had been a lie. He had not once mentioned that he had a fiancée; he had never even brought up Muriel's name. Indeed, if anything, he had seemed to avoid her, and when she had joined him yesterday afternoon, it had appeared to Constance that he had been irritated by her presence.

Most of all, he had flirted with Constance, had sought her out on several occasions and had talked to her as if he had no ties to any woman. Worse, far worse than that—he had kissed her! Morally and legally bound to one woman, he had made advances to another. His actions were those of a cad, and it was clear to Constance that Leighton's only interest in her could have been to seduce her.

He must be, as Lady Rutherford had said, a rake. And not just a libertine who sought the pleasures of the flesh with demireps or experienced ladies of the Ton, wives or widows who knew exactly what they were doing. He was the sort who seduced virgins, young ladies whose reputations would be ruined as a result. He was, in short, the kind of uncaring roué whom Constance would have sworn he could not be.

Her disillusionment was bitter. She felt wounded and betrayed. It hurt to know that Dominic was engaged to another woman, but it hurt even more to realize how mistaken she had been in her estimation of him.

Slowly, sadly, she got up and walked back through the garden and into the house. There was the sound of many voices, some of them masculine, coming from the sitting room as she passed, and she thought that the hunters must have returned. She did not pause, however, just quickened her steps until she reached the stairs.

Upstairs in her bedroom, she closed the door behind her and went to sit down beside the window. She wanted to leave, just pack her things and go, but that was impossible. She could scarcely explain to anyone why she no longer wanted to be there, and even if she could, she refused to admit that she had been so naive as to have been deceived by Lord Leighton or so foolish as to have been hurt by learning that he planned to marry another woman.

Clearly, she must stay. And just as clearly, she told herself, she must avoid Lord Leighton. But she could not remain in her room, as she wished to. That would be not only impractical, but also cowardly. Besides, she refused to allow anyone to see that his actions—or Lady Rutherford's news—had in any way bothered her.

Having made her decision, she went along the corridor to Francesca's room, where she offered to sit with the patient while Maisie took another break. Francesca awoke at Constance's entrance and smiled weakly.

"Oh dear, I have been a very bad hostess, I'm afraid," she said, stretching out a hand.

Constance smiled at her reassuringly and took her hand. "No, of course not. I have been doing very well on my own. There was the trip yesterday to St. Edmund's, which was quite enjoyable, and today I walked a bit in the gardens, and before that I visited with your mother and my aunt and Lady Rutherford."

Francesca made a face. "Oh dear. I am even more surprised that you are not angry with me, then."

Constance smiled and lied, "It was not so bad."

"You are very good to lie to me." Francesca sighed. "Maisie tells me I am better. I do not feel hot now, at least. But I am so very tired. Still, soon I will be well." She forced a faint smile. "And then I promise I shall be a more entertaining companion."

"Do not worry about it. Would you like me to get you anything? Or to read to you?"

"No, 'tis enough for you to sit here with me. Tell me what has happened."

"Why, very little, really," Constance said, sitting down in the chair beside her bed. She longed to ask

Francesca if it was true that Lord Leighton was engaged to Muriel Rutherford, but she could not think of a way to phrase it that would not reveal her own interest in Francesca's brother.

"Tell me about Mr. Willoughby and the others. Have any of them made any headway with you?"

Constance shook her head and let herself be diverted. "I fear you will find me a hard case, indeed. But I promise you that I will do my best to spend more time with them this evening and tomorrow."

After all, she thought, she would have to occupy her time somehow if she was to manage to avoid being around Lord Leighton.

With that aim in mind, Constance went down to supper later. She cast her eyes over the people in the room. She quickly spotted Dominic's tall figure standing on the far side of the room, talking to Mr. Norton and his sisters. He looked up and saw her, and a smile crossed his face.

Constance glanced away, searching for some other conversation to join. Out of the corner of her eye, she could see Lord Leighton leave the Nortons and start in her direction. Quickly she walked to her left. Her aunt was sitting against the wall, and she could join her, if nothing else.

Fortunately, Sir Lucien, who was chatting with Alfred Penrose, turned at that moment and saw her, and he smiled. "My dear Miss Woodley, do join us. You have met Mr. Penrose, have you not?"

"Yes, indeed. It is a pleasure to see you again, Mr. Penrose." Constance's smile was bright with relief, so much so that Penrose straightened a little and looked back at her with interest.

They chatted a little about the visit to the church, which Sir Lucien said—with a certain twinkle in his eye—he regretted he had missed.

"Indeed, sir, you missed a great deal," Constance told him. "It was very interesting."

Mr. Penrose looked at her in such astonishment that Constance was betrayed into a giggle.

"It was a dead loss," Penrose told Lucien bluntly. "Unless you're one of those poetic sorts who likes to hang about in graveyards. Or look at effigies of people who died four hundred years ago. Gave me the shivers."

"Ah, Miss Woodley, Mr. Penrose has shamed you with his candor. Now tell me, how did you actually enjoy the trip?" Sir Lucien grinned impishly at her.

Constance chuckled. "You will not lead me to criticize it, Sir Lucien. I fear I must be one of those ghoulish sorts who likes to look at effigies. It is quite an historical church. And as I had never seen it before, I found it enjoyable."

"Hear, hear, Miss Woodley. I am glad to see that you are a staunch supporter of our small country entertainments."

Constance turned quickly at the sound of Leighton's voice. He had walked up to the edge of their group and was standing just behind her. He smiled at her, and she felt the familiar flutter inside.

For an instant her resolution wavered. Surely Lord Leighton could not be the man Lady Rutherford had described. He could not be a cad who pursued young females while he was engaged to marry another.

But, of course, she reminded herself, a deceiver would not be so successful if his deception were written plainly on his face. She steeled herself and gave him a nod that was polite but nothing more. "Lord Leighton."

She turned back to Sir Lucien, who greeted Leighton warmly. So did Mr. Penrose, and Leighton took another step so that he was part of their small conversational group. Constance was careful not to look at him, and, fortunately, Sir Lucien engaged him in conversation so that she did not have to speak any further. When a few moments later the men's conversation lagged, Constance looked across the room to where her aunt sat and quickly excused herself so that she might speak to Aunt Blanche.

She gave a general nod to all three men. Sir Lucien and Mr. Penrose merely smiled and bowed. Lord Leighton, she noticed, was watching her narrowly. She turned and hurried away before he could speak. It would look odd and obvious if he followed her now, she knew, so she would be safe, she hoped, until they went in to eat.

She was forced to endure her aunt's chatter, of course, but she was correct in her estimation, and

Leighton did not join them. Later, at supper, she was at the opposite end of the table from him, safely ensconced between Sir Lucien and Cyril Willoughby. When she sat down at the table, she was aware of Sir Lucien studying her for a moment, then glancing up the table. She followed his gaze. It seemed to her that he was looking at Leighton, and she wondered a little apprehensively if he had guessed something about her and Lord Leighton. Had she been too obvious in the haste with which she had left the group after Dominic arrived?

But then Sir Lucien glanced at her and smiled, and Constance felt reassured. She turned and asked Mr. Willoughby about the hunt that morning.

The meal passed easily enough, as did the rest of the evening. She was careful to sit between Miss Cuthbert and her own cousin Margaret after dinner. Miss Cuthbert said almost nothing, and Margaret chattered far too much; however, Constance had not chosen her position in order to enjoy the evening, but to ensure that it would be impossible for Lord Leighton to take a seat next to her when the men returned to the drawing room.

When the men did return, Lord Leighton took up a post by the mantel, resting his elbow on it as he surveyed the rest of the room. Constance carefully did not look at him, though she was certain that she felt his eyes on her several times. She waited until Miss Cuthbert rose to excuse herself for the evening, then popped up with her, saying that she thought she would retire early, as well.

She could not keep from casting a quick glance at Leighton and found him watching her, a frown on his face, as she walked out of the room with Miss Cuthbert. She had to pay, of course, for leaving early by spending a lonely hour or two reading or gazing disconsolately out the window before she was ready to go to bed. And even then she found it difficult to sleep, her mind retracing the same track it had run all day.

She awoke the next morning, heavy-lidded and tired, and decided to miss breakfast, taking only tea and toast on a tray in her room. She put on the most attractive of her day dresses, thinking to lift her mood a trifle by looking her best, then went down the hall to Francesca's room for a visit.

Francesca, still stuffy-nosed and listless, was feeling somewhat better, and Constance stayed, reading to her for an hour or two until Francesca felt sleepy again. Then she made her way downstairs. She paused outside the cozy morning room where yesterday she had sat with the other women.

She started to go inside, but her gaze fell upon Lord Leighton sitting on a chair by the window, looking supremely bored. Quickly she slipped past the door, and hurried as quietly and quickly as possible down the hall toward the conservatory.

"Miss Woodley!" Constance heard her name called and glanced involuntarily over her shoulder.

Leighton had come to the doorway of the sitting room and was looking down the hallway at her. Without replying, Constance turned and whisked through the door into the conservatory. Almost running, she hurried through the large plant-filled room and out onto the terrace. She trotted down the steps and into the garden. She had almost reached the path she had taken the day before when she heard her name again, louder this time. Leighton had followed her onto the terrace.

She did not look back this time, but whipped around a hedge and down the path. Lifting her skirts to her ankles, she ran lightly along the path, following its twists and turns. She heard Leighton's footsteps on the gravel behind her, and she knew that it would be impossible to get away from him.

"Constance!" His voice was close behind her. "Bloody hell, will you stop?"

She whirled to face him. "What?"

"Why are you running from me?" he asked, his breath rapid from the haste he had made in following her, his brow drawn into a scowl.

"Why are *you* following *me?*" she retorted.

"Because you will not talk to me," Leighton answered, his scowl growing. "What the devil is the matter? Why have you been avoiding me?"

Constance drew herself up, saying coldly, "I am not in the habit of spending time alone with men who are engaged to other women."

"Engaged!" He stared at her blankly for an instant, and then anger darkened his face. "Engaged?" He took two quick steps to her and grabbed her wrist. "Does this look like I am engaged?"

Then he jerked her forward, and his other arm wrapped around her, holding her tightly against his long, hard body, as his mouth came down to cover her own.

CHAPTER TEN

CONSTANCE WAS TOO astonished to move or even protest. His arms were so tight around her that she could not move, and his mouth plundered hers, hot and consuming. She trembled, stunned by the desire that rushed through her at his kiss. She was suddenly on fire, wildly alive to every touch and sensation, her blood thrumming in her veins.

She had been thinking about his kiss for days, since the first time he had stolen a kiss from her in Lady Welcombe's library. She had thought about every moment of it, every aspect, recreating it in her mind. Indeed, she had even dreamed about it.

But none of that compared to the reality. Her heart thundered; her every sense was overwhelmed. His mouth sank into hers, his lips seeking, taking, giving such pleasure that she was almost drowning in it. The fury in his kiss drained away until there was only hunger and a passion so intense that it seemed to fill up every fiber of her being.

His arms loosened around her, and his hands slid

down her body, slowly gliding over her back and onto her sides, his thumbs brushing against the sides of her breasts as his hands moved down to her waist and over her hips. His fingers were spread wide, encompassing as much of her body as he could, and his skin was hot, searing through the muslin of her dress. He rounded his hands over the curve of her buttocks, caressing and squeezing, as he continued to kiss her. His fingers dug into her soft flesh, pushing her up and into him, so that she felt the hard length of his desire pressing into her abdomen.

Her flesh quivered, her loins turned pulsing and warm, and she yearned to press herself even more tightly against him until they melded together. An ache grew between her legs. She was not certain what she wanted, but she knew that she wanted it very much.

He pulled his mouth away, murmuring her name in a low, shaken whisper. He kissed her face and throat, his lips and teeth and tongue teasing and nibbling at her sensitive flesh as he made his way down the column of her neck. Constance let her head loll back, mutely offering up her throat to his mouth.

His hands slipped back up her body and cupped her breasts. She shuddered. Her breasts had ached for his touch, and now, as his fingers gently cradled the soft orbs, she was filled with a satisfaction that was equaled by an ever-growing hunger for more.

Dominic growled low in his throat, and his mouth

came swiftly up to claim hers again. His long fingers gently squeezed her breasts as his thumbs brushed across her nipples, exciting them into hard points. His tongue teased her even as his fingers played with her nipples, arousing her almost unbearably.

She moved restlessly, yearning for more but not knowing what to do. Her hands moved instinctively, sliding up his chest and around to the back of his neck, shoving up into his hair. His hair slid like satin through her fingers, caressing her skin as she caressed him. Constance felt as if she were sliding down into some fiery pit of hunger, helpless, yet longing for her own immolation.

There was the sound of high-pitched laughter and the murmur of feminine voices. Dominic stiffened, then quickly straightened and cast a look around him. Taking Constance's arm, he pulled her off the path and across the grass, then whisked her around a high hedge and into the shelter of a vine-covered arbor.

Deep in its shadow, they waited, every sense alert, as the sound of the voices drew nearer. Constance was standing only inches from him, her eyes level with his broad shoulders. She could feel the heat of his body, smell his scent, her skin so alive and sensitive that she could feel the very touch of the air on her flesh. His hands were on her upper arms, holding her in place, hot and heavy on her skin.

Constance looked up at him. His head was turned as

he peered back through the vines and leaves toward the path where they had stood earlier. She realized how exposed they had been, how easily they could have been seen if anyone had happened to stroll by. She knew the damage that would have been done if they had been discovered in that compromising position; her reputation would have been ruined.

But even knowing that, it was not the chill of fear that permeated her body down to its bones; it was the glow of passion that his kisses and caresses had awakened in her. Her body still hummed with pleasure, still throbbed with desire. He could have had his way with her just then, she thought, and she would have done nothing to stop him. Indeed, she was sure that she would have urged him on.

The thought filled her with anger, more at herself than at him. How could she be so weak? So ruled by her passions instead of her head? It was little wonder that he felt free to treat her like a doxy when she was so ready to act like one!

The Norton sisters and Lord Dunborough appeared finally, walking along a path a few feet from where Constance and Dominic had been standing. The three guests did not look around them, never even glancing across the grass and through the trees to the vine-clad bower where Constance and Lord Leighton were concealed.

Dominic watched the others until they disappeared

into the rose garden. He relaxed, his hands loosening on Constance's shoulders. She wrenched away from him and started out of the arbor, but he reached out and grasped her wrist.

"No, wait!"

"Let me go!" she spat, whirling around to glare at him. "Or do you intend to force me right here in your mother's garden?"

His mouth tightened, the skin around it turning whiter, and a light flared briefly in his eyes. "Of course not," he said tersely.

"Then let me go." She cast a pointed look at his hand wrapped tightly around her wrist.

He released her, holding his hands up and to the side a little as though to show his intention not to touch her again. "I apologize for my rash behavior. I was angry and I—'tis no excuse. I should not have seized you or…" His eyes darkened at the memory, and his gaze flickered for an instant to Constance's mouth.

She thought of what he must see, her lips swollen and soft from his kisses, dark with the blood called by her passion. She flushed and turned away.

"Wait, please," he said urgently, his voice lower and softer now. "Will you not at least give me a chance to speak on my own behalf? Are you so unfair as to condemn me without giving me an opportunity to defend myself?"

"How dare you?" Constance blazed, swinging back

to face him, her eyes bright with anger. "How can you act as though I am the one who has done something wrong? You are the one who is manhandling a woman, holding her here against her will!"

"I am not holding you now. Please. I am sorry for acting boorishly. I ask only that you listen to me."

Constance gazed at him for a long moment, aware of how very much she wanted to hear his explanation, how much she wanted him to explain away what she had heard, yet knowing that it was probably foolhardy to do so. It was clear that she could not trust herself around the man.

She crossed her arms across her chest. "All right. I will listen to you."

"Thank you."

He led her deeper into the garden, bringing her after a few minutes to a wooden bench that lay deep beneath the shade of a spreading willow tree. They were all but hidden from sight and far enough from any path that no one was likely to wander past. She and Dominic turned to face each other, standing several feet apart.

"Now, tell me," Dominic said. "What did you hear? Why do you think I am engaged?"

"Lady Rutherford herself told me," she replied. "She said that you are engaged to her daughter Muriel."

His eyebrows soared upward. "Did she now?" He looked away meditatively. "She must be very sure of herself. Or very desperate."

"It does not seem likely that she would lie," Constance said. "It would be far too embarrassing to be caught in such an untruth."

He nodded. "Yes. I can understand why you believed her." He came closer to her, reaching out to take both her hands in his, and looked intently down into her face. "But it *is* a lie, nonetheless. I am not engaged to Muriel Rutherford. I never have been and never will be. I can promise you that."

Constance's hands trembled in his as relief rushed through her. She felt suddenly breathless and light-headed, as though she might faint, and she moved away, sitting down abruptly on the bench.

"Constance? Are you all right?" Leighton went down on one knee in front of her, gazing at her with concern in his eyes.

She nodded. "Yes. I—" She shook her head, not knowing what to say.

"Do you believe me?" he pressed her. "I swear to you that I am telling you the truth. Ask Francesca. Ask my parents. I have not made Muriel an offer."

Constance looked at him. His face was grave, his blue eyes dark here in the deep shade of the tree and filled with an intensity that she had never seen there before.

The heavy weight that had pressed upon her chest for the past day was lifted now, and filling the space it had left was an uplifting joy. "Yes," she murmured, scarcely trusting her voice. "Yes, I believe you."

Relief flooded his face, and he smiled at her, then raised her hand and pressed his lips to it. "Thank you."

He sat down on the bench beside her, still keeping her hand in his. He raised it again and laid a kiss upon her palm, cradling her hand against his cheek.

Constance gave in to a moment of weakness and leaned her head against his arm. Then, with a sigh, she straightened.

"Why would Lady Rutherford make such a claim when she could be so easily found out? It would be humiliating to have you deny it."

He shrugged. "I presume she was hoping that you would not have the courage to ask me outright, that you would assume I had been deceiving you. Or perhaps she was hoping she could force my hand, that if she announced it, I would simply acquiesce. Give in to the pressure."

"Why would she think that?"

Dominic gave her an amused glance. "Because Lady Rutherford does not know me. She is used to bending others to her not inconsiderable will. Her husband and her children dance to her tune. I know how haughty and ill-natured Muriel is, how much she expects to get her way. But I can tell you that she does not cross her mother. I suppose that Lady Rutherford might have thought she could bully me, as well."

Dominic sighed and stood up, beginning to pace. "There is no engagement. Or even any sort of understanding between us. But it *is* my parents' dearest wish that I marry Muriel. They have been plaguing me with it from the day I became heir to the title. My parents wish it, and Lady Rutherford wishes it, which means that Lord Rutherford wishes it."

"If all these people wish it, does that mean that eventually you will agree?" Constance asked, her newfound happiness beginning to crumble around the edges.

"No!" he retorted sharply. "God, no! I would as soon take a viper to my bed as wed Muriel. Indeed, there would probably be little difference in the two."

"But do your parents not realize how much you dislike the match?" Constance asked.

Dominic let out a snort. "My parents do not care what my feelings regarding the matter are. That is not important. All that is important in their eyes is the estate. The family." He sighed and resumed his seat beside her. "Redfields is a large estate, but the lands have been much encumbered over the years. The family needs an infusion of gold, you see. My father has chosen me as the sacrificial lamb to bring about this happy result."

"And the Rutherfords are wealthy?"

"Very." He nodded. "Despite all their pretensions, Lord Rutherford's title is not an old one, and there is the taint of trade in their background. Lady Rutherford's grandfather, you see, made a fortune in the wool industry, enough to snare a nobleman's daughter for his son and a baron for his granddaughter. Now Lady Rutherford is eager to make her daughter a countess."

"I see."

"They cooked up the scheme between the two of them, my father and Lady Rutherford. It suits them perfectly, and the wishes of the persons involved do not matter. One must do one's duty. The family is all that is important."

"And what of Muriel?" Constance asked, though she was rather sure that she knew the answer to that question. Muriel had made it clear that she considered Leighton her property.

"I think she is agreeable. She is proud and ambitious, much like her mother. She aims for an earl only because there is little prospect of anyone higher. If she thought she had any chance of Rochford, believe me, she would try for him. No doubt I would be far down on her list were it not for the fact that she is beginning to feel desperate. She finds me…lacking in the proper respect for my position." He quirked a smile at Constance. "But no doubt she feels sure that she will be able to crush all levity out of me once we are married."

"I imagine she is capable of that," Constance agreed. "I must confess that I am glad you are unwilling to marry her. I cannot like Miss Rutherford."

"Neither can I. I knew that my father hoped to force the match upon me at this party. That is why I had planned to stay well away from it." He paused and looked at her. "Until Francesca told me that you were planning to attend."

Constance looked at him, then quickly away. The warmth in his eyes unsettled her. She was very glad to learn that Lady Rutherford's tale of his betrothal to her daughter had been nothing but a fabrication, but she was also well aware that the factors that had made his father pursue the match were still there. The family required an heiress for Dominic's bride. He was not for her any more than he had been a moment earlier. He had not deceived her; he had not acted the part of a cad. But, still, one day he would have to marry to please the family. Constance knew that it would be complete folly to let herself even start on that slippery slope that led to love.

"But you are not one to shirk your duty," she said quietly.

His gaze flickered over to her. He studied her for a moment, then answered just as quietly, "No, I suppose I am not. Though I have done my best to ignore it for the last two years."

Constance looked at him. His jaw was set, the usual amused expression utterly gone. Looking at him thus, she had little trouble believing him a man who had gone to war for his country, who had fought and bled and led men into battle. He had known sacrifice.

She reached over and laid her hand gently atop his. It was the same gesture of comfort and consolation that she had given him at the gravesite of his sister. He smiled, a bare curving of his lips, and he turned his hand, taking her hand in his and raising it to his mouth, gently pressing his lips against her skin.

A frisson of pleasure ran through Constance at the touch, and she quickly edged away, hoping that he had not seen her response.

"I was almost engaged once," she said.

She could feel him grow still beside her. After a moment's pause, he said, "Almost?"

"Yes. He proposed, but I told him that I could not accept."

"Did you not love the man?" Dominic asked carefully.

"I did. Or thought I did. Perhaps it is not love when one can recover from it as quickly as I did."

"But you refused."

"I could not marry him. My father was ill. I had to stay and nurse him through his illness." She looked at Dominic then. "I understand the call of duty and its precedence over other things."

"And what of the man? What did he do?"

She shrugged. "He accepted it. He went on with his life. He married a year or two later."

"He was a fool," Dominic growled, his eyes boring into hers. "He was a fool not to wait for you."

Constance's breath caught in her throat. Dominic's gaze, heated and intense, sent desire shimmering through her. She remembered the way his hands had felt upon her body earlier, the taste of his mouth against hers. Unconsciously, she leaned toward him.

In an instant his hands were on her arms, pulling her up and into his lap. One arm curved around her back, supporting her, and his other hand went to her chin, tilting her face up for his kiss. He kissed her long and deeply, and she clung to him, her arms wrapped around his neck. All modesty and shyness seemed to have fled from her. She pressed brazenly up against him, returning his kiss.

With his free hand, Dominic roamed the front of her body, caressing and exploring her as his mouth ravaged hers. He was hampered by the layers of her clothes, and impatiently his hand delved beneath the neckline of her dress, finding the smooth bare skin of her breast and curling around it. Constance started in surprise at the unaccustomed touch of his fingers on her naked flesh, but after that instant of astonishment, her skin responded, turning hot and tingling, her nipple tightening into a hard bud.

Nothing had prepared her for the things that Dominic was doing to her, the wild sensations he was arousing within her. She felt as if she were on fire, and everywhere his mouth or hands touched her, her flesh grew even hotter. When he caressed her breasts, they swelled, pleasure flooding through her, and at the same time, they ached even more, yearning for his touch.

She squeezed her legs together, for it was there that

the desire was pooling, molten and insistent. A pulse throbbed deep in her abdomen, and she yearned for more, though she was not sure what it was she wanted.

Constance kissed him harder, her tongue tangling with his, seeking the satisfaction she craved. She could feel him hardening against her hips, his desire prodding at her soft flesh, and she wiggled restlessly on his lap. Dominic made a choked noise, and his lips left her mouth, kissing frantically down her throat and onto the white plain of her chest. He found the soft white mounds of her breasts and kissed the quivering flesh gently, working his way across her breasts and down to the fleshy button of one nipple.

He kissed the bud gently, and pleasure shot through her, exploding in white-hot heat in her loins. She let out a moan of surprised pleasure, and she felt his soft, smugly masculine chuckle against her tender flesh. She might have resented the sound had it not been for the fact that it was followed an instant later by the hot, wet touch of his tongue, circling her nipple and curling over it, and she arched up in response, her whole body tightening.

Her hands dug into his hair. Just when she thought that she could feel nothing more intensely pleasurable than his tongue, he opened his mouth and closed it around her nipple, pulling the bud into the hot, damp cave of his mouth. Constance trembled at the sensations that shot through her. With each pull of his mouth, he seemed to pluck a chord that went deep into her loins. Each stroke of his tongue excited an even greater hunger, a deeper satisfaction.

His hand moved slowly down her front, caressing her through the material of her dress. His fingers flexed, then relaxed, bunching the muslin. She could feel him against her, taut as a bowstring, his muscles tight and hard, as though he could barely hold himself in check.

He murmured her name, his breath trailing over her breast, made moist by his mouth, and her skin prickled in response, something tightening between her legs and increasing the ache there. Dominic rubbed his face gently against the soft, swelling mounds of flesh, then lightly kissed his way across them. His lips were like velvet upon her sensitized skin, and she waited, her entire body anticipating the moment when he took the other nipple into his mouth and worked his magic on it. She tensed, breathless, whimpering a little as he paused to circle his tongue around the areola, then blew softly upon it.

He was arousing her past bearing, she thought, and she moved instinctively, her hips rocking against him, her back arching up, offering her soft white flesh to him. Dominic groaned in response to her movements, and his mouth clamped around her nipple, hot and wet, suckling her.

At the same moment, his hand slid down between her legs, firm and insistent, seeking out the hot center of her desire. Constance jerked, startled, and her legs closed tightly around him as though to deny him access. But his fingers moved rhythmically, stroking her through the cloth, teasing and testing, and her legs moved apart, mutely inviting his touch.

She lay in his arm, limp and dazed with desire, feeling open and exposed to him in a way that had little to do with actual bareness, for, except for her breasts, her body was shielded from his gaze by her dress. It was as if, layer by careful layer, he had stripped from her the familiar conventions, the modesty that had always shielded her, the cool surface of virtue and calm, exposing the heat that lay beneath, the sultry inner core of her self, throbbing with passion and heat. She pulsed, she ached, she yearned for the feel of his skin upon hers, for the heat and hunger of his mouth, and for a hundred other things that she did not know, did not understand enough to name.

She knew, somehow, that she wanted to be taken, that she longed to feel him as intimately as possible, that she wanted to be filled by him. She ached in some deep, primal way to belong to Dominic wholly, and the fact that her mind was rather hazy as to the details of that belonging in no way kept her from wanting it.

"Dominic…" His name was a sigh in her mouth. "Please…"

Her words shook him, and he lifted his head.

"Dominic?" Her eyes flew open, and she looked up at him.

Dominic's face was taut and suffused with desire, his eyes heavy-lidded and dark. He clenched his jaw, his struggle for control stamped plain upon his features.

"Sweet Lord." He let out a long, shaky breath and closed his eyes. "I must not. We cannot..."

Constance lay motionless for a moment, still too caught up in the roiling mix of desire and confusion to even move. Suddenly it struck her where she was and what she was doing. A faint breeze stirred the air, caressing her breasts. Heat flooded her face, and she sat up, hastily tugging her dress up over her bare breasts.

"I—I must go," she said, her voice shaky and suddenly close to tears. What had she been doing? What must Dominic think of her?

"Wait." His voice was low and harsh, and he reached out and grasped her shoulders, turning her around so that she had to face him.

"I want you," he said hoarsely, his eyes fixed intently on hers. "I want you more than I've ever wanted anyone or anything. But I cannot... I will not hurt you."

Constance did not trust herself to speak. She nodded and backed up a step, then whirled and hurried away from him. She walked quickly back toward the house, her hands going to her hair to smooth any loose strands into place and re-pin them, then hastily brushing at the front of her dress. She prayed that she would not meet anyone as she went; for however much she might put herself back in order, she feared that her face would reveal exactly what she had been doing.

Once inside the house, she whipped up the narrow back stairs that were normally used only by the servants. Relieved that she ran into none of the maids coming down the stairs, she hastened along the corridor and into her room. There she locked the door behind her and collapsed into the chair.

For a long moment she simply sat, letting the trembling of her limbs ease and her mind calm down. Finally she stood and walked to the mirror. Her eyes were bright, her cheeks pink with color, and her lips were dark and full, almost bruised-looking. She looked, she thought, exactly as she had feared, as though she had been thoroughly kissed. She also glowed, she realized, and she was lovelier than she had ever seen herself.

Clearly, she thought, wantonness agreed with her. She shook her head and turned away, going back to the chair.

All her life she had been warned about the sins of the flesh. Until today, she now realized, she had not known what those who warned her had been talking about.

She wanted to give herself to Dominic. Indeed, the fact that she had not done so had been entirely due to his restraint, not hers. She had been consumed by desire; it had whirled through her like a roaring blaze.

She thought again of the sensations that had run through her body, the flames that had curled in her loins, hot and eager, and she flushed all over again with the remembered heat.

It had never occurred to her that such a sensual, passionate nature resided in her. She had hurt, she had loved, but never had she felt the earth-shattering hunger that had poured through her today, the driving, willful desire that wanted to cast aside all else. It astonished her. It was, in fact, rather shocking.

But, she was honest enough to admit, it delighted her, as well. Perhaps it meant she was a lower creature than a lady should be, not refined or virtuous enough. But she thrilled to the passion humming through her veins. She would not want to give up this feeling. She wanted, quite frankly, to feel even more. She wanted Dominic to take her in his arms, to take her to his bed. She wanted to learn everything there could be between a man and a woman. And she wanted to learn it at Dominic's hands.

What would happen, she wondered, if she went to him tonight? If she gave herself to him? Would he pull her to him and kiss her until the world fell away, and the only thing that was real was their mutual delight? Or would he restrain himself again, unwilling to let her sacrifice her good name?

For that, she knew, was the only course open to her if she lay in Dominic's arms. The future Earl of Selbrooke could not offer her the protection of his name. Even though she believed him when he said that he would not marry Muriel Rutherford, she understood now that he had to marry someone of wealth. It was his duty to his name, to his family. He could not let their ancient estate fall into ruin. As the head of the family, he must do whatever was necessary to maintain the FitzAlans' position. Dominic was not the sort to shirk his duty. He would do what had to be done, she knew, and that meant marrying to advantage.

Marrying her would be ruinous. Indeed, she knew that she had no reason to think that he would even wish to marry her. There had been no words of love between them, only the hot, speechless swirl of desire. He wanted her; she had little doubt of that. But he did not love her; he could not let himself love her.

She must be clearheaded, Constance told herself. She wanted him. But was it enough to have his passion, knowing that she would never have his love or his name? Was she willing to risk everything for desire?

CHAPTER ELEVEN

THE CENTERPIECE OF THE FitzAlans' house party was the ball two nights later. Constance wore her loveliest gown, a confection of pale pink satin covered by a robe of white lace, opening on the side and looped back to expose the underskirt. The square-necked bodice was decorated in front with a stomacher of pink satin sewn with tiny pearls. Her hair was swept up, only to tumble down in a profusion of smooth dark brown curls, with pink satin roses and ribbons twined through them.

Looking at her own image in her mirror, Constance was sure that the money she had spent on this gown was well worth it. She smiled to herself, thinking of the look on Dominic's face when he saw her.

She and Dominic had behaved circumspectly since that afternoon in the garden. Though they had not avoided one another, neither had they been alone together. They had talked, but only in gatherings of several people, and he had been careful not to touch her in any way, even to take her hand in greeting or to offer her his arm to stroll down the hall.

He seemed determined not to compromise her, and she, unsure of her own feelings, made no effort to entice him into anything more. But whenever Leighton was in the same room with her, she was constantly aware of his presence, even if she did not look at him. When she did look up, her gaze unerringly went to him, often to find him watching her. Before long, he would work his way around to her side, pausing to engage her in conversation, even if only for a few moments. As they talked, his eyes would gaze into hers, and the air between them sizzled with tension.

Constance suspected that it was wrong of her to want to see his eyes leap with desire tonight when he saw her in this gown. But she could not bring herself to wear something else.

She swept down the hallway to Francesca's room, where she found Maisie putting the finishing touches to her mistress's toilette. Today was the first day that Francesca had spent out of bed, except for a nap in the middle of the afternoon, and she was still not feeling herself. However, she was past the worst of her illness, and she refused to miss the ball.

Francesca smiled as Constance entered the room. "Don't you look lovely tonight?"

"Not as lovely as you," Constance replied candidly.

She thought it would be rather difficult for anyone to outshine Francesca, who was a vision in black satin and tulle, with jet beading decorating both the bodice and the overskirt of her dress. The sleeves were long and sheer, her elegant white arms all the more enticing for their shadowy covering. Her blond hair was pulled up into a knot at the crown of her head, a riot of curls spilling out and a spray of jet beads ornamenting the smooth sweep of her hair on one side, vivid against the pale shade. The final touch was a choker of jet beads around her slender neck, highlighting its delicacy and whiteness.

Francesca smiled. "'Tis kind of you to say so, but I fear that you do not realize your own beauty. Come, let us go downstairs and dazzle everyone."

She linked her arm through Constance's, and they went down the stairs to the large ballroom at the back of the house. It, like the conservatory beside it, led onto the terrace, and tonight its doors and long windows were opened wide to let in the cool night breeze.

Decorated in white and gold, its walls heightened the glow of the three crystal chandeliers that hung in a row down the center of the room. Crystal drops also hung from the sconces that lined the walls. Musicians played at the far end of the room on a small stage, discreetly hidden from view by green plants. Roses stood massed in vases around the room, casting their sweet scent upon the air.

Constance drew a long breath and released it, thinking how very lovely a scene it was. It seemed to her the most beautiful of balls she had attended, though she could not quite put her finger on what made it so perfect. Perhaps, she thought, the beauty of it lay in the excitement and eagerness that filled her chest.

They made a circuit of the room, pausing to talk to everyone. There were more people here tonight than the guests who had been staying here all week, for many local people had been invited, as well as several who had come only for the ball and would be departing the following day.

Near one of the doors that led out onto the terrace, they came upon the Duke of Rochford, looking as severely elegant and formidable as ever. A young woman stood beside him, and though her face was animated where his seemed set in stone, there was a similarity in coloring and in features to mark her as a relation.

It did not surprise Constance when, after bowing slightly to her and Francesca in greeting, the duke said, "Miss Woodley, pray allow me to introduce my sister, Lady Calandra."

"My lady, it is an honor to meet you," Constance told the girl, who smiled brilliantly, her dark eyes sparkling.

"The pleasure is all mine, I assure you," Calandra replied, reaching out to take Constance's hand. "I have been looking forward to the evening with great anticipation. I have spent the last month in Bath with Grandmama, and it is deadly dull there. I was thrilled when Sinclair told me of the ball."

Unlike her brother, Lady Calandra was not tall, but

her hair was the same striking black, and her eyes equally dark. Her features were straight and well-formed and would likely have been termed elegant but for the vivacity that stamped them and the long, charming dimple that lay in one cheek.

She chatted with Francesca and Constance with a happy lack of self-consciousness and an openness that seemed at great odds with the Duke's formal manner. She was, clearly, much younger than Rochford, but she appeared not to be in awe of him, a fact that struck Constance with surprise, for she found Rochford to be an imposing figure.

"You must come to visit me," Calandra told Constance earnestly. "Rochford is not returning to London until next week, and I shall be all alone in that house until then—well, except for Rochford, of course, but he is poor company when we are in the country, always talking to the steward and looking at the books." She glanced over Constance's shoulder and smiled sunnily. "Leighton! How good to see you!"

Constance's stomach fluttered at the sound of Dominic's name, and she turned to greet him, careful not to seem eager. "Lord Leighton."

"Lady Calandra. Rochford. Francesca," Dominic greeted the others and turned to Constance. "Miss Woodley."

The look in his eyes was everything Constance had hoped it would be. A blush rose in her cheeks, and she cast her eyes down, in the way a girl was modestly supposed to do…although in her case, Constance knew that she did it more to hide the answering heat in her own eyes than to act in a proper manner.

"I hope you will do me the honor of the next dance, Miss Woodley," Dominic went on.

Constance knew that it would have been more appropriate for him to have asked the Duke's sister, as Lady Calandra was of much higher rank, as well as being a new guest, but Constance was very glad that he had not. It would have been painful to watch Dominic walk off with the beautiful, wealthy and well-connected Calandra, who would obviously be an excellent match for him.

Constance murmured her assent and took the arm he offered to lead her onto the floor. The three people they had left behind watched them take the floor and begin to dance.

After a moment, Rochford said in a faintly mocking tone, "Dear, dear, Lady Haughston, do you think it is sporting to win your bet in such a manner?"

The two women turned to him, puzzled.

"Whatever do you mean?" Francesca asked.

"Your bet, dear lady, to find our Miss Woodley a husband before the end of the Season. It hardly seems fair to have made a match for her with your own brother."

Francesca went still, staring at him. "What?"

"What are you talking about, Sinclair?" his sister asked. "What bet?"

"He's talking about nothing," Francesca told her quickly, color blooming in her cheeks. "We have a silly little bet, that is all."

"To make a match for Miss Woodley?" Calandra asked, looking interested. "But how nice!" She turned to stare across the ballroom at the couple in question. "They look very good together."

"No," Francesca protested. "Rochford, you are wrong. I have made no match between Constance and Dominic."

The Duke raised a quizzical eyebrow at her, and then, without a word, nodded toward the couple in question.

Irritation and alarm rising in her, Francesca followed his gaze to where Constance and Dominic were going through the intricate steps of a country dance. Even when they separated, their eyes went only to each other, and when they rejoined, palms up and placed together, to circle first one way and then the other, they seemed to form a perfect set, entirely apart from and oblivious to everyone else in the room.

Francesca sucked in a quick breath as the truth hit her. "Oh, no…" The words issued on a soft little moan. "Oh, dear God, what have I done?"

CONSTANCE WAS UNAWARE OF the glow that marked her face or the way Dominic's eyes never left hers. She knew only that she was blissfully happy. She could have no future with Dominic, but that did not matter tonight. She wanted to have this moment, this perfect memory to cherish forever. She could be sensible tomorrow and the next day and all the days after that. Later she would tell herself all the reasons she could not fall in love with him, all the sorrow that would follow if she did.

But right now she would have the pleasure of looking at him, moving with him, laying her palm flush against his as they circled, their bodies close enough together that she felt the heat of his flesh, smelled the scent of his skin.

The music came to a close, and Constance made her curtsy to him. She took his arm, but he did not lead her back to her companions, turning instead toward the open doors leading onto the terrace. She smiled and went with him.

Other couples had sought the fresh air outside, as well, strolling along the terrace and even descending the steps toward the garden. Dominic and Constance did not take the steps but stayed on the wide terrace, drifting along past the lighted windows and doors of the ballroom.

The heady scent of roses drifted upward from below, and shadows beckoned beyond the last window of the house. They stopped on the edge of the dark end of the terrace and gazed out over the garden. It was washed with the pale light of the moon, and Constance looked up to see the moon glowing in the velvety black sky, softer and warmer than the sharp white sparkle of the stars.

A breeze played across the bare skin of her neck and shoulders, lifting the stray hairs that curled around her face. She turned and looked up at Dominic.

He was very close to her, only inches away, his face thrown into sharp relief by the moonlight. Even in this light, the desire in his eyes was clear. She thought of the kisses they had shared the other day in the garden, the way his hands had caressed her body, arousing in her feelings she had never known before, even with the man with whom she had once thought herself in love. She could not help but wonder if the feeling that permeated her whenever she saw Dominic was not only desire but something much stronger, much larger. Could it be that she was falling in love with Dominic—indeed, had already taken that fall?

She wanted him to kiss her, no matter how improper that might be. She wanted to feel again the passion that had rushed through her body when he had kissed her before. She could not help but think of the life that awaited her after tonight. In a few days she would be leaving Redfields, and then, within weeks—she knew how the time would fly—her Season would be over. How many more times would she see Dominic once she left his family's home? Once her time in London had ended, she would never see him.

Was she to spend the rest of her life never knowing the taste of his lips again? Would she never know passion? Would she grow older, watching others court and marry and have children, never knowing any of those joys for herself? It seemed to her in that moment a horribly bleak existence.

A thought crept in. Would it not be better to experience the full depths of desire at least once? If she was collecting memories, did she really want to exclude the grandest, most glorious one she could hold?

She thought of kissing Dominic again, of sinking into his embrace and melding with him. She wanted to discover all the pleasures that lay hidden in his hard body; she wanted to know, to feel, everything her own flesh was capable of. Perhaps it was wicked of her, Constance thought, but she wanted to know what it was like to lie with a man—no, not with *a* man, but with Dominic. She wanted it with a fervor that made her tremble. And she could not help but think that if she denied herself that pleasure, she would regret it for the rest of her life.

Once again Constance considered casting caution to the winds, defying the conventions and seizing her moment of passion. It was a frightening, tantalizing thought.

Something of what she was thinking must have shown on her face, for Dominic let out a little half groan and pulled her into his arms. He kissed her tenderly, his lips gently pressing, nibbling at her lips, his tongue grazing the sensitive flesh, but as the heat rose between them, his mouth turned harder and more demanding, and his tongue entered her mouth, thrusting and hungry. His arms tightened around her, crushing her to him.

The growing fierceness of his kiss did not frighten Constance. Rather, it roused an equally fierce longing inside her, and she pressed up against him, her arms twining around his neck and holding him nearer, ever nearer. Desire clawed at them, sharp and insistent, and coiled hotly deep inside.

The soft murmur of voices penetrated through the haze of their passion, and hastily Dominic swept her back with him, deeper into the shadows. They turned and looked down the sweep of the long walkway, where a couple strolled, talking softly. Dominic released Constance, then took her hand and pulled her even farther back. She stood with him, waiting, watching the other couple, her heart thundering, her breath coming in quick pants.

The man and woman walked closer and lingered just beyond the edge of the shadows. Moments crawled by before finally they turned and strolled back the way they had come.

Dominic turned to her, his eyes glinting in the darkness. He took her hand and raised it to his mouth, kissing her knuckles.

"We must go back," he murmured hoarsely.

Constance nodded. There was nothing in her thrumming body that wanted to do what he said, but she was well aware of the dangers of remaining here. They had probably already caused talk by disappearing from the ball for as long as they had. Her hands went to her hair and gown, smoothing out any disarray she found. She only hoped the look on her face could be erased as easily.

She put her hand formally on his arm, and they strolled back along the terrace. Constance glanced up at him in the soft glow of the outdoor lanterns, and Dominic smiled down at her. She smiled back almost shyly, then looked away, afraid that too much of what she felt must show on her face.

He cleared his throat and said, "I would like to show you around the estate."

His words were quite ordinary, but the husky quality of his voice sent a shiver through her.

"Yes, that sounds most pleasant," she replied, fighting for an easy tone of voice.

They stepped inside, continuing to talk in a somewhat stilted way, making plans to go riding together. Constance hoped that the flush in her cheeks would cause no more comment than the pink in others' faces, brought about by exercise and the large number of people in the room.

"Let me fetch you something to drink," Dominic suggested, and she smiled at him.

"Thank you." With any luck, a cup of punch would cool the heat rushing through her.

He left her at one of the chairs that lined the walls of the ballroom and started making his way around the dancers to the refreshments at the far end. Constance waited for him, idly watching the dancers as she fanned her face. She did not see the person approaching her from the side until the shadow fell across her.

"What do you think you are doing?" a woman's voice hissed, sounding like drops of water hitting a hot stone.

Startled, Constance looked up to see Muriel Rutherford looming over her, a tall, slender column of cold fury. Her rail-thin figure was clothed in a simple, even girlish, white ballgown that did little for her looks. Constance presumed the style and color were meant to place Muriel among the young debutantes who made up the bulk of the marriage mart. However, she was clearly past the age of most of them, closer, Constance thought, to her own twenty-eight years than to eighteen or nineteen, and the girlish dress only emphasized the older set of Muriel's face, stamped with lines from years of disdain. The color, moreover, was not flattering to Muriel's very white skin, washing out her pallid tones even more.

She frowned at Constance, her face pinched in anger. Her light blue eyes were chips of ice. Her hands were curled so tightly into fists that Constance thought her fan might very well snap in her hand.

"I beg your pardon?" Constance asked coolly, rising to face the other woman.

"How dare you?" Muriel snapped. "I know my mother told you that Dominic and I have an understanding, yet still you chase after him. I saw you flirting with him, leading him out onto the terrace."

Anger sliced through Constance at the other woman's contemptuous words, and she was aware of a strong desire to box Muriel's ears, but she kept her voice calm and quiet as she said, "Careful, Lady Muriel. You overstep your bounds."

"Stay away from him!" Muriel shot back bluntly.

"If I were you, my lady, I would lower my voice. You would not want to create a scene in front of all these people."

"I don't care!" Muriel retorted rashly. "Let everyone know what you are up to!"

"I doubt that you would care to have everyone hear that you are not engaged to Lord Leighton despite what your mother has been saying," Constance answered, gazing back at Muriel with a quiet, unmoving confidence.

Muriel's eyes flashed, and Constance thought for an instant that the woman was actually going to slap her. But then Muriel seemed to gain control over herself, and she let out a harsh laugh that held no amusement at all.

"Do you actually think he will marry you?" Muriel

asked, her voice dripping with scorn. "Gentlemen like Lord Leighton don't marry pretty little nobodies like you. They dally with such women, that is all. They marry someone like me!"

"I suggest, Muriel, that you stop talking before you make more of a fool of yourself than you already have," cracked out a masculine voice.

Both women started in surprise and whirled to find Dominic standing beside them. Neither had seen him approaching. Constance wondered how much of their conversation he had overheard.

He held a cup of punch in his hand, which he handed to Constance with a small, polite bow in her direction. His face was set in a cool, courteous mask, but there was a hard quality to his blue eyes that betrayed his temper.

"D-Dominic." Muriel looked dismayed. "I did not see you there."

"Clearly." He looked at Muriel, and Constance felt a faint twinge of pity even for her, having to face Dominic's stony gaze. "You and your mother appear to be laboring under a misapprehension, Lady Muriel. You and I are not engaged."

Muriel looked as if she had sustained a blow, but she recovered quickly, letting out a little laugh and saying, "Of course we have not yet made the announcement...."

"There will be no announcement," Dominic retorted bluntly.

Muriel sucked in her breath sharply, her eyes widening. She opened her mouth, but nothing came out.

"Perhaps my father and your mother should have consulted me before they made their arrangements. I will give you the benefit of the doubt and assume that my father encouraged you and Lady Rutherford to think that I was amenable to my parents' plans for my future. However, I can assure you that I am not. I never gave the Earl any reason to think that I would marry as he directed. Nor have I at anytime said anything to you or your parents that would indicate that I had any intention of asking for your hand. That much, at least, I know you are aware of. I would have thought that fact would have restrained your mother or you from uttering the falsehoods that you have told Miss Woodley."

Muriel gaped at him. She recovered enough to say in a low, harsh voice, "Dominic! Do not be a fool. You know that people such as you and I marry for larger reasons than some mawkish sentiment."

"Muriel," he replied impatiently, "I am not going—"

"No!" Muriel flung up a hand as if to stop him, pasting on a brittle smile. "Please. Do not. I will not stay here and listen to you say something I know you will later regret, when you have gotten over…this foolishness." She cast a last dagger of a look at Constance, then whirled around and stalked off.

Dominic's jaw tightened, and his eyes flashed with a

dangerous light. Constance thought for an instant that he was about to start after Muriel, but at that moment Francesca swept up on Sir Lucien's arm, smiling brightly.

"Dominic, my love, there you are!" she exclaimed as if she had not seen him only half an hour earlier, linking her arm through her brother's and turning him away.

Dominic stiffened, then visibly relaxed his face and turned toward Constance. "I apologize, Miss Woodley."

Constance was trembling, her stomach quivering with nerves, but she managed to shake her head, pasting a smile on her lips, and said, "No, please, do not worry about it, my lord. I am fine, I assure you. I am growing accustomed to Lady Muriel's manner of speech."

"Then you are a much braver person than I," Sir Lucien told her. "Frankly, the woman terrifies me."

The others smiled, the tension of a moment earlier eased. Sir Lucien turned to Constance, giving her a graceful bow, and asked her for the dance that was about to start.

Gratefully, she accepted. She needed to be away from Dominic for a moment, to have a chance to recover her temper and her composure, and a dance with as capable and entertaining a partner as Sir Lucien was perfect for her purpose. Constance laid her hand on his arm and nodded a polite goodbye to Francesca and Dominic.

Francesca watched her friends leave, waiting until

they were on the dance floor and the music was starting before she turned back to her brother.

"Now," she said, crossing her arms and fixing him with her dark blue gaze, so like his own, "just what do you think you are doing?"

Dominic stiffened, his eyes sparking with anger. "What? You, too?"

He whipped around and strode off. Francesca stared after him for a moment, then sighed and followed him. She caught up with him outside the ballroom, reaching to grab his sleeve.

"Dominic, wait."

He pulled to a stop and turned to her, his face a polite mask. Francesca muttered an imprecation under her breath and, glancing around her, took his hand to drag him down the hall away from the music and the noise. Picking up a candlestick on one of the narrow tables along the hallway, she lit it from a sconce, then opened one of the closed doors along the hallway and whisked Dominic inside.

Francesca cast a quick glance around. They were in the small east-facing room that her mother used as a morning sitting room. It was empty of people, the only light in it the candle that she held. She set down the candle on a small table beside the door and turned to face Dominic.

"What do you want, Francesca?" he asked, his voice

cold. "Do you also hope for Muriel Rutherford for a sister-in-law?"

"Good Gad, no," Francesca retorted bluntly. "I should hope you would have good sense than to tie yourself to that icicle of a woman. I do not care whom you marry. But I warn you—I will not have you hurting Constance Woodley. I am very fond of the girl."

He let out a short bark of laughter that contained little amusement. "You think I am not?"

"I fear that you are too fond of her," Francesca replied. "I fear that you will lead her on, encourage her to fall in love with you, and then her heart will be broken."

"Why do you assume that I would break her heart?"

"Because you and I both know that you must marry money," she shot back.

"Why?" he responded, his voice laced with bitterness. "Why should I marry to please our wretched family? You and I both know how little our family is worth the sacrifice."

"Yes, and I also know you," Francesca told him. "You will do your duty. You always have, and you always will."

He gazed at her levelly. "Would you condemn me to that? You, of all people, know how it is to marry where one does not love."

Tears sprang into Francesca's eyes, and she turned away quickly.

"Oh, bloody hell!" Dominic crossed the room and took his sister's shoulders in his hands, saying in a softened voice, "The devil curse my tongue. I am sorry, Francesca. I should not have said that. You are the last person on whom I should take out my frustration. Please, forgive me."

She turned and gave him a watery smile. "No, I should ask your forgiveness." She slid her arms around him and laid her head against his chest. "Oh, Dominic, I do want you to achieve happiness. I truly do. I don't care about the family or Redfields or any of it, if only you are happy. You should not have to be the one to pay for all the foolish ways our ancestors wasted their money." She pulled back and looked up into his face. "Do you love Constance? Do you want to marry her?"

Dominic looked at her, his face torn. "I—I don't know. I am not sure if any of us are even capable of such an emotion. The FitzAlans are a sorry lot."

Sadly, Francesca nodded. "I fear you are right." She walked away from him, sitting down in the nearest chair. She smoothed down the material of her dress, saying in a low voice. "The truth is, I married foolishly—we both know that. I did not help myself or the family, either one. I do not wish to see you in such a marriage. I would be most happy if you married Constance. I cannot think of anyone I would more like to have as a relative."

Dominic shook his head. "No. You are right. I would be a cad to pursue Miss Woodley." He strolled over to the window and pushed aside the curtain, looking out into the dark night. His face was shadowy and unreadable in the dim light. "I know where my duty lies. I shall marry as I must."

CHAPTER TWELVE

CONSTANCE DID NOT SEE Dominic again that night, though she glanced discreetly around the ballroom several times. Francesca seemed preoccupied, and more than once Constance saw her frowning.

Constance felt sure that Francesca must be upset over the scene with Muriel. She feared that Francesca regretted bringing Constance into her family home. Dominic's parents expected him to marry Miss Rutherford; perhaps Francesca had expected that, too. Dominic had said that the family needed money, and Constance could not help but remember Francesca's skill at saving pennies when they were purchasing her own wardrobe. Perhaps Francesca, as much as any of them, needed Dominic to marry well.

What if Francesca, like Muriel, felt that Constance was to blame for Dominic's refusal to marry the other woman? Constance could not detect any change in Francesca's attitude toward her, but neither could she shake the feeling that Francesca was worried.

Constance went to bed feeling uneasy, and the next

morning, as she dressed for the day, she wondered whether she should offer to leave Redfields and return to London. She did not want to; her heart felt as if it would tear from her chest if she did. But she could not bring harm to Francesca. She could not repay all Francesca had done for her by being a part of the ruin of her family's fortune.

If she were not here, Constance thought, perhaps Dominic might be more agreeable to marrying as his family wished. Without the distraction of his attraction to Constance, he might talk to Muriel more, might spend time with her and find…what? That was the problem. Muriel was a cold, disagreeable snob. Constance could not imagine Dominic even liking her, let alone falling in love with her. And Constance's absence would do nothing to change Muriel's character. Nor would she condemn Dominic to a lifetime with Muriel, even if she had the power to do so.

She was resigned to the fact that Dominic would not be in her life in the future. They would part in a few days, and eventually he would marry some other heiress, one who was—she hoped—better than Muriel Rutherford. But right now, surely Constance's being here would not be ruinous to him or his family. Even if Francesca did have financial problems, Constance could not really believe that she would want her brother to marry someone like Muriel.

It would not matter in the long run, Constance told

herself, if she stole a few days of happiness with Dominic. There would be no harm, surely, in her riding about the estate with him today, as he had asked her to last night. The only harm, she thought, would come to her own heart.

She knew that she was perilously close to loving Dominic, that every moment she spent with him pushed her nearer and nearer to that state. Some part of her yearned to know that love, to feel all the happiness that such emotion could bring. Another part of her feared it. She had loved before and been pained to lose it, and she knew that what she had felt before for Gareth, both the love and the pain, would pale before what Dominic could bring to her heart.

Constance went to her wardrobe and pulled out the riding habit that Maisie had brought to her two days after their excursion to the village church. It was made of a deep blue velvet and had belonged to Francesca when she was younger. It had been left here at Redfields, and it had required only letting out the hem to fit Constance. Francesca, even though she had been ill, had set her maid to altering the outfit, an action that had touched Constance deeply. She had known Francesca only a few weeks, yet she was kinder than her own cousins or aunt. Maisie had also found an old pair of Francesca's boots in her closet, and, fortunately, Constance's feet were the same size, so she was able to wear them.

Constance hesitated, thinking again about Dominic's absence for the final portion of the last evening. Perhaps he would not wish to take her riding this morning. Perhaps he regretted what he had told her, or perhaps he had changed his mind about Muriel and realized that he must marry her, no matter what. Constance's heart clenched inside her at the thought.

At that moment Maisie popped her head in the door to see if Constance was ready to have her hair done. "Oh, going riding, are you, miss?" she asked, and came over to take the skirt and jacket from Constance's hands. "I'll just press this, then, while you're at breakfast."

"I—I am not certain I will be riding," Constance equivocated.

"No matter. 'Twill be ready. Now, what would you like for your hair today? Something simple and well-pinned, I should imagine, if you'll be riding."

Constance agreed and let the woman begin working her artistry.

Minutes later, when she walked into the dining room, Constance found more people around the long table than were normally there. Dominic was seated at the farthest end of the table, beside his father. Across from him, Constance noted, were Lady Rutherford and her daughter. Dominic seemed engrossed in talking to Mrs. Kenwick and her son Parke, who sat between Dominic and Francesca. Constance glanced at Dominic and quickly away, very aware of the eyes of the Rutherfords on her.

Next to the Rutherfords were the three Nortons and Lady Calandra, the Duke's sister. As Constance slid into the empty seat beside Francesca, Calandra swung toward her with a friendly smile.

"Hello," she greeted Constance. "Rochford finally gave in last night and let me stay over. He, of course, went home in the carriage." She rolled her eyes. "The estate manager and the books cannot wait, it appears."

"I am glad that you are still here," Constance replied honestly, having liked the lively young woman on sight.

"Oh, yes," Elinor Norton agreed emphatically. "The more the merrier for our ride."

"Ride?" Constance asked.

"Did you not know? Lord Leighton is showing everyone about the estate this afternoon," her sister Lydia chimed in.

"Sounds like a jolly good time," their brother, Sir Philip, agreed.

Constance's gaze went to Dominic for the first time. He looked at her rather ruefully, but said only, "Miss Woodley has already agreed. You cannot back out on me now."

"When we heard Lord Leighton was planning a tour of the estate, we could not help but want to join in," Elinor went on happily.

Constance looked toward Muriel, who gazed back at

her smugly. Constance had little doubt who had spread the word that Dominic was planning a "tour" of the estate.

"No doubt you will be going as well, Miss Rutherford," Constance said mildly, allowing none of her irritation to show in her voice.

"Yes, indeed," Muriel replied with a thin smile. "I would not miss it for the world." She stood up, pushing back her chair. "Now, if you will excuse me, Lord Selbrooke, I must see to some things."

"Of course, Lady Muriel." The Earl beamed at her and returned to his conversation with her father.

Constance swallowed her disappointment. Clearly Muriel had overheard Dominic's plans to take Constance around the estate, and she had seized the opportunity to deny them the time alone together. Given the stony set of Dominic's face, Constance did not think that Muriel had helped herself very much. She might have outmaneuvered him, but she would not have endeared herself to him.

It was better, anyway, that they had company, Constance told herself. She could enjoy the time together, but she would not have to worry about how to deal with the wayward passion that always threatened to overcome her when she was alone with him. It was much better. Really.

"Are you coming with us, Francesca?" Constance asked.

Francesca shook her head. "No, I think I am too

recently recovered. I shall stay with Mama and the other ladies."

Cousin Margaret was quick to inform them that she planned to go, as did Lord Dunborough, Mr. Willoughby and most of the young men. Indeed, it seemed that of all the young people, only the shy Miss Cuthbert and Cousin Georgiana, afflicted by a fear of horses, would be staying behind with Francesca and the older women.

"Lord Leighton has promised that we shall go to a promontory from which one can see the entire valley," Lydia Norton announced.

"I am not sure I should want to go so high," Cousin Margaret demurred.

"It is a bit of a climb," Calandra told them. "But when you get to the top, you can see the whole countryside."

"And we shall have tea in the summer house," Elinor Norton put in.

"It sounds wonderful," Constance agreed.

She applied herself to her food, letting the excited chatter of the others swirl around her, and attempted to adjust her expectations for the day.

Later Constance left the table with Francesca and walked with her up the stairs to their rooms. When they reached the door of Constance's room, she smiled a goodbye at her friend and started inside. But she came to an abrupt halt, sucking in her breath in a sharp exclamation of dismay.

There, on her bed, was the dark blue riding habit, which Maisie had obviously pressed and laid out for Constance to wear. But it would never be worn now, for dozens of long rips ran across the skirt and bodice, reducing the garment to shreds.

"What is it?" Francesca asked, hearing Constance's gasp and following her into the room. When she saw what lay on the bed, she let out an exclamation. "Sweet heaven! Who could have done such a thing?"

"I don't know," Constance replied, unable to keep the bitterness from her voice. "But I have a good idea."

"Yes, I do, too." Francesca walked over to the bed and looked down at the torn garment. Then she turned to Constance, a dangerous light now glittering in her eyes. "Don't worry. We will not allow Muriel to get the better of you so easily."

Constance smiled at her friend, warmed by Francesca's ready sympathy and eagerness to help. Clearly, any worries she had had that Francesca might prefer Muriel for her brother were not true.

"But how? We already used your old riding habit."

"You shall simply use the one I brought with me," Francesca told her. "Maisie can let out the hem in a flash. The party is not leaving for another hour or so. And I shall borrow my mother's riding habit. It will not matter if it is a trifle large. I have no one I need to impress today."

"But I thought you were not going," Constance replied.

"I wasn't," Francesca told her grimly. "But Muriel has changed my mind."

Francesca rang for her maid and showed her the shredded habit, explaining what she wanted her to do. Maisie, after exclaiming over the damage, immediately set to work on Francesca's riding habit, the light of battle in her eyes, and Francesca went to her mother's room to borrow her riding clothes. Fortunately, nothing had been done to the old riding boots, because Francesca's feet could not fit into her mother's boots.

By the time the others had gathered downstairs for the proposed ride, Maisie had managed not only to let down the hem of Francesca's riding habit, but also to tack and pin Lady Selbrooke's dress so that it fit Francesca.

Francesca and Constance went down the stairs to join the others, who were waiting in the entry hall, and Constance had to hide a smile at the expression of surprise, then anger, that flitted across Muriel's face at the sight of her. Constance gazed back at Muriel, unsmiling, a challenge in her eyes. Muriel's face tightened, and she whipped around to face the other direction.

The next few minutes were taken up outside mounting their horses, which the grooms had brought around to the front drive. Dominic came up beside Constance, saying, "I chose Grey Lady for you. She's a good little mare, calm and biddable, but not a laggard."

Constance turned to look up at him, her stomach fluttering, as always, at the sound of his voice. "Thank you. I have not ridden much in recent years."

Her mare, the horse she had ridden since she was fourteen, had grown old and slow, but Constance had not had the heart to replace her. And when the mare had died, her uncle had not purchased a new mount for her.

"I was not sure." Dominic led her to the mare.

Constance spent some time getting acquainted with her horse, stroking its mane and talking to it. Then Dominic gave her a leg up, and she settled into the sidesaddle and took the reins he handed her. Dominic's stallion was near hers, and he mounted, taking his place beside Constance.

The small company rode out of the yard and took the trail leading back to the farms that were part of the estate. Dominic rode in the lead, with Constance beside him.

She quickly realized why Francesca had been determined to join them for the ride when Muriel drew alongside them, looking her best on horseback, as Constance had noticed on the trip to the church.

"Come, Dominic," she said, not even glancing at Constance. "I am sure Arion wants to stretch his legs. Let's race to the stream."

"I cannot leave the rest of the party," Dominic responded equably. "I am the one showing the way, after all."

"Of course you cannot," Francesca agreed, trotting up beside them. "Come, Muriel, I will race with you."

Muriel's mouth tightened. Riding away from the group with Francesca was doubtless not what she wanted. On the other hand, she was rather caught by her own offer.

"All right," she said with little grace, and the two women took off with a burst of speed.

Dominic and Constance watched as the two horses streaked out ahead of the rest of them. It was little surprise that Muriel won the race, for she was an excellent horsewoman. However, Francesca turned out to have won the day, for she stayed by Muriel's side, even when Muriel dropped back to join the rest of the group. No matter how Muriel maneuvered to get closer to Dominic, Francesca managed to wedge herself between them. Constance could not keep from smiling to herself, warmed by Francesca's loyalty.

Constance could not remember when she had enjoyed a day as much. She and Dominic talked and laughed, sometimes alone, sometimes with others of the party around them. He pointed out the various farms and crops along the way, leading them through the edge of the woods and across the meadows. He knew the names of every person they happened upon, and he could tell the history of any part of the land. It was clear from his voice that he loved the estate. It made Constance wonder even more why he had kept himself away from it for so long. Surely it could not be solely because of his parents' desire to marry him to Miss Rutherford.

His parents were rather stiff, formal people. There was nothing in them of the easy, friendly manner that characterized Dominic and Francesca. But a difference in personality was often in evidence among family members, and it did not usually bring about the sort of distance Constance saw between Dominic and his parents. She had taken note of it throughout the week. Dominic was rarely with either Lord or Lady Selbrooke, and on those occasions when he had been in their company, he had remained there only a short time. At supper, he sat at the end of the table near his father, but that was only because the place cards situated him there. Never had Constance seen him carrying on what she would have termed an easy conversation with the older man. Anyone watching them would have supposed them mere acquaintances.

Something, she thought, must have caused a rift between them, but she had no idea what it had been. Dominic, for all his ease in talking, rarely spoke about the past or his family. The few times she had heard him mention the past, he had talked about his regiment and the days he had spent in the Peninsular Campaign. His memories of his fellow Hussars seemed much warmer than those of his family. Constance could not help but wonder what had happened.

They made their way back toward the house late in the afternoon and stopped at a small ornamental lake that lay within sight of Redfields. A summer house sat at the far end of the lake, with a pleasant path leading all the way around the small body of water.

They found two footmen and two maids in the summer house, putting the finishing touches on the afternoon tea that they had brought down in large wicker baskets from the main house. They had laid snowy damask coverings on two wooden trestle tables. On one table stood a large urn of tea, and on either side lay platters of tea cakes, biscuits, scones and crustless wedges of sandwiches.

After the afternoon's ride, the food was more than welcome, and everyone dug in eagerly. They sat around for some time afterward, lazily talking. Sir Philip and his sisters wanted to try out the two small boats moored at the pier beside the lakehouse, and young Parke Kenwick, who seemed rather smitten with Miss Lydia, volunteered to make a fourth with them.

Shortly afterward, Francesca persuaded Muriel to accompany her on a short stroll around the lake. Muriel seemed somewhat reluctant, casting an eye toward the other end of the table, where Dominic was sitting, surrounded by his friends. However, Francesca paid no attention to her hesitation and linked her arm through Muriel's, professing her desire to get Miss Rutherford's opinion of the decoration scheme she was planning for her music room. Muriel could do little but give in gracefully.

Next to Constance, Lady Calandra smothered a giggle. "Francesca seems to have developed an inordinate fondness for Muriel."

Constance glanced at her and found Calandra's expressive dark eyes dancing with laughter. She could not keep from breaking into a grin, as well. "Indeed, she has."

"Poor Muriel, I am sure it must be horribly frustrating for her. She wants to hang on Dominic's arm, but she is too much of a snob not to be flattered by Lady Haughston's attentions."

Constance did not know what to say to the young woman. Calandra seemed to have assessed the situation quite correctly, but Constance was unsure whether the girl was aware of the reasons for Francesca's actions.

"Well, we must make use of the time that Francesca has sacrificed herself to give you," Calandra went on merrily. She turned toward her host. "Dominic, you promised earlier to show us the promontory."

"Of course." Dominic smiled at Calandra. "You have only to ask." He cast a look toward the lake, where Francesca was slowly strolling arm in arm with Miss Rutherford. "Yes, I suppose now would be a good time."

"But what about Lady Haughston?" asked Alfred Penrose, who had, Constance suspected, developed something of a crush on Francesca. "Will she not want to come?"

"Oh, no," Calandra assured him quickly. "I feel sure she would not wish it. She has seen it many times, and she is still feeling rather weak from her illness. In fact, she might appreciate it if you were to join her and Miss Rutherford on their stroll."

"Why, yes, I suppose I could." Penrose looked quite taken with the idea, promptly standing up and excusing himself.

Once again Constance and Calandra exchanged glances, and it was all Constance could do not to laugh. "You wicked girl," she murmured to Calandra. "Lady Francesca will repay you for that."

Lady Calandra giggled. "I could not resist. Anyway, having spent the afternoon in Muriel's company, I suspect that Francesca will be thrilled to have anyone else to talk to."

After a bit of discussion, it was arranged that Mr. Carruthers and Mr. Willoughby, along with Constance's cousin Margaret, Constance and Lady Calandra would join the expedition to the promontory to see the view of the surrounding countryside. They set out immediately, curving away from the main house and entering the woods on the northern edge.

Calandra rode beside Constance for a time. Just behind them, Margaret was flirting madly with the blond, rather shy Carruthers. The other men led the way, winding through the trees. The ground soon began to rise, slowing them even further.

"Is Francesca helping you or her brother—or both of you?" Calandra asked.

"What? Why would she be helping me?"

The young woman smiled. "My brother is convinced that she is trying to make a match between you and Dominic."

Constance blushed. "I am sure she is not."

Calandra shrugged. "Well, Sinclair is not what I would call an expert in matters of the heart. After all, he is nearing forty, and he hasn't yet come close to marriage. Still, I must say, there is something about the way that Dominic looks at you…."

The little mare skittered, and Constance looked down, realizing that she had clenched the reins too tightly. She forced her fingers to relax. "I am sure you must be wrong. Lord Leighton has expressed no preference, said nothing…"

"Dominic would not do anything improper, I am sure," Calandra told her. "He is all a gentleman should be—no matter what sort of rumors you may have heard about him. They say he has lived rather wildly in London the past few years, but I know there is nothing bad about him." She paused, then added with a small smile, "I confess that when I was younger, I developed a mad crush on him."

"You did?" Constance looked at her. It occurred to her, with a heavy feeling in the pit of her stomach, that Lady Calandra, the sister of a wealthy and powerful duke, would make an excellent match for Lord Leighton.

"Oh, yes. You should have seen him in that Hussars

uniform. I can tell you, he cut quite a figure. But I got over that long ago." She made an airy wave of her hand. "He is not at all the sort of man I would wish to marry." She sighed. "Not that it appears I have much hope of marrying, anyway."

Constance chuckled. "My lady, I cannot imagine that you would have any dearth of suitors."

"Oh, indeed, there are a number who seek my hand. But so many of them are fortune hunters. It is dreadfully hard to tell, sometimes—except that I have learned that those who express undying love the most quickly are usually the ones who most adore my money. Not that it matters, for Sinclair scares them away." She sighed. "Unfortunately, he scares *all* my suitors away. Sin can be a bit…overwhelming at times."

Constance smiled faintly. She had herself felt rather overwhelmed by the formidable duke. "Surely that will not matter to the right man."

"Mmm. I hope you are right," Calandra said. "Otherwise, I fear I shall die a spinster."

The idea of this lively girl, both eligible and attractive, remaining unmarried struck Constance as so ludicrous that she laughed, and Calandra joined her.

"I know, I must sound quite foolish," Calandra admitted and fell to talking about fashion, a topic that satisfactorily occupied both women through much of the ride.

The climb had been growing steeper as they talked,

and now Dominic pulled his horse to a stop and turned to them. "We shall have to walk the rest of the way to the promontory."

At the prospect of walking, the idea of looking at the view quickly lost its enchantment for Margaret. As they all dismounted, she whined, "All the way to the top? But I am scarcely dressed for walking."

Her mouth turned down expressively as she looked at the train of her riding habit, looped over her arm, then turned toward Mr. Carruthers, looking up at him beseechingly. "I think I would prefer to stay here. It seems quite pleasant in this little clearing. If, of course, someone would stay with me…"

It was true that the heavy skirts of the women's riding clothes, with their trailing trains meant to appear at advantage draped over the side of the horse as they rode sidesaddle, were not easy to walk in. Nor were the supple riding boots. However, Margaret had known about the steepness of the climb before they left; she had expressed her doubts about it at the breakfast table. It was distinctly annoying that she had decided to come on the expedition to the promontory despite her laziness, and Constance felt rather certain that she had done it primarily to have a chance to be with Mr. Carruthers.

"I shall be pleased to remain here with Miss Woodley," Mr. Carruthers offered gallantly.

Constance sighed. "Perhaps I should stay, too."

She did not really want to stay here tamely in the clearing without even seeing the view from the promontory, but she felt it incumbent upon her not to leave Cousin Margaret alone with a man whom she scarcely knew. It was not inherently scandalous, of course, for a woman to be alone with a gentleman in the afternoon, even in this rather secluded setting, as long as it was not for a very long period of time. However, her cousin was quite young and also quite silly, and Constance was not at all certain what she might do if left to her own devices, especially given the way she had been flirting with Mr. Carruthers. She could not leave Margaret in a situation where she could damage her own reputation.

Calandra glanced at Constance, then at Margaret, and said easily, "Oh, no, you have not seen the view. I shall stay here. I am rather tired, and I have been to the promontory several times."

Constance cast the young woman a grateful look. "Are you sure you don't mind?"

"Of course not," Calandra told her. "I only came along because I did not want to be there when Muriel returned from her trek around the lake."

In the end, Mr. Willoughby, whose horse was showing signs of weariness, decided to remain behind, as well, so only Dominic and Constance continued to the top. They walked, leading their horses, and soon were out of sight among the trees. The path became steeper, and they fell silent, needing their breath for the climb.

They passed a small thatch-roofed cottage and shed, nestled against the hillside. It looked, Constance thought, like a cottage from a fairy tale.

"Who lives there?" she asked, pointing.

"No one. It's deserted. Has been for years," he answered. "We might as well leave our horses here." He tied their mounts to the low-hanging branches of a tree in front of the cottage.

"It is called the Frenchman's House," he went on. "I have no idea why. There are innumerable stories about it. Some say it was where they exiled some mad FitzAlan ancestor."

"Oh, no, it must have involved some tragically romantic story," Constance said in disagreement. "Just look at it."

Dominic chuckled. "Most likely it was where some favored old servant retired."

"That is much too mundane," she protested.

He smiled down at her, and suddenly Constance was very aware of her own body, of the pulse of blood at her throat and the pull of air into her lungs. Her skin was warm with the exercise of climbing, and she felt the caress of a breeze on it.

She was aware, too, of the fact that they were all alone in this secluded spot, something quite rare at any time, but especially in this large house party. Dominic's eyes traveled over her face, and he reached up to gently brush his thumb across her cheek. The brief, skimming touch seemed to awaken every nerve in her body, and Constance shivered.

"Are you cold?" he asked, and she shook her head.

"No. Not at all." Gazing back into his eyes, she knew that he understood why she had shivered—and understood, as well, that the heat in her body came only partly from the warmth of the day.

She thought that he was about to kiss her. She knew that she wanted him to. She wanted, Constance realized, far more than that. She wanted to feel his hands on her body again; she wanted his lips to travel over her. She wanted his mouth to close around her nipple and bathe her in damp heat. Her breasts ached a little just at the thought, her nipples tightening.

Dominic moved fractionally closer. He knew, she thought. He knew exactly what she wanted, and he wanted it, as well. For a moment they stood there, simply looking at each other, and the very air seemed to simmer between them.

Then he stepped back abruptly. "We should keep going. The others will not want to wait too long."

She nodded woodenly, thinking that it was better this way and yet not liking it at all. He struck out for the top, and Constance followed. The ground turned rockier, and the trees thinned out. Now and then he reached out to take her arm to help her up a steep spot, and she felt each touch all through her.

Finally they reached the top, a rocky cliff jutting out

over the countryside and offering a sweeping view of the land below.

"Oh!" Constance drew in her breath sharply. "It's beautiful!"

Dominic nodded, looking out over the vista. "This was always one of my favorite places. I would sit here and look out and dream…all sorts of foolish things."

"I am sure they were not foolish," Constance replied.

He shrugged. "Impossible, anyway." He looked at her and grinned. "Not much call these days for a knight or a corsair." He gestured out in front of him. "You see the stream going down to Cowden? And there's the tower of St. Edmund's in the distance." Closer to them, he indicated two of the farms that they had ridden past earlier this afternoon.

"You love this land very much, don't you?" Constance remarked.

He glanced at her, surprised. "What makes you say that?"

"It's in your voice. And in the way you know your tenants and their families. The way you asked after them."

The knowledge caused a sharp pain in her chest. It was clear to her that Dominic would do whatever was necessary to help the estate. No doubt that would include marrying an heiress.

"I am surprised that you have stayed away from it so long," she went on.

He glanced at her, his eyes bright and hard. "My father and I are…estranged."

Constance did not say anything, reluctant to pry into his affairs, and after a moment, he went on. "He and I had a falling out years ago. He ordered me off the land. After that I could not return—would not have, even if I could. I gave up all ties to Redfields then. I despised the place. I despised my family."

Constance made a small noise, and he looked at her. "You disapprove," he said.

"No. I—I am just surprised. I had not realized how much your past troubled you." She thought of his light manner, the easygoing smile. She had realized that there was a rift between him and his father, but she had not guessed at how deep it ran. The pain was still clear in his voice.

Dominic grimaced. "I have done my best to get away from my past, but I have found it a difficult thing to outrun."

Constance took his hand, and he smiled down at her. "Dear Constance," he said, reaching up with his other hand to cup her chin. "You are always so kind, so ready with your sympathy, your warmth. I fear you would be appalled if you knew what my family was really like."

"I am sure I am a great deal less kind than you give me credit for," she replied, with a rueful smile. "And whatever your family may be, I know you and I know your sister, and neither of you is wicked."

"Perhaps Francesca and I were not wicked, only negligent. Selfish…" He sighed, then tugged her toward a large rock. "Come, sit down here with me, and I will tell you about the FitzAlans."

CHAPTER THIRTEEN

"FRANCESCA AND I WERE close in age, only a year apart," Dominic began after they had sat down on the rock. He held Constance's hand in one of his, with the other tracing a light pattern over her palm. He watched his finger on her skin, not looking at her as he told his story.

"We had an older brother, Terence," he went on. "He was three years older than I. And we had a younger sister, Ivy." He smiled sadly. "She was the baby. Such a beautiful little girl. I remember, I thought she looked like an angel."

The loss in his voice pierced Constance with sorrow, and she took his hand in both of hers, bringing it up to lay a soft kiss upon it. For a long moment she cradled his hand against her cheek, then let their joined hands fall back to her lap.

"My brother, however, was anything but an angel. Terence was always a bully. He terrorized Francesca and me when we were young, but Ivy was enough younger than the three of us that he did not bother her.

Our governess knew what Terence was, and she did her best to protect Francesca and me from him. There was, of course, only so much she could do, for our parents would hear no ill of Terence." His mouth twisted with remembered bitterness. "Terence was the heir, the perfect son. As far as my mother and father were concerned, he could do no wrong. Fortunately, Francesca and I had each other, so we were able to join forces to combat him. And, even better, eventually he went off to Eton and we had to put up with him only at holidays."

He paused, gazing out across the vista before them. "Terence was better as we grew older. I never really liked him, but he left us alone more. I'm not sure if he gave up his bullying or simply confined it to school. At any rate, we did not have to be around him much. After Eton, there was Oxford for a couple of years, and when he grew tired of that, he did a tour of the Continent, then lived in London for a while. Finally, when he did come home to live, I was not often at Redfields. I had started Oxford by then, and after that I was busy being a young blade in London. Francesca was not home much of the time, either. She made her debut and got married. Neither of us realized…"

He stopped. Cold dread filled Constance's stomach. She almost hoped he would not continue.

"But finally, when Francesca was home visiting, Ivy confided in her. She was, of course, too frightened to tell our parents, too sure that they would not believe her.

She told Francesca that Terence had—had been forcing himself upon her for the past two years, since she was only fourteen. And she was in despair."

"Oh, Dominic," Constance breathed, and she put her arms around him, leaning her head on his shoulder. "I am so sorry."

He turned into her, sliding his arms around her and resting his cheek against her head. His voice was low and hoarse as he went on. "Francesca wrote to me. She urged me to come posthaste to Redfields and help them. She was frightened, but she hoped that while she was there, Terence would not try anything with Ivy. She had Ivy sleep in the room with her. But Terence tried to get around Francesca. He wanted to take Ivy riding with him, and she fled to Francesca, who confronted him, told him that she knew all about him and what he had done. He denied it, of course. He swore that Ivy was making it all up. Francesca went to my parents with Ivy and told them everything. And my parents…my parents sided with Terence. As they had always done. They would not believe Ivy. Francesca begged them to let Ivy come live with her, but they refused. They said it would reflect badly on them. They were afraid that Ivy would spread her 'lies' about Terence, about them."

Dominic released Constance and sprang to his feet, as though unable to sit still any longer. He paced away from her and back, and she watched helplessly, seeing his pain and wishing that she could take it from him somehow.

"Francesca assured Ivy that all hope was not lost. When I arrived, she told her we would get her out of there. But Ivy did not believe her." His mouth twisted, and moisture glimmered in his eyes. "And why should she have? All of us had failed her already. For two years she had been subjected to Terence and his attacks, and we had done nothing."

"You didn't know!" Constance cried out, jumping to her feet. "You couldn't be expected to know."

"I knew what he had been like. I should have paid more attention when I was home. I should have asked Ivy. Dear Lord, surely if I had just looked at her more closely, I would have seen her unhappiness! But I did not. I was having far too much fun cutting a swath through London." He swung around, staring off into the distance as he said, "Ivy killed herself shortly before I arrived. She stole my father's dueling pistol, and went out into the woods and shot herself in the head."

"Oh, Dominic!" Constance went to him, her heart aching with pity. She wrapped her arms around him from behind, resting her cheek against his back. "I'm so sorry. I'm so terribly sorry."

He crossed his hands over hers, holding her tightly to him. "That is why I attacked Terence at her grave-site. No doubt someone has filled your ear with that story. It will not surprise you, I am sure, to hear that my father again sided with Terence. He threw me out and told me never to come back. I told him I had no desire ever to set foot in the house again. I left. My uncle, my mother's brother, bought me my commission, and I went to the Peninsula. I never saw or spoke to my brother or my parents again until Terence died in a riding accident. My father had to take me back then. I was the heir. And I had to return. I never wanted anything less."

Constance squeezed herself more tightly against him, as though she could force some of his pain out of him. Dominic turned, wrapping his arms around her, and they stood that way for a long time. Constance could hear the steady thud of his heart beneath her ear; his warmth enveloped her. Her body was alive to him, as it always was, but she pushed such wayward feelings out of her mind. She wanted to comfort him; she wished she could somehow leach his sorrow from his body.

Dominic curved his head down over hers. She felt the brush of his cheek against her hair. He squeezed her gently, and his lips pressed into her hair for an instant.

"Thank you," he murmured.

"I only wish I could make it better," she answered, rubbing her hand against his back in a soothing circular motion.

"You do. Believe me, you do." He hesitated, tensing slightly, and Constance went still in response, waiting.

Then a fat raindrop plopped upon her shoulder, followed by another on her back.

"What the devil?" Dominic released her and moved back, looking up at the sky.

They had been so wrapped up in their conversation that they had paid no attention to their surroundings. The pillowy white clouds that had made the day cooler had massed into a gray, lowering cover.

"We had better get back." Dominic grasped her arm, and they started back down the hill, raindrops splattering on them with greater frequency.

The rain made the stony ground slicker, and they slipped again and again as they retraced their steps, slowing their speed. When they reached the trees, the branches provided more cover, but the wind and rain increased at such a rate that it scarcely mattered. Constance let out a little shriek and clutched at her head as the wind tore at her hat. She was too late, and the hat went sailing off through the trees.

She slipped and would have fallen but for Dominic's hand on her arm. His fingers tightened painfully and they stayed upright, but in two more steps, the smooth sole of his riding boot went sliding on the wet leaves. He slipped, and they staggered. He grabbed for a tree branch, and then they were on the ground, flat on their backs, sliding along until they were stopped by a knobby tree root.

Dominic sat up and looked down at her. Constance let out a giggle and reached up to pluck the twig that had caught in his hair. He grinned, then laughed, too.

The rain, coming faster now, sluiced down his head and face. He shoved his hair back with his hands and got to his feet, reaching down to pull Constance up. They scurried down the hillside to where their horses were tied. The rain was pounding down harder now. The horses jittered at the sound of thunder.

Dominic pointed toward the little cottage. "Go inside. We'll wait it out. It's getting worse. I'll put the horses in that shed."

Constance nodded, not eager to lead their horses down the rest of the hill and then ride for the summer house with the rain still pelting them. As Dominic untied the horses and led them to the shed, she ran for the cottage, keeping her skirts up as best she could. She didn't know why she bothered, she thought. Her velvet riding habit was already sodden with rain, and not only splattered with mud about the hem but also liberally striped with it down her side and back from their fall. And that wasn't even to mention leaves and twigs that had adhered to it as she slid along the ground.

She turned the latch and pushed, and for an instant the door stuck, but then it gave way with a creak, and she stepped into the room. She left the door open despite the rain; for there was little light inside the tiny one-room house. It was cool, too, in her wet clothes, and a shiver shook her. Constance wrapped her arms around herself and advanced farther into the room, looking around.

There was not much to see—it was a plain and sparsely furnished place. The entire house was but a single room. Two small windows, one almost completely overgrown with ivy outside, provided what light there was. A bed was pushed up against one wall, and there was a small table in the center of the room. A stool sat beside the table, and closer to the small fireplace, there was a wooden rocking chair. A braided rug lay on the floor beside the bed. Over everything, there was a layer of dust. She wondered how long it had been since the cottage had been inhabited. Years and years, it appeared.

Dominic entered the cottage on the run and stopped, taking in the place in a glance. "Not much here, I fear." He looked at Constance. "You're shivering."

"Just a little. It's the damp."

"Damp?" He raised an amused eyebrow. "You are soaked through."

Constance thought of how she must look, and she blushed, her hands going to her hair. Strands of it had come loose during their dash down the hill, almost a third of it on one side, and the locks straggled wetly around her face and down her back. Leaves and twigs had caught in it, as well, when they went sliding across the ground. Her riding habit was thoroughly wet and clinging to her, as well as being bedaubed with mud and stray leaves and twigs. She must look, she thought, a complete fright.

Dominic went over to the fireplace and dropped down to one knee in front of it. "Hope this still works," he commented as he felt for the flue handle.

He began to build a fire with the small stack of logs beside the hearth. Constance busied herself with removing all the twigs and leaves she could find from her hair, while Dominic roamed the cottage and outside, collecting enough small dry twigs and bits of wood to use for kindling. It took some time, but eventually he got a small fire started in the fireplace, and, miraculously, it drew well enough to keep the smoke from flooding back into the room.

She took the remaining pins from her hair and set them on the table, then squeezed the water from her locks. Combing her fingers through her hair as best she could, she watched Dominic coax the little flames into a steady fire.

He turned toward her. "Here, come sit by the fire."

Constance went closer, stopping beside him. He smiled down at her and reached out to take an errant leaf from her hair.

"I must look a mess," she murmured.

"You look like a wood nymph," he replied, and his smile widened. "A very wet wood nymph."

"I *am* very wet," Constance admitted, and another shiver shook her.

"You should get out of your clothes," he told her. Their gazes locked. His words seemed to hang in the air.

Constance felt suddenly breathless. "I…um…"

Her mind was crowded with images of pulling off her clothes in front of Dominic, and, bizarrely, the heat that washed through her at the thought was less from shame than anticipation. She thought of Dominic's fingers on the buttons of her bodice, peeling back the material, and the tremors that raced across her skin were no longer caused by cold.

He turned away abruptly and glanced around, then walked across the room, his moves a trifle jerky. A small trunk lay at the foot of the bed, and he opened it. Reaching in, he pulled out a blanket. He shook it out.

"Here, this should be a good bit cleaner than what's on the bed. Take off your dress and wrap this around you. We shall spread your things out on the chair to dry."

He slid off his jacket as he spoke, as though demonstrating, and hung it on the back of the rocker. His fingers went to the buttons of his waistcoat, and Constance found her eyes following their movements. She watched his long, supple fingers undo the buttons; it seemed as though she could not look away.

"Come," he said, his voice husky. "You must. You will catch cold. I—I will go outside while you undress."

"No, you'll get wet. It is raining even harder," Constance protested.

"I am already wet through," he pointed out.

He was right, of course. Her gaze went to his white

shirt, which clung to his chest, the thin lawn almost transparent. She could see the dark circles of his nipples, the lines of his musculature, the faint shading of hair in a V across the center of his chest. His riding breeches were molded just as wetly to his legs, suggestively outlining every taut muscle of his thighs and buttocks. It was almost worse, she thought, than if he had actually been naked, since she could think of nothing else but what her imagination was picturing beneath the clothes.

She realized that she was staring, and a hot flush spread up her neck and stained her cheeks. She had to say something, she thought, but her tongue seemed glued to the roof of her mouth. "I-If you will turn your back…"

He nodded and swung around, going back to the chest at the foot of the bed and digging in it for another cover. Constance turned back to the fire and began to unbutton the bodice of her riding habit with unsteady fingers. Then she unbuttoned the skirt; it was heavy with water and slid swiftly downward, landing on the floor with a wet plop. She grasped the sides of her bodice and started to pull it off.

She thought of Dominic behind her and wondered if he had in fact turned away or if he were watching her undress. The heat that blossomed in her loins at the thought of him watching her made her wonder which she would actually prefer. She slid the jacketlike bodice off, then stopped. Unable to resist, she peeked over her shoulder.

She should not have looked, she thought. It was quite wrong, for Dominic was behaving just as a gentleman should, his back resolutely toward her. He had pulled off his boots, then taken off his shirt. His back was bare, his wide shoulders tapering down to the long slender line of his waist. She watched the muscles ripple across his back as he hooked his hands in the sides of his breeches and pulled them down his legs. It was not an easy task—they were thoroughly wet, and he had to peel them from his skin.

Constance knew she had been wrong. Seeing him naked was worse, much worse, than seeing him in his soaked clothes. She could not take her eyes away from the smooth taut curve of his buttocks as they flowed down into the firm muscles of his thighs. His legs were long, and his muscles, though hard, were lean. She had never seen a man naked; she would have blushed even to have thought of what a man looked like without clothes. But she knew that she would not have expected him to look so compelling. She would not have thought his naked form could have drawn her eyes this way, could have made her loins melt or turned her mouth dry as dust.

She must have made some small noise, because just then he turned his head, glancing over his shoulder, and his eyes met hers.

Constance knew that she should whirl back around and face the fire. She should be humiliated at being caught watching him. She should wait until he looked away again, and then she should shrug off her bodice and wrap the blanket around herself.

Instead, she found herself turning to face him. Slowly, deliberately, her eyes on his face, she pulled her bodice the rest of the way off her arms and let it fall to the floor. She stood in front of him clad only in her chemise and petticoat.

He pivoted slowly to face her. His face was sharp and drawn, the skin stretched tautly across his bones. He watched her, his eyes dark, his hands curling into fists against his legs.

Her eyes took him in slowly. He was hard and powerful and masculine. She could see the lines of his ribs, the curve of muscle beneath the smooth skin of his arms and chest, the flat plain of his stomach. Blond, curling hairs lightly furred his legs and arms and formed a narrow V on his chest, running in a line down from his navel to explode in a glinting riot of curls around his burgeoning manhood. It was the sight of that smooth-skinned shaft, lengthening and swelling, that drew her eyes downward. She had had no idea what to expect, had never dreamed that the sight of his awakened desire would stir her own need so much.

Constance's breath came shallow and fast. Her heart was hammering in her chest. She was scared and excited and a hundred other pounding emotions. Anyone would have told her, she knew, that she should not be doing this. She should stop. She should pull her clothes back on and run from this house.

But she had no intention of doing that. She was, perhaps, acting impulsively, but she was not thoughtless. This was what she wanted. Dominic was *whom* she wanted. She knew that he would not, could not, marry her. She knew that others would label what she was about to do a mistake. But she did not care.

She wanted Dominic. She wanted this moment. Whatever else happened in her life, she wanted to make love with him. She wanted to open herself to him, to let him take her in his arms and teach her everything that could be between a man and a woman. The rest of her life might stretch out in bleak emptiness, but she would, for this moment, know passion. She would, for this moment, lose herself in Dominic's arms.

Constance pulled the end of the blue bow at the neckline of her chemise, and the bow fell apart. Slowly, one by one, she unfastened each tie until the two sides were separated all the way up and down, exposing a narrow ribbon of skin down the center of her chest. She reached up to grasp the sides.

"Constance…" Dominic grated out. "No. You should not."

"I want to."

He swallowed, gazing at her for a long moment, and

when her name came again on his lips, there was no warning in it, only a low sigh of hunger. "Constance…"

He started toward her with the slow, smooth stride of an animal on the hunt. Watching him, she pulled her chemise off and dropped it to the floor. He drew nearer, and she untied the side of her white muslin petticoat and let it slide down to the floor. He stopped only inches from her. She moved to the tie of her pantalets, but Dominic reached out and touched her hands, stopping her.

A faint smile playing at his lips, he took the narrow bands in his fingers and undid them. He laid his hands flat against her sides, fingers splayed out over her skin, and slid them down, his hands moving under the cloth of her pantalets and shoving the cloth downward. His palms glided down her flesh, searing her with their heat and exposing her skin inch by inch.

Constance sucked in her breath at the feel of his skin upon hers. His fingertips and palms, roughened by years of riding, were light on her soft skin, awakening the sensitive flesh to a tingling awareness. Her skin tightened all over, and an ache bloomed between her legs, low and pulsing.

Dominic's eyes fell to her breasts, where her nipples had hardened in response to his touch. His smile deepened with masculine satisfaction, and he pushed her undergarment the rest of the way down, letting it pool around her feet. He stood still for a moment, his hands resting on her hips, his eyes exploring her body.

Then his gaze came back up and caught hers. He continued to hold her attention, his eyes hot and intense, as his hands moved up her sides, slow and soft, coaxing every tiny bit of sensation from her flesh. He caressed her breasts, fingers and thumbs teasing at the tight buds of her nipples and sliding across the pillowy softness of her breasts. His hands roamed her back, sliding down and curving over her hips, squeezing and separating her buttocks before gliding onto the tops of her thighs.

His shaft prodded gently against her abdomen. Constance caught her lower lip in her teeth, amazed at each new pleasure his fingers brought. Then, startling her even more, he slipped one hand between her legs. She gasped even as she unconsciously widened her stance, opening herself to him. His fingers teased at her tender flesh, gently stroking and separating the sensitive folds.

Constance brought her hands up to his arms, her fingers digging into his skin at the new, intense pleasure that was coursing through her. She swallowed, surprise in her eyes as she gazed up at him. He continued to look into her eyes as his fingers worked their magic on her flesh, taking in the subtle changes in her as each new sensation blossomed within her.

She had never felt anything like the feeling that he was evoking in her, had never dreamed that such heat or such intense pleasure could consume her this way. He had not even kissed her yet, and she was trembling with an almost overwhelming need, a delight so intense that she thought she might shatter under its pressure.

And then she did shatter, a small cry escaping her lips as passion rocked her. It burst at the center of her being, washing out in waves. She moved against him, her body so taut she shook all over.

She melted. There was no other word for it, she thought. She simply melted inside and out, her body sagging, knees giving way, so that she was kept upright only by the arm Dominic looped around her waist. She leaned her head against his chest, her arms going around him. His heart hammered; his skin was hot and moist beneath hers; she could hear the harsh rasp of his breath.

"Dominic…" She lifted wondering eyes to him. "That was…more than I… It was wonderful. But what about—I mean, you…" She stumbled to a halt, blushing.

He grinned down at her, his eyes gleaming as he picked up the blanket from the chair and shook it out, settling it onto the floor. "Don't worry, darling," he said, picking her up and lowering her to the blanket, then lying down beside her. "We are only getting started."

And, at last, he leaned in and kissed her.

CHAPTER FOURTEEN

HE KISSED HER AS IF HE had all the time in the world, his mouth soft and slow, seeking out every pleasure. There was no hint of haste, no hurry to satisfy his own need, only a quiet, lingering exploration. Constance, stunned and replete, returned his kisses with a languid pleasure, content, she felt, to lie here with him forever doing nothing more.

She slid her hands lazily up his arms, enjoying the feel of his skin beneath her palms, tracing the curve of muscle that lay beneath the skin. The tension that did not show in his kisses lay in his body, she realized. His forearms, supporting him, were as taut as stretched wire, and his skin, where she touched it, quivered. And she knew that desire raged in him, that his slow, tender lovemaking was the result of his iron control.

It pleased her to realize the intensity of his passion, to know that he wanted her so much. She stroked her hand down the center of his chest, and the shudder that shook him in response awakened a new heat in her.

She would not have thought that she could be aroused

again so soon after the cataclysm she had already experienced, and the fire that licked down through her startled her. She must have made some movement in her surprise, for Dominic raised his head and looked down at her.

His eyes were heavy with desire, his lips dark and swollen from their kisses. He saw the surprise in her eyes, and he smiled in a way that made the warm ache between her legs grow.

"Did you think that was all you would have?" he murmured, and when Constance nodded, he bent and pressed a kiss to the corner of her mouth. "There's more." He kissed the opposite corner. "Much more." He trailed the tip of his tongue along the line between her lips. "I promise you."

He kissed her cheeks, her chin, her brows, the petal-soft lids of her eyes, then settled at last on the lobe of her ear, kissing, then tonguing it, then taking it gently between his teeth and worrying it. Bright shivers of sensation darted through her, gathering hotly deep in her abdomen. Constance moved restlessly beneath him, unable to keep still under his teasing ministrations. The rough wool of the blanket was scratchy under her back, and its roughness seemed to accentuate even more the pleasure of the sensations his mouth aroused in her.

Constance let out a shuddering breath and skimmed her hands down his side and up his back. She found the textures of him exciting—the smoothness of skin and the firm muscle beneath, the hard lines of his rib cage, the bony points of his shoulders and collarbone, the wiry curl of the hairs upon his chest.

His tongue stole into her ear, and she jerked, desire slamming down into her loins and spreading out. Her breath rasped in her throat. He rolled on top of her, his legs between hers, spreading hers apart. He took much of his weight on his forearms, but his flesh was pressed against the length of her torso, and she could feel him against that most tender, intimate part of her, hard and heavy, pulsing.

He kissed his way down her neck, nibbling on the tight cord, pressing a kiss as soft as butterfly wings on the hollow of her throat. He curved his hand around her breast as his lips trailed over her chest and touched upon the gentle swell of the rounded orb. He kissed the soft flesh, moving with infinite patience over the arc of her breast, coming at last to the pebbled flesh of her nipple. His tongue traced the outer rim of the areola, slowly circling again and again, moving fractionally closer, until at last he touched the hardened tip at the center. He stroked it, teasing it so that it lengthened and hardened.

Constance wanted him to take the fleshy nub into his mouth; she remembered the pull of him, hot and wet, around it, each tug of his mouth tweaking a cord that ran straight down through her into her abdomen. With each little lick of his tongue, she wanted his mouth more. She yearned for it, ached for it, unconsciously digging in her heels and rising up.

She raked her nails lightly down his back and dug her fingers into the flesh of his buttocks. He let out a groan, giving in at last and taking her nipple into his mouth. He suckled as she kneaded his flesh. Her breath was almost sobbing in her throat, and the heat was building in her loins again, so pleasurable, so intense that it was almost a pain.

Constance whispered his name, turning her head to press her lips to his arm, propped beside her on the blanket. She kissed him, nipping at his skin as the pleasure turned ever more intense.

When she thought that she could bear it no more, that she would explode from the build-up of pleasure, he released her nipple. He hung his head for a moment, his breath harsh, his muscles clenched. After a moment he pressed a kiss between her breasts and then fastened his mouth around her other nipple.

Constance groaned, arching up against him. Desire throbbed between her legs, turning her wet and aching. His hand came down, slipping into the slick folds. She had thought that her yearning could grow no more intense, but now it did, burgeoning under the matched strokes of mouth and finger. She moved her hips against him and heard the ragged groan from his throat that signaled his last tenuous grasp on his control.

He moved, lowering himself, moving her legs farther

apart. She felt the probing tip of him against her center, the pressure, the fullness. Constance moaned, parting her legs farther and lifting up to take him in. There was a startling flash of pain, and she let out a stifled cry. He paused, his body rigid and trembling with the effort. But she did not care about the pain, could not bear the waiting, and she stroked her hands down his sides and onto his hips, urging him on.

Dominic thrust inside her, and she gasped, amazed and delighted. He filled her, stretching her to her limits, and it was wonderful, as if some emptiness inside her had at last been filled. Yet at the same time, she wanted more. She wanted to take him deeper inside her, to possess him and be possessed by him.

He began to move within her, and this, she realized, was exactly what she wanted. He pulled back slowly, and she almost protested at his leaving her, but he did not; instead he thrust back into her, harder and deeper. She let out a little hiccup of sound, part moan, part laughter, at the sheer pleasure of his movements. He stroked within her, moving in a steady rhythm, growing harder, faster….

And she moved with him, matching her movements to his, feeling the pleasure build and build within her, a huge hot ball of pleasure, with each stroke turning tighter and more intense. She dug her fingers into the blanket beneath her, gripping the cloth as though to keep from flying away.

This time the feeling ratcheting up in her was familiar, and knowing how the passion would burst inside her only made her want it more. Except that now the building pleasure was even stronger, even wilder, filled as she was with him, joined to him in this long, driving dance of hunger.

Then, at last, it came…the pleasure ripping through her, white-hot at the center and exploding outward to every inch of her body. She cried out, arching against him as he thrust deeply into her, his own hoarse cry joining hers.

Constance wrapped her arms around him, their bodies clamped together, melded into one in the mindless storm of passion.

Dominic relaxed against her, his face against her neck. Constance could hear his breathing gradually slow, feel his body lose its former tension. She hadn't the energy or the will to act or speak; indeed, she could scarcely bring enough thoughts together to form a coherent sentence, much less say it.

He pressed a kiss where her neck joined her shoulder, then rolled his weight from her, his arm going beneath her neck and around her shoulders, cuddling her to him. Constance found that her head fit quite perfectly in the curve of his shoulder. She stretched her arm across him, her fingers idly stroking his skin, threading through the hairs on his chest. She felt filled and used and slightly sore…and utterly content.

This, she thought, was what it was to love a man. She had never really known before—and how could she? She had never before felt the full extent of love—the way the heart and soul and body wrapped around another person, threaded through him, touched him in every way. It was raw, and it was beautiful. It was not nearly so sweet or ideal as everyone made it out to be. Yet it was a thousand times more wonderful—shocking, sweaty, intense and achingly real.

She knew that everything had become infinitely more complicated, but she would not think about that now. Right now, she wanted only to revel in this moment, to soak up every last bit of contentment and joy.

Dominic turned his head and kissed her forehead. He stroked his hand down her arm and twined his fingers through hers, lifting her hand to his mouth and kissing each finger.

"You are the most beautiful woman in the world."

She giggled, knowing he was foolish to think so and extremely glad that he was. He went on to enumerate each detail of her loveliness, until she had to kiss him, laughing, to stop him. And then some minutes passed before either even thought about saying anything else.

"Constance," he said at last, and she heard the hint of finality in his voice, the tone of thought and reason. She was quite certain that she did not want to hear what he was about to say.

"No," she told him quickly, rising up on her elbow and putting a silencing finger across his lips. She bent and kissed his cheek, then laid her face against his and whispered, "Let's not talk about it now. Later will be time enough."

"We have to go back."

"I know."

It took enormous effort to pull away from him, but she did, careful not to look at him, knowing that to do so would weaken her. She stood and gathered her undergarments, which had wound up perilously close to the fire. At least they were close to dry now, and she quickly put them on. The riding habit, spread across the chair, was, unfortunately, still quite damp; for the thick material had absorbed a great deal of water. Still, there was nothing for it but to don the skirt and bodice again.

The fire had died, but after he dressed, Dominic stirred and poked through it to make sure no errant sparks were left. Constance watched him as she combed through her hair and did her best to twist it up into a simple knot and re-pin it. There was too much hair and too few pins left, and the lack of a mirror made it even more difficult. She finally managed to get all her hair pinned, though she could only hope it would stay that way.

She still looked a mess, she supposed—her clothes damp and wrinkled and streaked with mud where she had fallen, her hair loosely pinned and, for all she knew, askew. But she could not bring herself to care. She was too filled with the rosy afterglow of their lovemaking.

Dominic turned from the fire at last, and their eyes met. His mouth softened, his eyes darkening, and he took a step forward, saying huskily, "Constance."

He reached for her, and she went to him without hesitation, raising her face to his. He kissed her, pulling her tightly against him, and her arms closed around his neck. He lifted his head from hers at last and drew a long breath, resting his forehead against her head.

"We must go," he said without conviction.

"I know."

"I can think of nothing I want to do less."

Constance smiled, her heart filling with pleasure at his reluctance to leave. "But we must." She stepped back from him, taking his hand. "They will be waiting."

He sighed. "You are right." He bent and kissed her, hard and brief, then walked with her out of the house.

Dominic got their horses from the shed, and they started down the hill, leading the horses by their reins. It was quiet and peaceful, the air smelling sweetly of rain. The clouds had lifted, and the sun was setting, casting a muted golden glow across the landscape.

They held hands as they walked, turning now and then to look at one another. It felt, Constance thought, as if they were the only people in the world. Everything would change when they rejoined the others, she knew, but she refused to think about it, holding on fast to this sweet moment.

When they reached the place where they had left Margaret, Calandra and the others, they found no one there. It was not surprising, given the downpour in which they had been caught. Doubtless they had ridden back to the summer house to take shelter.

Frankly, Constance was happy to find them gone. It would give her a few more minutes alone with Dominic, she thought as they mounted their horses for the rest of the return journey. When they rounded the curve a few minutes later and saw the white summer house in the distance, she was aware of a distinct sense of disappointment.

The brief interlude was over. She and Dominic would have to return to their normal lives. Unconsciously, she let out a sigh.

"I know," he said, glancing over at her. "I don't want to return."

Constance smiled, pleased to hear him say it, but her spirits were sinking rapidly. She was remembering all the reasons why Dominic would never marry her. Could never marry her. Soon they would return to London and this would all be over. Even before that, when they rejoined the other guests, they would have to watch how they looked and acted. He could not take her hand or pull her into his arms. She could not look at him with her heart in her eyes. Even an engaged couple's movements were restricted, and as to a man and woman who were not betrothed…well, they simply could not show a decided partiality for each other, let alone do something so scandalous as to touch in any but the most formal way.

As they drew nearer to the summer house, Constance saw that everyone else in their party was standing on the steps, watching them approach. Her stomach fell to her feet. She cast an anxious glance at Dominic. He was watching the group on the steps, and his face was stony.

Constance realized suddenly that they were in an even worse position than she had realized. She and Dominic were teetering on the edge of scandal. They could not help that it had rained, of course, nor that they had had to take shelter. But there was no getting around the fact that they had spent at least two hours alone together, half of that shut up in the privacy of a cottage.

It would not have been as bad, in all likelihood, if Calandra and Margaret and the others had remained at the place where they had left them. For one thing, they would not have been alone together quite as long. But more than that, they would have been able to ride with them back to the summer house, and if Calandra, Margaret and the two men had not revealed that Dominic and Constance had left the group, they could have kept that fact hidden altogether. That was, of course, a big if, but given that Margaret was her cousin and therefore had a vested interest in protecting their good name, and that Calandra was a nice person and a friend to Francesca and Dominic, Constance thought it would have been a likely possibility.

As it was now, there was no hiding the fact that they had been alone.

What little hope she might have kept that a storm of scandal might not erupt was squelched when she saw Muriel marching down the steps toward them, her face coldly furious.

"Bloody hell," Dominic muttered under his breath as he swung down from his saddle. He did not glance at Muriel as he moved around to help Constance down from her horse.

After a moment Muriel, unable to contain herself, asked shrilly, "Where have you been?"

Dominic stepped forward, putting himself between Constance and Muriel. His eyebrows lifted in an expression of aristocratic hauteur. "The storm caught us by surprise, I fear."

"Yes, I can see," Muriel retorted, looking expressively at Constance.

Constance flushed, one hand going instinctively to her hair. She was very aware of everyone's eyes on her. She was also aware of the unfortunate state of her garments—muddied and damp——and of the untidy mess of her hair. She was even hatless, since the wind had blown her hat clean off her head.

"I am sure that you were worried about Constance and me," Dominic went on, looking levelly at Muriel. "I apologize."

"Yes, we were afraid that something dreadful might have happened to you," Francesca said quickly, hurrying down the steps to join them. "I am so glad you are both all right." She reached out and hugged Constance. "Poor dear, you must have had a terrible time."

Constance's eyes filled with tears of gratitude. Francesca was clearly wrapping the mantle of her approval around Constance. If such a one as Lady Haughston found nothing wrong with what had happened, if she still clearly liked Constance, then who were the others to talk?

"We were quite drenched," Dominic agreed. "But we were lucky enough to find shelter from the worst of it."

"Shelter?" Muriel repeated, looking puzzled, but then a flash of understanding crossed her face, and her eyes sparked fire. "That cottage? On the way to the promontory? You were alone together in that cottage?"

"Muriel, hush," Francesca murmured.

But Muriel was beyond stopping now, apparently. A smile of wicked triumph lit her face. She whirled toward Constance, declaring in ringing tones, "You were with Lord Leighton alone in a cottage for hours! Your reputation, Miss Woodley, is in ruins."

Constance stiffened. Behind Muriel she heard the low murmurs of the other guests. Her first instinct was to bark back that nothing had happened in that cottage, but, of course, that would not be the truth. If she said it, would everyone see the lie in her face?

"Muriel, be quiet," Francesca snapped. "They were caught in a thunderstorm. What would you have had them do? Stand out in the rain the whole time?"

"A woman who was careful of her good name would not have ventured up there alone with a man," Muriel sneered. "And they were gone rather longer than the storm, were they not? Who knows what might have happened in all that time?"

Constance was aware of everyone's eyes upon her. She flushed with embarrassment. Muriel was obviously intent upon Constance's public humiliation.

She looked straight at Constance, her eyes glittering maliciously, her voice gleeful as she went on. "Your name is besmirched now. Your reputation is in rags. No one would think of mar—"

"Lady Muriel!" Dominic's voice lashed out, hard and cold, stopping even Muriel in the midst of her rant. "I am sure that if you but think over the matter, you will realize that there is no harm whatsoever to Miss Woodley's reputation just because she took shelter from a storm with the man to whom she is *betrothed.*"

A shocked hush fell over the crowd. Francesca and Constance both turned to gape at Dominic. Muriel simply stared at him, the blood draining from her face as she realized what she had just done.

"No, Dominic…" she breathed, her voice barely audible.

He gazed at her calmly, his eyebrows faintly raised, then turned toward Constance. "Sorry, my dear, to announce it so informally. But, as you must realize, I could not allow anyone to get the wrong idea."

He swung back toward the guests assembled behind Muriel, his hard gaze sweeping over them. Their faces ranged in expression from shock to avid curiosity, but at Dominic's steely stare, they all quickly settled into the sort of courteously blank face that was the cornerstone of polite British behavior.

It was Calandra who broke the frozen moment, saying, "What delightful news! Francesca, you sly thing, you did not let the slightest indication slip."

"I could not," Francesca replied easily. "I was sworn to secrecy."

"Congratulations, Dominic," Calandra went on, coming down the steps to join them. "And, Constance, I am delighted that you will be living close to us in the future. The neighborhood is already brighter."

She took Constance's shoulders and leaned in to lay her cheek against Constance's, murmuring, "Are you all right?"

Constance nodded, saying, "Thank you."

It was a trifle difficult to speak past the lump in her throat. Bless Calandra and Francesca for their aplomb and kind natures. They had eased the awkward situation and, perhaps, even lent some air of truth to Dominic's words.

"Dominic, don't be a fool!" Muriel snapped, her voice strained.

Francesca turned to her, her smile grim. "I am sure you are as surprised as everyone else, Muriel, at this good news."

She walked over to Muriel, gripping her arm and turning her aside. In a low voice underlaid with iron, Francesca told her, "Pray, do not make yourself look any more foolish than you already have. You have managed with your maneuvering to bring about the last thing you really wanted. I suggest that you close your mouth before you do any more damage to yourself or your family."

Francesca's smile never wavered as she looked meaningfully into Muriel's eyes. Muriel jerked her arm away, her face etched with anger. She shot a look of pure venom at Constance, then turned on her heel and strode over to her horse. She jerked its reins from the hand of the astonished groom who was holding it. He recovered quickly enough to give her a leg up into the saddle, and Muriel thundered off without a backward glance.

"I suppose it is time we *all* went back to the house," Francesca said calmly, turning toward the other guests, as if Muriel's behavior was perfectly ordinary.

"You must ride with me, Constance," Calandra said. "I want to hear all about the wedding plans."

Francesca and Calandra flanked Constance the entire ride home. Despite Calandra's words, they did not in fact speak about the supposed wedding or engagement. In fact, beyond an inquiry or two into whether Constance felt chilled in her damp clothes, the two women said very little.

Constance was immensely grateful. As she was sure Calandra had intended, no other prying person could quiz her about the scene that had just transpired as long as Calandra and Francesca rode on either side of her. And at this moment, Constance did not think she could talk to anyone, even Francesca.

Earlier she had been floating in a dreamy state of love, muzzily refusing to think about reality. But the scene with Muriel had awakened her with a vengeance. Constance could not believe how foolish she had been. She had known that the amount of time she and Dominic had spent together would just skirt the edge of scandal. But she had not stopped to think it through clearly. She had not thought about how much her ragged looks would intensify everyone's suspicions. And she had assumed that their friends would smooth over any intimations of scandal; it had never occurred to her that someone like Muriel would do her very best to make the situation look the worst it possibly could.

Constance knew that she should have been more careful, though she was not sure exactly what she could have done. But she should at least have been better prepared to deal with Muriel Rutherford's attack. Because she had not, Dominic had moved in swiftly to save her reputation. And that was what made her feel the worst.

The embarrassment of everyone's stares and whispers would have been bad enough, but the social humiliation was nothing compared to the guilt she felt over Dominic's announcement of their engagement. She did not fool herself into thinking that he had said what he did because he actually wanted to marry her. No, he had simply acted as any gentleman should. Seeing that Muriel would make certain that Constance's reputation was shattered, he had said the only thing that could save it—that they were engaged.

Having said so, he could not back out of it now. A gentleman could not honorably break off an engagement, especially in a case such as this, where the jilted bride's honor was under such a shadow. He was committed to it now and would have to marry her.

Constance glanced over at Dominic, riding a few feet on the other side of his sister. His face was grim, his jaw set. It was clear that he was furious. Looking at him, Constance felt perilously close to tears. Less than an hour ago he had gazed at her with desire—even, she had thought, with love. Now, she was certain, his only feeling toward her was anger.

An even worse thought came to her: what if Dominic assumed that she had maneuvered him into such a situation, hoping for exactly the result that had come about? She had heard rumors about women who had done exactly that, placing themselves in a compromising position with a man so that he would be forced to marry them. She did not think she could bear it if Dominic held such a low opinion of her.

When they reached the house, the grooms hurried out to take their horses. Dominic came to Constance's side to help her down. When he set her down on the ground, she looked up into his face anxiously, but she could read nothing there.

"I am sorry. I must take my leave," he told her quietly. "I have certain business that I must attend to."

Unease rippled through her. She feared that this "business" must be something to do with his declaration that they were engaged.

"Dominic, no…" she said in a low voice, charged with emotion, and reached out toward him.

"Francesca will stay with you," he said, glancing over at his sister, who had come up beside them.

"Of course," Francesca promised.

"Good." He took Constance's hand, bowing over it. "We will talk later."

Then he was gone, striding away toward the house.

Constance looked after him in consternation, then turned toward Francesca in agitation. "I did not mean this! I did not wish for anything like this to happen! Oh, this is such a terrible mess. What are we to do?"

Francesca calmly linked her arm through Constance's and smiled, saying quietly, "Why, nothing, my dear. Just keep your back straight, and your face pleasant and composed. You must not let anyone guess that Dominic said anything less than the truth."

Constance wanted to protest, but she knew that the other woman was right. They could not stand about discussing the matter in public. She had to put a good face on it until she and Francesca could get away from everyone else.

So she smiled back and went with Francesca. As they walked toward the house, the other riders turned toward them. Some offered her their best wishes on her engagement. A few tried to ask questions. But Francesca neatly evaded any prolonged conversation, laughingly telling them that she must get her future sister-in-law out of her wet clothes before she caught cold. And Calandra, she noticed gratefully, took the Norton sisters, who were obviously abrim with excitement and curiosity, off with her, chattering away about the storm, her own tiredness after such an adventure and anything else that came into her head.

Francesca whisked Constance into the house and up the stairs. Constance was glad to see no sign of Muriel anywhere. They went into Constance's bedchamber, closing the door behind them. Francesca released Constance finally, going over to the bellpull and tugging.

"Francesca, please believe me," Constance told her

earnestly. "I never imagined that such a thing would happen."

"Indeed," Francesca replied. "Who could have imagined that Muriel would behave so foolishly? I am sure that her mother will ring a peal over her head for letting her spite lead her to damage her own cause so severely. It is no more than she deserves, certainly, but I cannot help but feel a little sorry for her. Lady Rutherford is a demon when her ire is raised." She paused, then added consideringly, "Of course, Lady Rutherford frightens me even when she isn't angry."

"But it isn't right! It isn't fair that Dominic should have to pretend that we are engaged. It is not his fault. We talked at the promontory, and we let the time get away from us. We did not notice that the storm had built up. Then when we were caught in the rain, we took shelter in that cottage. Nothing happened." At such a bald-faced lie, Constance could not meet Francesca's gaze. She turned away, saying, "Dominic in no way wronged me. He should not have to marry me. Please, you must believe me, I had no intention of forcing Dominic to marry me."

"I am quite aware of that fact," Francesca replied calmly. "Do you think I do not know by now what sort of person you are?"

A maid entered at that moment in answer to Francesca's summons, and Francesca sent her to draw a hot bath for Constance and bring her a pot of tea.

When the maid had bobbed a curtsy and left, Francesca turned back to Constance. "Now, I think we had better get you out of those clothes."

Constance nodded, her fingers going to the buttons of her bodice. "Perhaps I should have something brought up to my room instead of going down to supper."

"Oh, no," Francesca replied decisively. "That is precisely what you must not do. I know it is difficult to face everyone, but it is important that you make it clear that you have nothing to feel ashamed of. That you did nothing wrong. You have to give Dominic and Calandra and me a chance to show that we do not care what the gossips may say."

Constance knew that Francesca was right. If a duke's sister and an earl's daughter supported her, showing that they did not believe the gossip, then it would do much to quell the rumors that were no doubt flying around right now. But she hated the thought of having to smile and chat with everyone and pretend that nothing was wrong.

"I know. It is just… It is so unfair! The wind blew my hat from my head, and my hair went every which way. It was so wet, and then I could not put it back up right. I know I looked a mess. But it was not Dominic's fault," Constance insisted.

"It is an unfortunate circumstance that your absence was so long and so public. Even more unfortunate that your cousin dropped out of the party, and Calandra and the others had to stay with her," Francesca commented. "And it is even more unfortunate that Muriel is such a spiteful fool that she would do everything she could to hurt you, even at the risk of losing precisely what she wants."

"Why would she do such a thing?" Constance exclaimed.

"I am sure she would not have if she had realized what Dominic would do. However, she misjudged my brother, because she does not know him at all. She assumes that everyone else in the world has the same lack of honor and scruples that she does. I think that Muriel must have thought that if she branded you a loose woman, Dominic would distance himself from you. She did not understand, of course, that he would not let your reputation suffer, that he would, of course, act in an honorable manner."

Francesca helped Constance out of her riding jacket as she spoke, then began to work at the buttons of her skirt.

"Muriel is desperate, of course. That may have clouded her thinking. No doubt she sees my brother as her last hope of marriage. Her family's fortune ensured that she would have ample suitors, but her cold, unforgiving temperament has frightened them all off. And, of course, the number of available men whom she would accept was rather low to begin with, as she refused to look as low as a baron for a mate. Muriel sees little point in marriage unless one improves one's standing."

Constance shook her head. "Dominic must not marry that woman," she said fervently.

She slipped her skirt down and let it fall to the floor, then sat to remove her boots. Francesca went to the dresser and took out Constance's dressing gown, coming back to hold it up as Constance finished skinning off the rest of her clothes and slid her arms into the robe.

Constance felt warm for the first time since she had dressed in the cottage, and she hugged the dressing gown to her gratefully. She turned to Francesca.

"But Dominic must not marry me, either," Constance told Francesca earnestly. "You know that better than I. He told me about the encumbrances on the estate. I know that he must marry to help his family. He cannot marry someone who has not even a decent dowry, let alone a fortune. I cannot let him make such a mistake."

Francesca looked at her for a long moment. "Dear girl, you must let Dominic decide for himself what he will do. Quite frankly, you have no other choice. No one can make Dominic do what he does not want to, I am certain of that. He has always been his own man."

Still, Constance could not help but fret. She could not allow Dominic to ruin his life out of a sense of obligation to her.

After Francesca left, as Constance lay soaking in the

soothing warmth of the tub and later, as Maisie helped her dress and do her hair, she continued to worry over her problem.

She could not bear to have Dominic forced into marrying her. What made it all worse, of course, was the fact that she wanted to marry him. She had realized today how very much in love she was with him. It was for that reason that she had made love with him in the cottage. When she allowed herself to think of being his wife, her heart thrilled inside her.

But, of course, she could not give in to that longing. She could not sacrifice Dominic's future for her own happiness. He was a man of duty, and if he married her, he would be ignoring that duty. More than that, she was certain that he did not want to marry her; he had announced that they were engaged only to protect her honor. He did not love her. Even when they had been making love, he had not told her that he loved her. He had wanted her; she was quite certain of that. But he did not love her as she loved him.

It would have been a different matter if he had asked her to marry him because he could not bear to live without her. If he had ignored his duty to his family because he could not face the unhappiness of never having the woman he loved, then Constance knew that she would have tossed all caution to the winds. She would not have cared if she had to live the rest of her life in poverty, as long as she was with Dominic.

But he did not love her. He had not asked her to marry him. And she did not want him without love any more than she wished him to be forced into marriage.

Something must be done, she knew, and she was the only person who could do it. She glanced at the clock on her dresser. There was still time before supper. She must do what she could to right this wrong.

Taking a deep breath, she strode purposefully out of her room.

CHAPTER FIFTEEN

CONSTANCE MADE HER WAY down the corridor to her aunt and uncle's room. She knocked softly at their door and entered at her aunt's response.

Her uncle was sitting in a chair, waiting for his wife, who was fussing over her hair and jewels in front of the vanity mirror. Both of them turned to look at Constance in some surprise.

"Well, come in, girl," her uncle said jovially. "You need not look at us like that. We are not angry with you. You took something of a risk, I must say, but it has turned out well."

"I have come to ask you to let me return home," Constance told him.

"What?" Her uncle stared at her, dumbfounded.

"Whatever are you talking about, you silly girl?" Aunt Blanche added. "Why would you want to return home? Oh, there may be a little whiff of scandal, but Lord Leighton has done the proper thing, and it will all pass in no time. Unless, of course, you draw attention to it by running away like a scared rabbit."

"I know that Lord Leighton said that we were engaged," Constance went on. "But it isn't true."

"Mayhap it was not when he said it, but it is now," Uncle Roger retorted smugly. "He came to me tonight as soon as he got in and asked for your hand, just as he should. Of course I gave him my approval. I would never have thought you were such a sly minx, Constance." He smiled at her as though they shared a secret. "But you have done very well for yourself."

"I did not do anything sly!" Constance protested. "Do you think I arranged it so that Dominic would have to marry me?"

She might have known, she thought, that even if Francesca knew her to be the sort of person who would not do such a thing, her own family would not.

"If not, you were very lucky indeed," Aunt Blanche put in.

"I cannot marry him," Constance shot back. "Dominic does not wish to marry me. He said that only because Muriel Rutherford was doing her best to create a scandal."

"Stupid girl," her aunt commented, giving a shrug. "Ah, well, her loss is our gain. Just think...we will have a countess in the family!"

She beamed, looking positively starry-eyed. "One cannot help but wonder at such a man, of course—why, he paid not the least attention to Margaret and Georgiana, and they are, of course, of a far more eligible age. But still...Margaret is quite hopeful of that charming

Mr. Carruthers. His attentions have been most marked the last few days. And once the girls are related to an earl, the possibilities will be endless. You will be able to introduce them to the very cream of society when you are Lady Leighton."

"I shan't be introducing them to anyone," Constance told her sharply, "as I will not be Lady Leighton."

Her aunt stared at Constance, her eyes bulging. "What? What are you talking about? Have you run mad?"

"I am not mad. I am instead, I am beginning to think, the only one here who is quite reasonable. Dominic does not wish to marry me, and I will not make him."

"Make him?" Sir Roger trumpeted. "What are you talking about? He has already offered for you."

"Only because he felt he had to," Constance retorted. "Can you not see the difference? He feels constrained to marry me."

"Of course he does. Quite right, too. A gentleman cannot play fast and loose with a young lady's affections," her uncle declared.

Constance sighed. It was clear that her aunt and uncle would never understand her objections to the nature of the proposal. They were far too intent on seeing the advantages of a marriage to Viscount Leighton. She could not look to them for help. She must turn to Dominic. He had to be made to see reason.

"I apologize for bothering you," she said, turning away and starting toward the door. "Pray excuse me."

Her uncle mumbled some reply, but her aunt called out sharply, “Constance!”

She turned back. “Yes?”

“Just remember this, my girl,” Aunt Blanche said sternly. “If you should turn down his offer, your name will be ruined. You will never get another offer. You will not, in fact, even be received.”

Constance just nodded and continued out the door. She went down the stairs. It was almost time for supper, but perhaps she could manage to catch Dominic alone for a few minutes.

When she entered the anteroom where everyone routinely gathered before dinner, she was aware of a pause in the conversation as everyone’s eyes flickered over to her. Dominic started toward her, and immediately the others began to talk again, though Constance was certain that all the guests were still watching her and Dominic, whatever they were talking about.

Dominic gave her an elegant bow; he was, she was certain, emphasizing his regard for her. “Constance, it is good to see that you are looking well. I hope you feel well, also.”

“Yes, I am quite all right.” She smiled tightly at him. With everyone eyeing them from all over the room, she did not feel comfortable talking to him, at least about anything but the merest polite nothings. “And you? I hope you did not catch a chill.”

He shook his head. “No. Not at all.” He extended his

arm to her. "Come say good evening to Francesca and my parents."

His parents were perhaps the last people she wanted to see—well, other than Muriel or Lady Rutherford—but she knew that this meeting was probably the most important one for tamping down gossip. Presumably his parents would be polite to her, not wanting a scandal, but she could not help but be afraid that they would cut her, shaming her in front of everyone. They could not be happy, she was certain, to have learned that their son was engaged to a near-penniless woman instead of the heiress whom they had chosen for him.

Fortunately, however, they greeted her politely, if with a degree of coolness that convinced Constance that they had as little liking for the match as she had supposed they would. Neither of them, she noticed, offered her any felicitations on the match. Francesca, at least, greeted her with her usual warmth and proceeded to keep the conversational ball rolling with little enough help from anyone else. Neither Lord nor Lady Selbrooke seemed inclined to talk, and though Constance would have liked to help Francesca, she was too aware of the fact that everyone in the room was watching her.

So she looked at Francesca, pretending to listen, but hearing not half of what she said. The smile on her face felt frozen. Lord and Lady Selbrooke remained in the small circle of conversation, which surprised Constance. She imagined that they found the exchange as stilted and uncomfortable as she did. But after a while she realized that they, too, must be hoping to avoid talking to anyone else—or to let Constance talk to anyone. She suspected that they reasoned the less said about the surprise engagement, the better their chances were of somehow disposing of the awkward matter.

Of course, marooned there with his parents and Francesca, there was no opportunity to broach the subject of ending their engagement with Dominic. She knew that she would have to wait until after the meal was over.

At last they were called in to supper, and Constance was able to leave Dominic and his parents. Of course, she was now also away from the protection of their presence, which meant that the other guests would be free to ask her questions.

She took some comfort in the fact that at least Lady Rutherford and Lady Muriel were not there; for surely they would have asked the more penetrating and embarrassing of questions. The Norton sisters would merely want to hear all the details of the engagement, and since she knew none, that would doubtless prove to be difficult, but at least with them there would be no intent to wound her.

Mr. Willoughby, much to Constance's relief, was as polite and gentlemanly as ever, and after murmured felicitations, did not bring up the subject of the engagement again. Nor did he mention this afternoon. Sir

Lucien, on her other side at the table, had clearly been instructed by his friend Francesca, for he talked wittily and at length about almost everything but the engagement.

But the gentlemen, of course, left after the meal was over, and Constance had to face the other women.

"It is so exciting!" Miss Elinor Norton said, coming up and linking her arm through Constance's as the women trailed out of the dining room. Her sister posted herself on Constance's other side.

"I had no idea that there was any understanding between you and Lord Leighton," Miss Lydia added. "How long have you been engaged? How did he ask you? Did he go down on bended knee?"

Constance felt herself coloring. "Please, it isn't really… I mean, I have known Lord Leighton for only a short time."

"How romantic!" Elinor exclaimed, pressing a hand to her bosom. "Did you look at him and know immediately that you loved him?"

"Um, well…" Constance looked around a little desperately, wishing that Francesca or Calandra would save her.

"Oh, Elinor, you are embarrassing her," Lydia scolded her sister. She squeezed Constance's arm, saying, "Don't mind Elinor. She is quite mad at the moment about weddings and betrothals."

As Constance could see scarce a ha'penny's difference between the two sisters' interest, she was unsure how to respond. Finally she said, "It is really much too soon to say anything. Lord Leighton should not have brought it up."

"A secret engagement," Elinor contributed breathlessly.

Constance was not sure but what she was making things worse. A secret engagement sounded a little havey-cavey. "Well, um, I don't know that it was secret, exactly."

"Well, of course your aunt and uncle knew," Lydia offered. "Lady Woodley was telling me all about it."

"She was?" Constance asked, rather alarmed at this news. Heaven only knew what Aunt Blanche might take it upon herself to say.

At that moment Francesca joined them, saying, "Miss Norton, you must play for us, as Lady Muriel is not with us this evening."

The sisters were diverted momentarily from their interrogation by a discussion over which of them should play. Francesca suggested, beaming, that each of them play several tunes, adding, "And your sister may turn the pages for you."

The girls bade Constance a quick farewell, and Francesca took her place at Constance's side. "I am dreadfully sorry," she apologized. "I could not get away from the Duchess. And if I offend her, I will never hear the end of it from my mother."

Constance smiled. "You need not apologize. Indeed,

I should beg your pardon for putting you in this position."

"It will not last much longer, I hope," Francesca said. "Once you and Dominic have a chance to confer, you will know what to say in answer to their questions."

They sat down near the door of the music room, and Constance was relieved when Calandra came over to take a seat on her other side.

"At least we will not have to listen to Lady Muriel's playing tonight," Calandra remarked cheerfully.

"Or at all," Francesca added. "I understand that she and her mother are leaving at dawn tomorrow."

"Really?" Constance asked.

"She can hardly stay," Calandra pointed out. "Not after what she did this afternoon. I heard Lady Rutherford talking to her when I went past their room coming down to supper." She gave an exaggerated shiver. "I almost felt sorry for Lady Muriel. Her mother was shrieking at her like a fishwife. She said that Lady Muriel had ruined all her chances."

"She never had a chance with Dominic," Francesca stuck in. "But she has chased off a number of other suitors. She will have to find someone whose pockets are completely to let."

"And marry him posthaste before he has an opportunity to get to know her better," Calandra added.

Francesca smiled, saying only, "Callie, you are unkind."

Calandra shrugged. "Muriel threw her cap at Sinclair, you know."

Francesca's eyebrows vaulted up. "Indeed. When?"

Calandra shrugged. "I am not entirely certain. When I was much younger. Well, you can imagine how she would enjoy snaring a duke. But of course she hadn't the slightest chance. I remember her discoursing to Sinclair on how a child should most effectively be reared. Of course, in her opinion, I was growing up in the worst way."

A grin flashed across Francesca's face. "I am sure Rochford took that well."

"You can imagine. He gave her such a set down that even Muriel turned scarlet with embarrassment."

Miss Lydia began to play at that moment, and they fell silent. Her skill at the piano did not approach Muriel Rutherford's, but the tune was livelier, and when the two sisters began to sing, it was altogether more enjoyable.

The men rejoined the women more quickly than was usual. Constance, seeing the way Dominic and his father studiously ignored one another, suspected that the atmosphere in the Earl's smoking room had been rather chillier than the guests liked.

Constance felt another pinprick of guilt. Because of Dominic's decision to marry her, the tension between father and son was worse than ever.

After another song or two, the party began to break up, with several of the older guests retiring. Lady Selbrooke, looking not so much tired as unhappy, was among the first to leave. The people who were left in the music room began to drift into groups, several of them gathering around a table for a card game, and Mr. Carruthers and some others hanging about the piano with the Norton sisters. With their singing and the chatter from the card players, there was ample noise to cover a private conversation. So when Dominic made his way over to where Constance sat, she seized the chance to talk to him.

They took a stroll about the long rectangular room, and she pulled him to a halt at the farthest end. "Dominic, we must talk."

"Yes, we have to decide when and where I asked you to marry me," he said, smiling faintly.

"No. No, that is not what I meant. Dominic, you must not do this."

He looked at her quizzically. "Mustn't I?"

"Yes. Don't be difficult. You know as well as I do that marrying me is the last thing you should do."

"It is precisely what I should do," he countered. "You must see that."

"I will not let you sacrifice yourself just because Muriel Rutherford caused a scene this afternoon."

"Constance, I'm not sure you understand what the consequences of that scene are. Your name will be besmirched if we do not marry. I realize that this is perhaps not what you would wish for."

Not wish for it? Constance thought. If only Dominic knew, marriage to him would be exactly what she would most wish for. But not under these circumstances. Not with him forced to marry her.

Dominic went on. "Certainly the style of my proposal lacked romance, but I thought it vital that I act quickly to forestall any further comments from Muriel."

"I do not care about the style of it," Constance retorted. It was exasperating the way Dominic was turning this conversation around, implying that it was Constance who did not want to marry, who must be convinced of the necessity. "I know that my reputation will suffer from it, but that is not important, either."

"It is important to me," Dominic told her quietly. "Do you honestly think that I would act so dishonorably? After what happened in the cottage?"

Constance's cheeks flooded with color. "I did not…do that to get you to marry me!"

His face softened. "I know you did not. But that fact does not alter my responsibility. I have spoken to your uncle, and he has given me permission to ask for your hand."

"You did not actually ask for it," Constance pointed out.

He smiled faintly. "I know. I must apologize for that omission. Shall I go down on my knee to you now?"

He started to move, and Constance quickly grasped his arm, whispering, "Dominic, no!" He chuckled, and she snapped, "Well, I am glad that you at least find amusement in this predicament!"

"It has to be done," he said, his face sobering. "If you mislike the idea, I am sorry. But if you do not care how you will be seen by the world, I do. I will not play the cad."

"You would not have to," Constance replied. "Surely if we just stop talking about the engagement, people will after a time forget about it. There has been no announcement, after all. If someone questions you, you could say it was a…a misunderstanding."

"There would always be a cloud over you," Dominic told her firmly.

"Then you are adamant?"

"I am. I have spoken to my parents. We will have another ball at the end of this week, the night before all the guests leave. And we will make the formal announcement then."

Constance sighed. Clearly there was no budging Dominic. Of course he would do what any honorable gentleman would. She should have expected nothing less of him, really.

But she could not bear to put this burden upon him. The family, the estate, would suffer because of their momentary indiscretion. It would be entirely different if he had wanted to marry her, she knew. If he had chosen love over the money the estate needed, she would have agreed in an instant. She would have been happy to live with him in penury, if that was the consequence of their marrying. If he had but once spoken of love, if he had told her how happy it would make him to marry her, she would have been overjoyed.

However, it was quite clear that he had acted out of honor, not love. She was his "responsibility." He would not "play the cad." How could she marry him, spend the rest of her life with him, loving him so much that she felt her heart might burst with it, when all that time he did not love her? When he had married her only because he was too honorable not to?

She wished that she knew what to do. It would be easiest, of course, to simply stop resisting, to agree to the announcement and the marriage. It was what everyone wanted. She would not have to face the ruin of her reputation. And perhaps, over time, Dominic would come to love her as she loved him. Did not people grow into love sometimes? Surely there had been couples who had married because their families had arranged it, yet afterward they had fallen in love.

But, no, Constance could not deceive herself. There was a vast difference between marrying because it was expected of one and marrying because one had been forced into it. Especially when marrying that person meant going against one's family. When it meant that one would be living the rest of one's life in straitened circumstances…and condemning one's family to live that way, as well.

In Dominic's situation, she thought, the marriage would be a constant source of irritation to him. Each time he saw her, he would be reminded of the fact that he had not done his duty by his family, that he hadn't the money to free his lands from their debts, that he could not provide as he would want to for his children—and all because of Constance. He could hardly grow to love her under those circumstances. Indeed, in all probability, he would come to hate her.

She could not give in and marry him, Constance decided. She had to be firm. But what could she do? If she remained, Dominic would stubbornly go ahead with his plans to announce the engagement at the end of the week; she could not stop him. And once it was announced, it would be much more difficult to turn back. People might overlook his hasty remark today in the face of Muriel's accusations, but one could not overlook a formal announcement. It would be a scandal if either of them refused to go through with the wedding after that.

Constance knew that she needed to keep him from announcing their engagement, and the only way she could think of to do that would be to leave Redfields. Clearly, talking with him had not worked. But he could not very well announce the engagement if she were not there. He would realize then how serious she was about not wanting him to have to marry her.

The problem, of course, was how she was to get

away. Her aunt and uncle had refused to take her back to London; they were much too eager for the wedding to do that. And Constance did not have enough money to lease a carriage to take her there. She had spent all but a few pennies on the clothes and accessories she had purchased in London. To get anything more, she would have to access some of the money she had invested in the Funds, and to do that would require several days. She considered borrowing the money from Francesca; it would not cost too much, surely, if she took the mail coach instead of hiring a post chaise.

But she had the niggling suspicion that Francesca would not be eager to help her. Had she not said only a few hours ago that she should trust Dominic on this issue?

Calandra had been very friendly with her, of course, but Constance could not imagine asking the girl to lend her money to run away. The same was true of anyone else visiting Redfields.

She excused herself from the evening early. It was difficult to be friendly and polite when her mind was running over her problems, and she was getting tired of smiling and avoiding everyone's questions.

To her surprise, as she started toward the stairs, one of the footmen intercepted her. "Miss…?"

She paused, looking at him inquiringly.

"His lordship requests your presence in his study," the fellow told her, bowing slightly.

"Lord Leighton?" Constance asked, confused. She

had left him in the music room, talking with Sir Lucien and Francesca.

"Oh, no, miss, beg pardon. Lord Selbrooke, I should say."

Constance gaped at him, even more surprised. "I—yes, of course. Thank you."

Some of her confusion must have shown on her face, for he then asked, "Shall I show you the way, miss?"

"Yes, thank you." Constance followed the liveried footman down the hallway, her thoughts in a tumble. What could Dominic's father want with her?

The footman knocked and opened the door for Constance, then withdrew, closing the door behind him. Constance looked across the room to where Lord Selbrooke sat behind a large mahogany desk. He rose and gestured toward one of the straight-backed chairs that faced his desk.

"Miss Woodley, please sit down."

Constance did as he said, her stomach knotting. The room was imposing, all dark wood and massive furniture, and she could not help but think that the Earl had meant her to feel that way. He was equally imposing, his face stern and his demeanor haughty. After she took her seat, he sat down once again behind his desk, leaving the large expanse of wood between them.

Perversely, the thought that the man purposely sought to intimidate her stiffened Constance's back. Even if her insides were jittering, she was not about to let him see it.

He did not speak for a long moment, letting the silence sink between them. She maintained a polite expression, waiting.

"No doubt you know why I wished to see you," the Earl began at last.

"No, my lord, I am afraid that I do not," Constance answered evenly.

"You must realize that this is a match that I would not wish for my son."

"Yes."

"Dominic is headstrong, as always," he went on.

"He is a man of strong principle," Constance agreed.

"Phrase it how you like," the Earl said with a shrug. "I think it will be easier to deal with you than with my son. You, I trust, will be more understanding about where your best interests lie."

He was, she thought, going to try to talk her out of marrying Dominic. It seemed ironic that he intended to convince her to do what she had already decided to do. She should agree, she thought, and ask him for the use of his carriage back to London. However, his manner, both toward her and regarding Dominic, had the effect of making her want to do the opposite of what he asked.

"I realize that you stand to gain a great deal from this marriage," he said, resting his elbows on his desk and steepling his hands together. "Of course, I would not expect you to give that up without some compensation. I am prepared to provide it."

Constance gaped at him. "I beg your pardon? Are you offering to *pay* me not to marry Dominic?"

"Naturally." He pulled a small leather pouch from a drawer and plopped it down on the desk in front of him. Pulling the drawstrings apart, he poured a handful of gold coins out on the desk.

Constance's gaze went to the coins, then back to the Earl. She was so appalled at his suggestion that she could not speak.

Lord Selbrooke gave her a tight smile. "Of course. I can see that you do not consider that enough. I did not expect it to be."

He pulled out a piece of velvet and laid it on the desk beside the coins. Carefully, he unfolded the cloth to reveal a necklace of rubies and diamonds, glittering against the soft background of black velvet.

"It is a FitzAlan family heirloom," he explained. "It has been in my family since the time of the second earl. My grandmother had her portrait painted wearing this necklace." He looked at her. "It is worth a great deal. You can sell it and have a healthy nest egg. But without the encumbrance of a husband."

Constance rose from her chair. She was trembling with anger, and she clasped her hands together tightly so that he could not see their shaking. "That is what you think of me?" she asked. "That I would take your money not to marry Dominic? I don't understand you, my lord, and clearly you do not understand me. You cannot buy me. I will not barter my good name for coins and jewels."

She whirled and stalked to the door. She turned and looked back at him, her eyes flashing. "I do not plan to marry your son. I would not let Dominic's honor force him into a marriage he did not want. But I would never spurn him for money. Or to please you. Goodbye, my lord. I will leave your house as soon as possible."

Constance stalked out of the room. She hurried down the hall, struggling to hold back the tears of anger that threatened to flood out. She felt furious and humiliated, and she wanted to leave immediately.

The only problem, of course, was how to do it. If she had to, she thought, she would pack her things and walk to the village. From there, she was not sure what she would do. She would have to ask Francesca for a loan for the mail coach fare, although she dreaded facing her friend's questions. Perhaps if she did not tell her why she needed the money…

But what if the mail coach did not come through the village tomorrow? What would she do? She suspected that if Dominic learned she had left, he would come after her. He would refuse to let her ruin her good name. She must get away—far away and quickly.

She hurried up the stairs and started down the hall toward her room, her head down in thought. Suddenly she stopped. She stood for a moment, thinking, then turned and strode purposefully down the hall. She rapped sharply on the door, and a voice called to come in. Constance opened the door and stepped inside to face Muriel Rutherford.

CHAPTER SIXTEEN

MURIEL'S BROWS DREW together thunderously. "What are you doing here? Did you come to gloat?"

"No," Constance replied evenly. "I came to ask for your assistance."

"My word, you have a lot of gall," said an older woman's voice, and Constance turned to see Muriel's mother, seated in a chair to the side of the bed. "You think that we would help you? When you have made my daughter a laughingstock?"

Constance held on to her temper. "Lady Rutherford, I have done nothing to hurt you or your daughter." She did not think it wise to add that Lady Muriel had made herself an object of ridicule, if anyone had. "I am quite aware of how you feel about me. However, I think you might be willing to allow me this one favor."

The older woman narrowed her eyes shrewdly. "Why?"

"Because I believe you would find it to be in your best interests."

"Whatever are you talking about?" Muriel snapped.

"I have heard that you are planning to leave Redfields tomorrow. Is that true?"

"Yes," Muriel replied bitterly. "We will sneak out of here at the break of dawn. The fewer who witness my humiliation the better. What does that have to do with you?"

"I am asking you to let me travel with you to London."

The other two women stared at Constance as if she had taken leave of her senses.

"What? Are you mad?" Muriel asked.

"Why?" her mother added sharply.

"I have no desire to harm Lord Leighton," Constance replied. "I know he must marry well. His words today were generous and kind. But he should not have to pay for the remainder of his life because he acted the gentleman." She refused to admit to Muriel and her mother that she could not marry Dominic because he did not love her; that was entirely too much to ask of her.

"You don't want to marry him?" Muriel looked stunned.

"I am doing what is best for both of us," Constance said flatly.

"Or are you playing a cunning game?" Lady Rutherford murmured.

Constance turned to look at her. "I don't know what you mean."

Lady Rutherford studied her for a moment. Constance was sure that she was considering the possibilities this request presented for Muriel. She would realize, Constance felt sure, that if Constance left Redfields before the engagement was formerly announced, there would be little likelihood that Dominic would persist in the charade that they were engaged. If Dominic was once again free, she could hope that there was some possibility that she and Lord Selbrooke could maneuver him into marriage with Muriel. Constance did not feel inclined to tell her that she was certain that Dominic would never marry Muriel, no matter what she herself did.

"So…" Lady Rutherford said finally. "You wish to sneak out of here in secret? No one knowing that you have gone?"

"Yes." Constance felt tears flood her eyes, but she struggled to hold them back. It was almost more than she could bear to think of leaving Dominic with no word of explanation. But she could not tell him or even Francesca, who she feared would be sure to inform Dominic. She had to slip out secretly, or Dominic would try to stop her.

"All right," Lady Rutherford told her almost pleasantly. "We are leaving before breakfast tomorrow. Be sure you are ready."

Constance nodded and left the room. She walked back to her bedchamber and began to pack her things. Her heart felt like lead in her chest.

She tried to concentrate on making her plans. When

she reached London, she would go to her aunt and uncle's house. Even without her relatives there, she knew the servants would admit her. She would have to go somewhere else soon, of course. Aunt Blanche and Uncle Roger would be furious with her for creating a scandal and ruining the possibility of their connection with an earl. But she could stay at their house long enough to withdraw some of her money from the Funds and get enough cash to travel to Bath.

She had another aunt who lived in Bath. She and her father had visited her often when her father was ill, and Constance thought that Aunt Deborah would be happy enough to take her in. As Aunt Deborah's widow's portion was not large and she lived in a very small place, it would not be a suitable living arrangement for long, but at least it would give Constance some time to recover and figure out what to do with her life.

She would have to earn some sort of income, she thought; the amount of money she received from her small inheritance would not be enough to live on. She supposed that she might be able to be a hired companion, though that seemed a dreary life. Of course, that prospect might not be available if there was too much scandal attached to her name. Perhaps if she and her aunt pooled their resources, they might be able to get a slightly larger place and eke out a living.

It did not take her long to pack, sped along by her unhappy thoughts. Her trunk was soon filled, as was another small bag. She stopped and looked around the room, and for a moment it was all she could do to keep from crying.

She thought about the fact that she would not see Dominic again—never see his smile or hear his voice, never glance over to see his eyes on her. It seemed so hard, so unfair, and she could not but wonder how she could bear it. Would he hate her for leaving abruptly, without any sort of explanation? Or would he breathe a sigh of relief?

She wanted to write him a note to explain what she was doing and why. She would hate to think that he believed her uncaring or ungrateful.

But Lady Rutherford was right in guessing that she needed to sneak out without anyone knowing. If Dominic knew where she had gone, he might very well pursue her. He could be, she suspected, a very stubborn man when he thought he was in the right. Though it was not a long journey to London, a man on horseback might be able to catch up with a carriage before it reached the city.

But if she left early in the morning and Dominic did not know right away, she could be in London or very near it before he even realized that she was gone. Once she was in London, she would instruct the servants that she would not receive Lord Leighton, and within a day or two, she would be on her way to her aunt's, and he would have no idea of where to reach her.

She had to leave secretly. She could not tell him anything. After she left, she could write him a letter, she thought. Or she could write a note for him and entrust it to one of the maids, telling her not to give it to him before noon. But even that was not very safe, she knew, for if Lord Leighton was asking for her among the servants, a maid would be frightened of the consequences of not telling him what she knew. No, it was safest to write nothing until she arrived in London. Leaving in such a way would doubtless make him angry with her, and she hated the thought of his thinking ill of her, but, really, it would be for the best. He would be less likely to try to make her change her mind.

Or perhaps, Constance thought, she was fooling herself with the idea that Dominic would even pursue her. He wanted to marry her only because he thought it was the right thing to do, not because he loved her. He might be happy when he found out she had left and he had been freed of an unwelcome obligation.

With these unhappy thoughts running through her head, Constance began to get ready for bed. She pulled the pins from her hair and brushed it out perfunctorily, then slipped out of her clothes and donned her nightgown.

She sat down on her bed, pulling her knees up to her chin and wrapping her arms around her bent legs. For a moment she thought of Dominic and of what had passed between them this afternoon. Whatever had happened since then, it could not ruin her memories of their lovemaking. She loved Dominic with all her heart, and the happiest moments of her life had been his arms. She had felt more truly alive then than she ever had before.

She realized that she could not leave without seeing him again, without experiencing one more time the joy she had known earlier. She stood up and slipped on her dressing gown, belting it around her waist. She would go to him tonight. No matter how bleak the rest of her life would be, she would at least have this one last moment of love.

Constance picked up a candlestick from her bedside table and lit it from her oil lamp. Then she opened her door and peered out into the hall. The hallway was dim, all the doors closed. She could hear no voices. It appeared that while she was packing, everyone else had gone to bed.

Quietly, one hand in front of the candle's flame to shield it from drafts, she glided quietly down the corridor. Stopping in front of Dominic's door, she looked carefully up and down the hall. She thought about knocking, but it seemed safer to simply turn the handle and go inside. It might be a trifle rude, but, she thought with a smile playing about her lips, she hoped that she could quickly persuade him not to care about the lack of courtesy.

Turning the knob silently, she opened the door and whisked inside, closing the door behind her.

"What the devil?" Dominic was standing beside his bed, and at the sound of her entrance, he whipped around. When he saw her, he relaxed, his fists unclenching. "Constance…what are you doing here?"

He had already started undressing and was wearing only his breeches, his feet and chest bare. Constance felt the now-familiar heat stirring in her loins at the sight of him.

"I wanted to see you," she said quietly, setting her candlestick down on the dresser beside the door.

"You should not be here. Someone might see you."

"Would you rather I leave?" Her hand went to the sash of her dressing gown, and with a boldness that she would not have thought herself capable of, she opened it and shrugged her robe back off her shoulders, letting it slide down her body and onto the floor.

Dominic's eyes followed the path of her dressing gown, then returned to her face. Even in the dim light of the room, she could see desire stamped plainly on his features.

"No," he replied, his voice low and vibrant with hunger. "No, I don't want you to leave."

He walked across the room to her, reaching behind her to turn the key in its lock. His body was only inches from her; she could see the ripple of muscle under his skin as he stretched around her to lock the door. He leaned in close to her, taking a long, slow breath.

"You smell like heaven," he told her, and the deep

vibration of his voice set up an answering tremor inside her.

Constance leaned yearningly toward him; she wanted to melt against him. He brushed his lips against her hair. His hands came up to grasp her arms lightly, holding her still as he nuzzled his face into her hair. His lips sent a shiver through her, and she could feel herself loosening, opening to him in her most intimate core.

"Are you sure?" he asked. "You feel…all right? I do not want to hurt you."

"You will not hurt me," Constance replied confidently. "I want to be with you again."

She pulled back a little, raising her face to look at him. She loved the look of him, his eyes hard and bright, intent upon her, his skin stretched tautly across his bones, his mouth softening with desire.

"I want you," she said simply.

His jaw tightened, and he let out a little groan. His hands slid around her, pulling her to him, and he lowered his face into the curve of her neck, kissing the tender flesh there.

"Ah, Constance, Constance, you destroy all my best intentions," he murmured against her throat, his breath sending shivers across her skin.

His lips traveled up her neck, and he pushed back her hair with one hand so that his mouth could explore unimpeded. He kissed along the line of her jaw, little featherlight kisses that teased her nerve endings awake, until he came at last to the lobe of her ear. He took the fleshy lobe delicately between his teeth, nibbling, then slid his tongue along the edge.

Constance drew in a quick breath, and her hands went to Dominic's sides. His skin was smooth beneath her fingers, and beneath it she could feel the hard ridges of his ribs. She slid her hands around to his back, sweeping up over the hard pads of muscle, then back down, coming to a halt when she touched the cloth of his breeches. Her fingers edged along the waistband, fingernails tracing a narrow, delicate line, then insinuated themselves beneath the waist, sliding down under the cloth, the pads of her fingertips touching the rising curve of his buttocks.

She felt a tremor take him at her movements, and she smiled in sensual satisfaction at the knowledge that she stirred him. Dominic's hands slid down to her hips, clenching on the material of her nightgown and bunching it up inch by inch, while his mouth played havoc with her senses.

He kissed her ears, her neck, her face, moving ever closer to her lips, until at last his mouth fastened on hers. With a small sigh of satisfaction, Constance met his kiss with fervor. Her arms wrapped around his neck, and she went up on tiptoe, pressing her body against his.

Dominic's hands slid up beneath her nightgown, caressing the soft skin of her buttocks. His fingers traced the bony ridge of her spine, his palms gliding over her back. The skin of his hands was rougher than her soft flesh, evoking tingles of awareness everywhere they touched.

His lips moved against hers, his tongue exploring her mouth with lazy pleasure. Her fingers twined through his hair, fingertips pressing into his scalp whenever a new sensation rocked her. Hunger was growing in her loins, hot and demanding. She rubbed her body against him, seeking the satisfaction she craved. He shuddered in response, his hands going down and digging into her buttocks, pushing her up and into him.

She felt the hard length of his desire against her, and it intensified her need. She moved instinctively, and Dominic groaned deep in his throat.

He pulled back from her, seizing the hem of her nightgown in his hands and sweeping it up and off over her head. He tossed it on the chair closest to them, then bent and swept her up in his arms. Constance let out a startled noise; then a small, pleased bubble of laughter escaped her, and she curled her arm around his neck, resting her head on his shoulder.

Dominic carried her to his bed and laid her down upon it. He started to step back, his hands going to the buttons of his breeches, but she reached out to his hands, stopping them. He looked a question at her.

"Let me," she whispered huskily, kneeling on the bed and setting to work on the buttons.

His hands slid into her hair, stroking and caressing the

soft waves, as her fingers manipulated the buttons. She could feel his flesh pressing insistently against the cloth, throbbing with the movement of her fingers, and she smiled, pausing to stroke her hand down the material.

He made a noise, his hands clenching in her hair. "Are you trying to kill me?"

Constance turned her face up to him, a slow, sensual smile curving her lips. "No, only to please you." She trailed one fingernail back up the rigid line of him. "Do you not like it?"

"Vixen." He bared his teeth in a wolfish grin. "Yes, I like it. I will show you just how much I like it."

His hands went to her shoulders as though to bear her back against the sheets, but she shook her head. "No, no, let me finish."

She unfastened another button, then slipped her fingers beneath the cloth, parting it and wiggling her fingers down inside. Her fingertips tangled through the wiry hair she found there, brushing over the satiny skin of his manhood and exploring the intriguing contrast of hard and soft.

His breath labored in his chest, and the sound stirred her. She brought her hands back out and traced a line down each side, close to but not quite touching the flesh that strained against the material. Her index fingers moved back up and outward along the joinder of his legs to his torso, then came back to meet on the last two buttons.

His engorged shaft sprang free of the confining cloth

as she pushed his breeches down, her fingers skimming over the curve of his buttocks and down onto the backs of his thighs. She gave a final push, and the cloth fell down his legs in a last caress. Dominic stepped out of his breeches and kicked them aside, his body taut with desire.

Constance curled her hand around him, her fingers teasing up and down the hard length. He sucked in his breath and, after one small jerk of surprised pleasure, stood still under her ministrations, though she could see the quiver of strain along his thighs, indicating what the effort cost him. Seeing that, she was drawn to reach out and slide her hands over his thighs.

Everything about him was so new and intriguing—the textures of his skin, the sounds of his hunger, the shape and strength of his musculature, the myriad signs of his arousal. She wanted to taste and touch and explore them all in this one night, to take every precious memory of him that she could.

She pulled her eyes from her contemplation of his beautifully masculine body and looked up at him. His face was heavy with passion, his eyes slumberous and dark, his lips full and slack.

"When you look at me like that…" he breathed, then stopped, swallowing. "It is all I can do not to explode."

"I love to look at you," she told him honestly, and her answer brought a laughing groan from him.

"Constance, you will have me tumbling you like a green lad," he warned hoarsely.

"I would not mind," she murmured, her fingertips stroking up the length of his surging manhood and teasing onto the heavy sac that lay behind.

He made a muffled noise and moved his legs apart, giving her questing fingers access to him. She cupped him as though measuring his weight. Then she released him and lay back on the bed, her arms stretching languorously above her head.

She smiled up at him as he gazed at her, his eyes roaming hotly over her body. She was amazed at her own boldness, at the delight she felt to have his eyes upon her naked body.

Dominic climbed onto the bed and straddled her. Leaning back on his heels, he placed his hands upon her chest and moved them slowly down her body. He took his time with her, caressing and stroking, seeking out each little spot that caused her to moan or sigh or writhe with pleasure.

He slipped his fingers between her legs, opening her to him. He watched her face as he caressed her, his fingers separating the slick folds, teasing and stroking, circling the tiny nub until she dug her heels into the sheets beneath her, arching up off the mattress, almost sobbing with the need that thrilled through her.

The pleasure built in her, propelling her toward that shattering conclusion that she remembered so well, but just as she approached it, he slid his hand away.

"Not yet," he murmured, and bent to kiss her breasts.

She was hot and pulsing, aching for release, and she groaned in protest at the delay, but the touch of his tongue and lips on the soft flesh of her breasts was a delightful counterpoint to the heavy throb of need between her legs. Each flicker of his tongue, each pull of his mouth upon the hard bud of her nipple, elevated her desire, yet it was teasingly not enough to send her racing to completion.

Constance moved her hips restlessly on the bed, sighing his name. "Dominic...please. I want you. I want to feel you inside me."

His answer was a groan of pure lust, and he moved between her legs, lifting her hips and sliding into her. Constance was aware of a faint soreness, but her body was too eager for him to pay heed to that. She took him into her, wrapping her legs around him and luxuriating in the way he filled her.

Then there was no holding back, only a hard, slamming race to fulfillment, their bodies hungry and demanding, moving together to the completion they both desired. Dominic let out a hoarse cry as he shuddered to his climax, and Constance turned her head, sinking her teeth into his arm to hold back her words of love as she, too, found her sweet release.

He collapsed upon her, breathing raggedly. "Sweet Jesus," he murmured against her skin. "I think you have finished me."

With a low growl, he nuzzled her neck, rolling over

onto his back and carrying her with him, so that she lay stretched out on top of him. Constance chuckled and raised her head, looking down at him. She felt that she could have gazed at him forever. His face was soft with contentment, his eyes lambent, his cheeks flushed. Love rose up in her so fiercely that it was all she could do to hold back the words. But she knew she must not say them. She could not offer that most precious piece of her heart to him and face the pain of not having her feelings returned.

So she simply smiled and bent to place a tender kiss upon his chest, then laid her head upon it. They lay in contentment, unwilling to move, extending the moment of pleasure. He twined his fingers idly through her hair, wrapping it around his hand and bringing it to his lips. Constance drew lazy circles on his arm.

She could feel him relax beneath her, his hand growing heavy and sliding from her hair. Carefully, she rose onto her elbow and looked at him. He was asleep, his face relaxed, his eyelashes casting shadows on his cheeks. Her heart squeezed tenderly in her chest.

How could she bear to leave him?

In that moment she was horribly tempted to stay. To take her things back out of her bag and put them away, to let the Rutherford women depart on their journey to London without her. Dominic might not love her, but she had brought him pleasure. Surely that was enough to build on. It seemed too much to ask of her to give all this up.

With a sigh, she turned and lay back on the bed. She

stared up at the tester above them. She knew she could not do what she was thinking. She loved Dominic too much; she could not let her desires override what she knew was right. She could not hold him to the pledge his gentlemanly code of conduct had forced him to make. She had to set him free.

She propped herself up on her elbow again and studied his face. It was late, and she knew that she should get some sleep, but she did not care. She could sleep tomorrow. Right now, this moment, was the last that she would ever have of Dominic.

So she watched him sleep, sometimes dropping her head to his shoulder and lying against him, feeling the warmth of his body, the steady rise and fall of his chest beneath her head.

Finally, when she began to fear that the servants might soon be up, she eased from the bed and tiptoed over to where her clothes lay. She pulled on her nightgown and dressing gown, belting it securely. Picking up her candle, burned down now to a stub, she cast one long look back at the man sleeping in the bed. Then she opened the door and looked cautiously outside.

There was no sign of anyone, so she slipped out into the hall, shutting the door noiselessly behind her, and hurried down the corridor to her room. She reached it and closed the door behind her before the tears came.

CHAPTER SEVENTEEN

WHEN CONSTANCE FINALLY dried her tears, she washed up and put on the brown bombazine carriage dress that she had set aside for the journey. She knew that it was useless to try to sleep before she left. She was too sick at heart to go to sleep, and in any case, an hour or so of rest would do her little good.

She folded her nightshift and dressing gown away in a bag, then sat down to pen a letter of thanks to the Countess, a polite necessity despite the Earl's behavior toward her. Nor did she feel that she could leave without writing a note to Francesca to thank her for her friendship and her many kindnesses. Constance knew that she was taking a risk, but she simply could not be so rude as to leave without a word. She would leave the missives on the table in the entry where the servants put the mail and calling cards. Francesca would not be likely to arise until late in the morning, and by the time she went past the table or a servant brought the envelope to her, Constance would be almost to London. And Lady Selbrooke, she reasoned, even if she received the letter earlier, would be happy that Constance had left and would not bring up the subject with Dominic.

So, having worked her way around to it, Constance decided that it would be no riskier to leave a letter for Dominic himself. After all, the same logic applied to him as to Francesca—he would arise late—and anyway, if Francesca knew she had left, she would tell Dominic immediately. So she wrote a letter to Dominic, which she could not manage to do without a tear or two, but she blotted them away and persevered.

When she was all done, she sealed the three notes and went quietly downstairs to leave them on the table. Afterward, she returned to her room and sat down beside her trunk to wait for the Rutherfords to awaken.

The servants were up before Lady Rutherford appeared at Constance's door, and her maid looked with surprise at Constance's trunk and bag sitting at the foot of her bed. Constance gave Nan a coin and pressed her not to tell anyone about Constance's departure, assuring her that she had written to the Countess. The maid looked somewhat doubtful but nodded as she slipped the coin into her pocket.

A few minutes after Nan had left the room, Lady Rutherford appeared in the doorway. Constance jumped to her feet, picking up her smaller bag.

"I must send for a footman for the trunk," Constance said.

"Oh, no, you needn't bother. Just leave your bags

here. My coachman and groom will bring them down for you when they fetch our things," Lady Rutherford replied so graciously that Constance was taken aback.

Of course, she reasoned, Lady Rutherford had every reason to make it easy for her to leave, thinking that it would advance her plans for her daughter. She went downstairs with Lady Rutherford and climbed into the carriage. She sat on the seat facing Lady Rutherford and Muriel, the less-preferred spot, as it faced the rear.

Constance did not care for that. She had no interest in watching the scenery, anyway. Her intent was to close her eyes and at least pretend to sleep; that way, she would not have to try to carry on a conversation with Muriel or her mother.

Constance looked out the window. She had hoped to have a last look at Redfields, but it was still dark outside, and the building was little more than a blacker outline against the sky. The front door was open and the entryway lit, as was the corridor window above it. She watched as the coachmen and the groom carried out the Rutherfords' luggage and her own, and fastened it to the back and top of the carriage.

Her stomach was a knot of nerves as she waited, fearing that Dominic would awaken and somehow know that she was leaving—and at the same time wishing just a little, deep inside, that he would. But as it happened, no one appeared at the front door. The luggage was loaded, and the carriage rolled slowly away from the house.

Constance closed her eyes, not trusting herself not to cry and determined not to do so in front of Muriel and Lady Rutherford. She had not believed that she could sleep, but with the motion of the carriage and the rumble of its wheels, she began to slide gradually into slumber.

She was awakened by shouts. She opened her eyes, confused for an instant. The carriage was slowing down. Realization of where she was and what she was doing came back to her in a rush. She straightened up.

"What is it? Why are we stopping?" she asked, looking over at Lady Rutherford.

"I haven't any idea," the older woman said coolly, drawing aside the curtain over the window and looking out.

Constance, too, pushed back the curtain beside her and peered out. Dawn was breaking to the east, a line of gold across the horizon, with pinkish clouds above it. The carriage had come to a standstill, and two men on horseback were outside the carriage door. One of them swung down off his horse and walked over to the carriage.

"My lady?"

"Yes?" Muriel's mother leaned out the window. "What is it? What is all this shouting about?"

"Lord Selbrooke sent me, ma'am. He wishes you to return to Redfields at once," the man answered, sweeping off his hat and bowing respectfully.

Constance drew in a sharp breath. No! They could not return!

"Return? Whatever for?" Lady Rutherford asked.

"I don't know, ma'am. But he requested it most urgently. He said it is of the utmost importance."

"I see. Well…I suppose we must, if it is of such import."

"Lady Rutherford! No!" Constance could not keep from crying out. Her plan would be in ruins if they returned now.

"Turn around and go back," Lady Rutherford called up to her driver. As the carriage began its unwieldy turn, she pulled her head back inside the carriage and looked at Constance coolly. "Don't be silly, girl. How would it look if we did not return?"

"I don't know," Constance retorted honestly. "But it will ruin everything. I can't…"

"Don't be nonsensical," Lady Rutherford told her shortly. "Dominic cannot force you to marry him. If you don't want to, just say so. I shall tell him that I will take you back to London with me, and that will be that."

"But why is Lord Selbrooke calling us back?"

Lady Rutherford shrugged. "We shall soon find out. Perhaps Lord Leighton has seen the error of his ways." Her eyes glinted malignantly at Constance; then she turned to look back out the window.

Had her letters been discovered early? Constance wondered. Did Dominic and his parents know that she had fled rather than announce their engagement? Or perhaps the maid, despite the coin Constance had given the girl, had rushed straight to the butler with the news that Constance had left. But even if that had happened, why would Lord Selbrooke call her back? She was doing what he wanted without his even having to bribe her.

Perhaps it was Dominic who had sent the servant, not the Earl. Perhaps he was angry with her for leaving with only a note of explanation when he had been ready to sacrifice his entire future for her.

Constance's hands knotted together in her lap. She did not think that she could bear to face a furious Dominic. She remembered the anger in him when he had told her what his brother had done to their sister. Constance did not want to have such a gaze turned upon her.

She wished desperately that she had not left the letters.

The ride was an agony of nerves for her, and by the time they arrived back at the stately old house, she was almost numb with dread. Reluctantly she climbed down from the carriage after Muriel and Lady Rutherford, and followed them to the front door. To her surprise, she saw that two footmen had come out and were unloading their luggage from the carriage.

She walked into the house to find Lord and Lady Selbrooke standing in the entryway. Lady Selbrooke's face was a cool mask of hauteur; Lord Selbrooke looked thunderous. Constance glanced to one side and saw that several people had come down the stairs, most of them in various stages of dishabille. Dominic was in front, on the bottom step. He was dressed in a shirt and breeches, though clearly his clothes had been hastily donned, for his jacket and waistcoat were missing, and his shirt was not tucked in. His hair was still rumpled from sleep in a way that even in her present state of anxiety she found rather endearing. He appeared, she realized, not angry but puzzled.

Francesca was a few steps up from Dominic, wrapped in a brocade dressing gown, her hair tumbling loosely down her back. Behind her several more guests ranged up the stairs. Constance noted Calandra and Lord Dunborough, as well as all three of the Nortons. Everyone looked sleepy and confused, as though they had been pulled from their beds.

Constance turned her gaze back to Lord Selbrooke, feeling even more puzzled than before. She had no idea what was going on, but the look of calculation as well as anger in his eyes was enough to convince her that he had some sort of mischief in mind.

"Well!" he exclaimed, looking straight at Constance. "Miss Woodley! So this is how you repay our hospitality?"

"Father, what is going on?" Dominic asked sharply, coming down the remaining stairs and taking a few steps forward. "Constance? Why are you with Lady Muriel?" His eyes swept down her, taking in her gloves and bonnet and traveling dress. "Where have you been?"

Constance straightened, shooting a glance toward the other guests standing on the stairs. She could not explain this in front of everyone.

But she did not need to worry, for Lord Selbrooke was going on, giving her no chance to speak. "I will tell you what is going on. I awakened this morning to find that we had been robbed!"

There was a collective gasp from the guests on the stairs. Constance stared at the Earl blankly. Whatever she had envisioned the man saying, it had not been this.

The tableau was broken by the entrance of the two footmen who had gone out to unload the carriage. They carried a trunk between them, and Constance and the Rutherfords automatically parted to let them walk through. They set the trunk down on the floor in front of Lord Selbrooke. Constance saw with some astonishment that it was her trunk.

"Lady Selbrooke's ruby necklace is gone," the Earl proclaimed, gazing straight at Constance. "What have you to say for yourself, Miss Woodley?"

Constance gaped at him.

"Are you mad?" Francesca cried from the staircase, and she ran down the steps toward her father. "Surely you cannot think that Constance took the necklace?"

"I am certain of it," the Earl retorted, still looking only at Constance. "Why else did she run away like this? A trifle odd, is it not, that Miss Woodley disappears on the same morning that the necklace does?"

Again there was a murmur from the staircase.

Anger shot through Constance, stiffening her spine, and she said clearly, "I took nothing from this house, my lord."

Out of the corner of her eye, she could see Dominic look consideringly from her to his father. Pain seared through her. Surely he could not suspect her!

"Indeed?" The Earl cocked one eyebrow and nodded toward one of the footmen, who knelt and unfastened her trunk, opening the lid.

There, on top of her folded clothes, lay a small box. The footman turned toward the Earl, and he nodded. The footman handed him the box, and the Earl opened it. Inside was a folded piece of black velvet.

The cloth looked quite familiar, and Constance felt suddenly sick inside.

The Earl placed the velvet material on the palm of his left hand and opened up the folds with his other hand. An elegant ruby and diamond necklace shimmered against the dark velvet.

"Then how do you explain this, Miss Woodley?"

Constance's head swam. The Earl had placed the damning necklace in her trunk. It was the only explanation.

"You planned this!" she gasped. "When I would not take that necklace as a bribe, you put it into my trunk! You knew I was leaving, didn't you?" Constance turned toward Lady Rutherford, realization breaking through.

It was no wonder Lady Rutherford had been so unexpectedly pleasant to her, even accommodating. She must have seen the possibilities Constance's flight from the house offered and had gone to the Earl to suggest a way to rid themselves of the problem Constance presented to their betrothal plans.

"You planned this thing together!" Constance's gaze went from Lady Rutherford to Lord Selbrooke. She could not understand why they had done this to her. She was leaving Dominic and the house; surely that was enough for them.

But, no. They must have been afraid that Dominic would persist in his plans, that he might go after her and persuade her to return. If they managed to disgrace her in front of everyone, if they convinced Dominic that she was a thief and made her name a subject of scandal, then he would not insist on marrying her. They were making certain that she could not marry Dominic. And they did not care that they would ruin her in the process.

"Young lady!" Lady Rutherford exclaimed. "Mind your tongue. How dare you speak to me like that?" She whipped around to face Lord and Lady Selbrooke. "It is clear that you have nursed a viper to your bosom, my lord. Lady Sybil, my heart goes out to you. What a blow this must be. And to think that she was almost your daughter-in-law."

Lady Selbrooke did not respond but looked aside. At least she, Constance thought, had the grace to look embarrassed at this charade.

An awkward silence fell on the group. Constance could feel the eyes of everyone upon her. She realized, with a sinking sense of horror, that she had no idea how she could disprove any of what Lord Selbrooke had just said. No one knew of their conversation last evening in his study. And who would think that an earl would do such a thing? Who would believe her over him?

"I did not take that necklace," Constance said, angry at the tremor of emotion in her voice. "You offered it to me, and I told you no. But I left Redfields anyway. You had what you wanted. How could you do this?"

She glanced over at Dominic. He was not looking at her; his eyes were on his father. Her heart twisted within her chest. If Dominic believed his father, she thought that her heart would break.

There was a long silence. Then Dominic spoke at last, his voice like ice. "Is this the best that you could do, Father?"

Lord Selbrooke turned an affronted gaze on his son. "What do you mean? This young woman stole one of our family heirlooms! Surely you cannot be so foolish, so naive, as to believe her protestations."

"No, I am not foolish," Dominic replied levelly, his

blue eyes like shards of glass. "Nor, I imagine, is anyone else in this room foolish enough to believe this tale you have concocted."

The Earl's eyes widened. "How dare you—"

"No, Father, how dare *you?*" Dominic exploded, stepping forward to face his father, putting himself squarely between the Earl and Constance. "How can you have allowed your greed and animosity to lead you to so strip yourself of all honor?"

His father swelled up in indignation and opened his mouth to speak, but Dominic stepped forward and took the necklace in his hand, which seemed to rob the Earl of speech. Lord Selbrooke sputtered and reached in vain to take it back, but Dominic had already turned and was holding it out in his hand toward the guests on the staircase, who were all gazing at the scene with avid interest.

"I realize that none of you know Miss Woodley as I do. You may not be certain, as I am, that the idea of stealing anything from anyone would never occur to her. You probably have no idea that she tried to argue me out of marrying her because she felt that I had a duty to my family to marry otherwise."

He paused for a moment. Everyone's eyes were glued to him. Constance's heart warmed within her chest at his words, and tears pressed against her eyelids. Nothing else mattered, she thought, as long as Dominic believed in her.

"However," he went on, "even if you do not know Miss Woodley, I would think that anyone with a modicum of sense—anyone, at least, whose mind was not clouded by his own greed—would quickly see that if a woman were about to marry the future Earl of Selbrooke and would then have not only this necklace but every other jewel in the Redfields safe to wear, as well as having this house and these lands and a rather large amount of gold and silver plates at her disposal, she would not throw it all away to steal one paltry necklace."

The silence after his words was deafening. Finally, in a faint voice, the Earl offered, "The necklace would have given her immediate gain. She would not have to wait. She would not have to marry."

"No. Nor would she if she had taken your offer last night," Dominic answered smoothly. "Would she? And if, by chance, she had actually chosen to steal a necklace that she could have had only for agreeing not to marry me, it seems odd that she would not have hidden it but would instead put it her trunk in plain sight of anyone who might open it. Without even a lock upon it. Not a particularly clever action for someone who must have been smart enough to break into the safe in your study. But then, I suppose her carelessness in not concealing what she stole is no odder than the idea that, having broken into the safe, she stole none of the other jewelry there, even the earrings and bracelet that match this necklace. Speaking of peculiarities, I find it strangest of all that you happened to discover that this necklace was missing at dawn this morning. And that you had such an unerring instinct as to where it was hidden. You did not have to bring in any other bags or search her reticule. You just looked in this trunk."

Dominic's gaze remained on his father for a long moment. Then he turned to Constance. "My father offered you this very necklace last night in return for your refusing to marry me?"

"Yes."

He looked back at his father. "I would not have thought you would stoop so low as to try to bribe a young girl with this."

He turned his hand to the side, letting the necklace slide from his grasp. It hit the floor, and as everyone watched in astonishment, Dominic raised his foot and smashed down on the necklace with his heel.

"Paste," he said flatly, lifting his foot to reveal the mess of powder and chain.

Gasps echoed all over the room, and everyone's eyes were now focused on the Earl. All color had drained from his face. His mouth opened and closed spasmodically.

"I think we all realize what happened here," Dominic went on, his voice deadly quiet as he turned to his father. "But I think it would be best if you admitted to everyone what you tried to do to Miss Woodley, so that there will be absolutely no threat of any stain to her good name."

His father set his jaw rebelliously, and Constance was certain that he was about to refuse.

Dominic quirked one eyebrow and said without inflection, "Or perhaps you would like me to continue to enlighten everyone about our family."

The Earl's nostrils flared. Bright spots of color flamed in his cheeks, and hatred shot from his eyes. But he turned toward the crowd gathered on the staircase and said, "Leighton is correct. I was wrong to accuse Miss Woodley." He swallowed, casting a last venomous look in Constance's direction. "She did not steal the necklace. The servant put it in there when he carried down the trunk."

Lady Rutherford's servant, Constance thought, and turned to look at the woman. Lady Rutherford was staring at the Earl, her face livid.

"Selbrooke, you are a fool," she said flatly. She whirled around, saying, "Come, Muriel."

She strode out of the house, followed by her daughter.

When Constance turned back around, she saw that Lord and Lady Selbrooke had also disappeared from the entryway. There was silence as everyone else turned to look at each other.

"Well," Francesca said, "after that, I think the only recourse is breakfast."

She proceeded to urge everyone down the stairs and along the hallway to the dining room. Constance was aware of a number of eyes upon her as people drifted past, but Dominic's stony gaze encouraged no one to stop and talk.

At last the only ones left in the entryway were the two of them. Constance, who had turned away during the group's passage, turned back to Dominic. The sorrow she saw in his face tore at her heart.

"I am sorry, Dominic," she whispered. "If I had had any idea that this would happen, I would not have left. I did not mean to hurt you or your family."

"Did you so dislike the idea of marrying me that you had to run away?" he asked, his face grim.

"No!" Constance cried, horrified, tears springing to her eyes. "No, it was not that! It was never that I did not want to marry you. I love you!"

She had not intended to admit it to him—ever—but she found she could not hold back the words, so hurt was the look in his eyes.

Dominic's eyes widened in surprise. He crossed the floor to her in two quick strides and took her hands. "Do you mean that? Truly?"

"Yes. Yes, of course I mean it."

"Constance..." A grin broke across his face, and he lifted her hands to his lips, kissing them, then released them and gazed at her with a foolish grin upon his face. "I had hoped. I had thought that you might—that you would, perhaps, come to love me in the future—but then..." He paused, frowning. "Why did you run away? And with the Rutherfords, of all people! You must have been desperate."

"I was afraid that if I stayed, you would persuade me to marry you."

"Why would that have been so bad?"

"Dominic, you know why. I told you—I could not bear to be the cause of your misfortune. To have you and your father turned against each other even more fully, your duty to your family unfulfilled, your estates remaining encumbered, all because you made a poor marriage."

"Constance!" He stared at her in exasperation. "I told you it would be all right, that I would work it out. And I will."

"But how? I haven't anything but a pittance to bring to our marriage."

"You have yourself, and that is more than enough," he told her quietly. "Listen to me. I have no need for a great deal of money. During the war, I lived on what I could forage in the countryside often enough. And we will not be penniless. We may have to economize, but I don't care for that. I have a small estate in Dorset. It was left to me by my uncle, the same one who purchased my commission for me. It has a very pleasant manor house, with a small estate farm that produces enough for us to live on. I invested what I received when I sold out of the army, and it will give us a little more income. It will be a good enough life for me, if it is for you."

"It would be a wonderful life!" Constance assured him. "But what about Redfields? And your parents?"

"I would not be concerned about my parents if I were you," Dominic said caustically. "But, of course, that is not your nature. I have already told my father that if he agrees to my plan, we will move into Redfields and institute it immediately. If not—or if, as I presume after what he did to you today, you are unwilling to live in proximity to them—we will live at my manor house until I inherit the estate, and then we will move here. We will sell the house in London, as it is not entailed, and we will use it to help pay off a good portion of the debt. We will then institute a number of economies, primary among them not going to London for the Season. I have no need to live in London, if you will not be too unhappy with a simple country life."

"I will not be unhappy at all. A simple country life is what I lived the whole of my existence until this summer."

"If we have to, I will sell what my uncle left me, but I would prefer to keep it as a property for a younger son or a daughter. I can use my investments, too, against the debt. I have been talking to the estate agent's son since I have been here, and he has a good many ideas for better farming methods that will increase our income. There are a number of other things that we can do to decrease our expenses. The FitzAlans have overspent their incomes for centuries. Decreasing the expenses will also increase our profits. The added profits can be used to pay down the debt. We can sell a number of horses. We have far more than we need. And there is no reason to keep three different family carriages. We can sell two of them. That will help to pay the debt, as well. Forrester and I agree that I can cut the encumbrance on the estate by half within the first five years. By the time I pass it on to our son, we will have paid it off entirely."

Constance smiled, enjoying his enthusiasm. It made her warm inside to hear him speak of "our son." If only…

"It will not be a bleak life, though," he assured her hastily. "You must not think that there will be no luxuries. No joy."

It would be joy enough, Constance thought, to live with Dominic. The thought of sharing a life, making plans, raising a family together, filled her with such longing that she wanted to cry.

"It would be easier to marry into money," she said softly.

He grinned. "Yes, not nearly as much fun," he retorted. "Besides, I don't think I would want it if I could not have you."

"What?" Constance stared at him. "Do you mean that?"

"Of course I mean it." He looked at her oddly. "Why else would I ask you to marry me?"

"But you did not say that!" Constance cried. "You never said that you *wanted* to marry me."

"I didn't?"

"No. Indeed, you did not even ask me to marry you. You just told everyone that we were engaged. And you did that only because Muriel forced your hand. You did it to keep me from being plunged into scandal. That is not reason enough to marry me! I want your love, Dominic. I do not want to spend the rest of my life in love with you, knowing that you married me only because you were too much a gentleman not to. Knowing that you regretted it. You would come to hate me. And I could not bear that."

He stared at her. "Hate you! Constance, don't you know that I could never hate you? I love you. I would never regret marrying you. I am sorry that I did not ask you properly. Muriel did force my hand, and I regret that it happened the way it did. For then I had to blurt it out to everyone without having a chance to ask you first."

"Do you mean that you intended to ask me to marry you before Muriel said that?" Constance asked, amazed.

"Yes, of course. You say I was too much of a gentleman not to marry you so that there would be no scandal. Did you think I would, as a gentleman, take you to my bed unless I already planned to marry you?"

Constance let out a breathy little laugh. "Did you not

also think, my dear, that you might have let me know that at the time?"

"I am a fool," he said. "I freely admit it. I have no excuse other than that your beauty rendered me incapable of thinking."

He took her hand in his and dropped down onto one knee. "Miss Constance Woodley, you are the heart of my heart. The only woman whom I have ever loved or ever will love. I offer you my heart, my hand, my fortune—or lack thereof. I will count myself a rich man, indeed, if you will but consent to entrust your hand and your heart to me. Will you marry me?"

"Yes," Constance said, laughing and crying all at the same time. "Yes, yes, I will marry you. I love you. Oh, stand up, you foolish man, and let me kiss you."

"Gladly," he said, and he did.

And she did.

EPILOGUE

DOMINIC AND CONSTANCE WERE married in St. Edmund's church in Cowden at the end of July. It was, some said, not as grand as the FitzAlan family weddings in years past, but all agreed that none had ever been more beautiful, nor had the bride and groom been happier. It was, after all, a love match.

Lady Calandra and Lady Francesca were her attendants, and though both were beautiful women, neither could match the bride in radiance. Her love shone from her eyes as Constance walked down the aisle to where Lord Leighton stood with the rector. And Leighton gazed back at her with a look in his eyes that made more than one woman in the church heave a sigh and turn to her husband, wishing that he looked at her in such a way.

They left the church as husband and wife, cheered by the villagers and their tenants, and rode back to Redfields, where the wedding supper awaited them and their guests. All the late summer flowers had been stripped from every garden around to provide decorations for the ballroom, and both food and drink were in ample supply.

If the Earl of Selbrooke and his countess were not happy about the marriage, as was widely rumored, the two of them hid it well enough, smiling, feasting and dancing with as much enthusiasm as they were ever inclined toward. After their honeymoon trip to Scotland, Lord and Lady Leighton intended to return to Redfields to live. Lord and Lady Selbrooke would by then have removed themselves to the dower house a few miles away, which Lady Selbrooke had spent the past two months renovating to her liking and furnishing with her most valued pieces of furniture. Lord Selbrooke said that it was for the best that way, as Dominic was eager to take up the duties of management that would one day be his.

There would be a great many changes coming, as everyone knew, and, frankly, most were quite eager to see them. The FitzAlan family had figured in much of the village history, and the people of Cowden were proud of them. But the present Lord and Lady Selbrooke were not especially well-liked. Lord and Lady Leighton, it was clear, would be different.

Their marriage had also increased the reputation of Lady Haughston as a matchmaker. It was rumored, not only here in Cowden, but also in London—and throughout the most aristocratic families in the rest of the country—that Lady Francesca had discovered the new Lady Leighton at a party and had immediately envisioned her as the perfect bride for her brother. She had an intuition about such things, people said—and quite a few agreed that she was not above giving a couple a timely push or two if the pair was a bit slow about finding their destiny.

Certainly, Lady Francesca had a look about her that reminded one of the proverbial cat who had consumed a canary—and gotten away with it unnoticed, as well.

At the wedding party, Francesca stood to one side of the ballroom, observing the bridal pair as they waltzed around the floor. Dominic was smiling down at Constance, his blond head lowered to catch what she said. Constance's face was turned up to him, and there was a glow on it that made Francesca's heart stumble a little in its beat.

"You have done it again, my lady," said a deep male voice just behind her.

Francesca turned to face the Duke of Rochford. She was not surprised to find him there, though she had not seen him since the house party here over a month earlier. He had traveled to one of his other houses to oversee some business or other, as he was wont to do, and Francesca had gone to London to help Constance choose her wedding gown and trousseau. But she had known the Duke would be at the wedding and would seek her out. He was always a gentleman, even when he lost.

Indeed, perhaps even more so when he lost.

She smiled at him. "Yes, Your Grace, I have."

"Not only engaged before the end of the Season, but even married before then, as well," he went on in his usual sardonic tone. "Perhaps I should give you a bonus."

"What we agreed upon will be enough," Francesca responded.

He reached inside his jacket and pulled out a square box. She took it and slipped it into her reticule.

"Not even going to look?" he asked.

"I trust you."

"Do you?" He looked at her consideringly for a moment.

"Of course. You can be quite odious about many things, but you always pay your debts."

"Mmm. Some take far longer to pay than others, I fear."

"You are in a very cryptic mood," Francesca said.

He shrugged. "I may pay my debts, dear lady, but I never like to lose."

With a polite bow to her, Rochford left. Francesca looked after him until he disappeared in the crowd. Her fingers were itching to dig the box out of her reticule and open it, but it wouldn't be seemly. She had to wait until she could retire to her room. And that meant waiting for the bridal pair to leave.

Fortunately Dominic and Constance seemed eager to begin their honeymoon. They did not linger at the wedding supper, but slipped upstairs to change their clothes, then left the house. Francesca watched them climb into the carriage, a lump in her throat.

She watched through the window of the carriage as Dominic leaned over and kissed Constance and her hand came up to curve around his cheek. For a moment they were lit by the setting sun slanting through the window, and their faces glowed with a golden light.

Francesca had to press her lips together hard to keep the tears from overflowing her eyes.

She waved until they had disappeared out of sight down the drive. Then she turned and made her way through the crowd of well-wishers and up the stairs to her room. The party would continue, but she had done her duty and could retire.

Maisie was in her room when Francesca entered, and she came over with a smile. "Surely you're not done yet, my lady."

"Actually, I think I am. I'm a bit tired, Maisie."

"And no wonder. Shall I take down your hair?"

Francesca nodded, and Maisie went to work on the hair pins, removing them and setting them aside in their crystal dish. Soon the heavy weight of Francesca's blond tresses tumbled down, and Maisie picked up the silver-backed brush and began to pull it through her hair.

Francesca took the box from her reticule and set it on the vanity table in front of her. She opened it and drew a sharp breath when she saw the bracelet.

It was exquisite, a dainty concoction of sapphires as blue as her eyes, strung with diamonds in between. She ran a finger over the precious stones.

"Ooh, my lady," Maisie breathed. "That's beautiful, that is."

"Yes, it is," Francesca agreed absently. Rochford's card lay inside beneath the bracelet, his strong, angular hand clearly visible.

She took out the bracelet and laid it over the back of one hand. The diamonds caught every stray bit of light, flashing it back at her. The sapphires were dark and mysterious. It was beautiful, and clearly expensive. Exactly what she would have expected from Rochford.

"Shall I take it to the jewelers to sell for you?" Maisie asked. It was their custom after Francesca was gifted by the grateful mother or father of the bride whose path to the altar Francesca had been instrumental in clearing.

"No," Francesca said after a moment. "I believe I will keep this one."

Maisie looked down at her mistress, somewhat shocked. But Francesca did not notice her. She was too busy gazing at the bracelet.

Francesca rose and walked over to the dresser, where a large teakwood box lay. She opened the lid and moved the shelves out, revealing the wooden bottom of the small jewelry chest. Pressing a rosette carved in the bottom of the front of the box, she slid out the thin wooden layer that appeared to be the bottom of the jewel case. Beneath it lay a compartment.

Inside the compartment were two sapphire-and-diamond earrings. They were as beautiful as the bracelet, though they were years older. They also clearly matched the new piece of jewelry.

Francesca laid the bracelet gently in the compartment beside the earrings, then slid the wooden layer closed, concealing it.

"I think it is time, Maisie," she said as she pushed the shelves back in and lowered the lid of the jewelry case. "We must start considering who we shall take on next."